City Heat

LACEY ALEXANDER

ELLORA'S CAVE
ROMANTICA PUBLISHING

An Ellora's Cave Romantica Publication

www.ellorascave.com

City Heat

Content Advisory:

S – ENSUOUS
E – ROTIC
X – TREME

Ellora's Cave Publishing offers three levels of Romantica™ reading entertainment: S (S-ensuous), E (E-rotic), and X (X-treme).

The following material contains graphic sexual content meant for mature readers. This story has been rated E–rotic.

S-*ensuous* love scenes are explicit and leave nothing to the imagination.

E-*rotic* love scenes are explicit, leave nothing to the imagination, and are high in volume per the overall word count. E-rated titles might contain material that some readers find objectionable — in other words, almost anything goes, sexually. E-rated titles are the most graphic titles we carry in terms of both sexual language and descriptiveness in these works of literature.

X-*treme* titles differ from E-rated titles only in plot premise and storyline execution. Stories designated with the letter X tend to contain difficult or controversial subject matter not for the faint of heart.

Also by Lacey Alexander

ຄ

Behind the Mask (*anthology*)
Brides of Caralon: Seductress of Caralon
Brides of Caralon 1: Rituals of Passion
Brides of Caralon 2: Master of Desire
Brides of Caralon 3: Carnal Sacrifice
Hot For Santa
Hot in the City: French Quarter
Hot in the City: Key West
Hot in the City: Sin City
Unwrapped

About the Author

ຄ

Lacey Alexander's books have been called deliciously decadent, unbelievably erotic, exceptionally arousing, blazingly sexual, and downright sinful. In each book, Lacey strives to take her readers on the ultimate erotic adventure and hopes her stories will encourage women to embrace their sexual fantasies.

Lacey resides in the Midwest with her husband, and when not penning romantic erotica, she enjoys history and traveling, often incorporating favorite travel destinations into her work.

Lacey welcomes comments from readers. You can find her website and email address on her author bio page at www.ellorascave.com.

Tell Us What You Think

We appreciate hearing reader opinions about our books. You can email us at Comments@EllorasCave.com.

CITY HEAT

ଚ୨

LYNDA'S LACE

CARTER'S CUFFS

Dedication

❧

The City Heat series is dedicated to my editor, Heather Osborn, and all the great people at Ellora's Cave!

LYNDA'S LACE

હ્ય

Trademarks Acknowledgement

ॐ

The author acknowledges the trademarked status and trademark owners of the following wordmarks mentioned in this work of fiction:

James Bond: Danjaq, LLC.

Chapter One

ဆာ

Lynda Phelps stood behind the counter of her French Quarter shop, Cajun Lady Antiques, on a quiet Wednesday afternoon. Bad weather had run the tourists indoors, and she found herself peering out the window into the dreary rain, just wishing.

Wishing for fun.

Wishing for sex.

She knew rain made some people sleepy, but it only made *her* bored, and despite herself, she found herself longing for the wild, hedonistic kind of sex she'd been merrily indulging in ever since her divorce twelve years ago.

At the tender age of twenty-one, Lynda had rushed into marriage with Charlie the Loser, a traveling salesman type who'd found a lot of time for *pleasure* on his so-called business trips. When she'd called Charlie on his cheating ways two long years into their marriage, he'd shown no remorse, offered no apology, made no excuses. He'd simply said, "Baby, the way I see it, you go around once in this life. I figure you gotta grab all the fun you can, so I've been grabbing it."

She'd swiftly left him, but had also learned a valuable lesson from her smarmy ex. She didn't approve of his methods, but he was right. You only lived once. So ever since the day Lynda had signed her divorce papers, she'd been living. As in bedding anyone she took a notion to.

In between sexual encounters, she'd also worked hard to keep her store afloat, and she took care of the large Garden District house she'd gotten in the divorce settlement—all of which added up to a busy but satisfying life. One thing about Charlie—he was a pig, but a high-income pig, so she'd come out of the marriage with a valuable home and enough money to start her own business. Thus she'd always thought perhaps the whole thing was meant to be. For all his faults, Charlie had helped her achieve a life full of things she loved—her home, her shop...and a sex life to be envied.

And as for the sex, she'd never hesitated to take it to extremes. She'd had sex with men and sex with women. Sometimes she had sex with both of them at the same time. Once, she'd taken part in a full-blown orgy, the kind where she hadn't been quite sure who she was touching or who was touching her—she'd only known it felt good. Having convinced herself she didn't care about silly emotions like love or commitment, the sex had been...gloriously freeing.

Lynda now considered herself a veritable connoisseur of fucking. She knew what she liked and she knew what most *other* people liked, too. Friends and acquaintances even came to her for advice on their sex lives. She'd come to fancy herself the Sex Queen of New Orleans. And even if, in a city like The Big Easy, there was a lot of competition for such a title, she didn't know anyone who dabbled in, experimented with, or just plain enjoyed sex as much as she did.

As Lynda's pussy rippled with memories and a lusty bit of nostalgia over some of her more satisfying conquests, the bell above the door jingled. And like an answer to a sinful prayer, a totally hot and sexy younger man walked in off St. Peter Street, his sandy locks darkened and curling from the rain.

"Hi," he said, and she immediately felt his eyes dancing over the low-cut V of her gauzy, fitted top, belted at her hips.

She smiled. "Wet out there." *And in here, too,* she thought, the crux of her thighs going moist.

"Hope you don't mind if I step in to dry off for a minute. It's really coming down." Indeed, what had before been a drizzle had just progressed to a downpour, cocooning them in the static sound of hard rain.

"No problem," she said with a look she knew radiated heat.

He gave his head a short shake to rid his hair of moisture as droplets trailed down his jacket. "So, are you the Cajun lady?" he asked, motioning toward the gold lettering on the opposite side of the old glass door. He couldn't have been more than twenty-five, and his smile held instant flirtation.

Her nipples tightened on the spot, puckering her thin bra and top as she gave her stock reply to such inquiries, particularly when they came from good-looking men. "Well, I'm not really Cajun, and as for whether I'm a lady, that depends upon your definition." Then she winked, just before provocatively lowering her chin and flashing a small but inviting smile.

A sparkle lit his green eyes. "Well, whether or not you're a lady, I bet you're a hell of a good time."

She grinned, confident and sensual. "Honey, you have no idea." This was exactly what she'd been thinking about, wishing for so wistfully.

He tilted his head, the move tossing slightly scruffy hair away from his face to reveal an expression brimming with interest. "Maybe you should show me."

Everything inside Lynda trembled in anticipation. She needed this—so, so bad. An encounter with a hot stranger, a release of her inhibitions. Inhibitions she'd been holding inside lately.

But—God, what was she doing?

You're being your old self, that's all.

Because she'd forgotten for a moment. Or maybe she'd just *chosen* to forget. Just for a naughty and very tempting minute. But the reality was—the Sex Queen of New Orleans was currently on hiatus.

Three months ago, she would have set up a rendezvous with Mr. Young, Cute and Wet for later, after the shop closed—or she simply would have drawn him into the back room, lifted the long peasant skirt she wore, and indeed, shown him. Her whole body ached for the feel of his masculine hands on her breasts and his stiff cock between her thighs.

Yet, working hard to push back the waves of desire threatening to engulf her, Lynda replied, "I wish I could. I'd take you on a ride you'd never forget. But...I can't."

He narrowed his eyes in disappointment. "Husband?"

"Yeah," she lied. Because it was simpler that way. Simpler than explaining that she'd recently started dating the most handsome, debonair man on the planet and his only flaw was not quite being wild enough for her in bed, but that she still didn't want to cheat on him because she really thought she cared for the guy.

Five minutes later, after she'd let the delicious young man walk back out into the rain, she found herself glancing again out the plate-glass window, this time toward a storefront across St. Peter and up a few doors. The sign hanging from the awning read Spy Games and the shop belonged to her lover, Jordan Ellis III.

She'd never expected to date a man with a number behind his name. And even if he sold spy gadgets for a living, he was easily the most sophisticated guy to ever cross her romantic path. A James Bond of retail. She smiled a little at the silly thought—but then her breasts resumed aching and her pussy spasmed slightly from thinking of *him*, not the blonde cutie from a few minutes ago. And it made *much* more sense to want Jordan. He was a man, not a boy. And he treated her so wonderfully.

She bit her lip and focused more closely, imagining her dark-haired Adonis inside, perhaps tinkering with some high-tech mini-camera concealed in a lighter or some microscopic listening device nearly invisible to the human eye. She thought of his broad chest, his sweeping smile that burned all through her. She thought of his enormous cock—and at nine solid inches by her estimations, it actually went a long way toward making up for what she was missing in the bedroom.

God, I want you.

Of course, she'd *had* him—many times. Only, as time passed, she wanted him in a different way. An *animal* way. She wanted him up against the wall, or spread on the floor, clothes askew. She was the Sex Queen, after all.

But it's a tradeoff, she reminded herself. *And you knew that going into this.* It just wasn't possible to get animal sex and such high-sheen class in the same package—life didn't work that way. Moreover, you couldn't get animal sex and tight leather and sex toys along with something warm and comforting and meaningful. And somewhere along life's path, the latter was what Lynda had decided she really wanted.

Oh sure, she told her friends she'd sworn off relationships in lieu of hot sex. But then her thirty-fifth birthday had recently rolled around and something had changed—she'd realized she didn't want to grow old alone. She wanted a companion, a lifemate. Her nasty divorce all those years ago had made her think love wasn't for her and never would be, but as she'd blown out all those candles she'd realized that she was finally starting to change her mind.

Enter Liz, her ex-neighbor and friend. Lynda had introduced Liz to her yummy P.I. husband Jack—sort of—so Liz had decided to do some reverse matchmaking herself. Jordan was a friend of Jack's, not surprising since they were both in the business of spying on people, and Liz had invited Lynda and Jordan to dinner at the apartment she shared with Jack on Bourbon Street.

A man could look at you with enough sin in his eyes to make your pussy quiver, and that's exactly what had happened when Lynda had met Jordan. At thirty-eight, he was dark and handsome, olive-skinned, sporting just a hint of gray around the edges of raven hair. His warm brown eyes had taken possession of her on sight. In that moment, she'd have sworn they'd end up hot and sweaty together before the night was through.

Only then he'd kissed her hand. And pulled out her chair.

He'd asked about her business, talking only briefly of his.

He'd complimented her perfume, as well as her necklace—an antique piece from her grandmother, sporting small rubies.

And as the night had worn on, she'd felt herself falling a little bit in love with him. Lust, too, but she'd quickly discerned that despite the fiery heat she'd witnessed in his gaze, Jordan was the consummate man of style and sophistication, not a guy who ripped off a woman's clothes in the heat of passion.

She'd instantly been torn between loving that measure of class she'd never had in a man before and hating what she'd almost immediately known the relationship would lack. For Jordan Ellis III clearly needed a prim, sophisticated lady on his arm, and despite herself, Lynda wanted to be that woman.

Even if there was no animal sex.

And there hadn't been.

Instead there'd been fancy dinners, and lovely gifts, and sweet, romantic kisses that had led to sweet, romantic lovemaking. Sweet…and vanilla.

Of course, to be fair, they did moan and groan together, sometimes even talking a little bit dirty, and Jordan knew exactly how to touch her to get her off—he had great hands and knew how to use them. The bedplay wasn't boring. Hell, the man made her come—what more did she want?

Animal sex, a quiet little voice whispered inside her.

She wanted whips and chains and leather.

Screaming and begging and commanding.

Sweat and clenched teeth and spanking. God, she couldn't remember the last time she'd gotten a good spanking—or given one, either.

But when she'd met Jordan, she'd figured she'd sown enough wild oats and could give all that up now. And the deeper truth was—no matter how tempting Mr. Young and Wet had been a few minutes ago, over the past year or so she'd actually started finding her particular brand of sex a little meaningless, experiencing the urge to look into her lover's eyes afterward and know they had truly *shared* something, something relevant and vital. Which was exactly what she'd found with Jordan. So it had made perfect sense to change her ways and invite this new, staid sort of lover into her life. After all, he was everything a woman could want.

Except for the animal sex part.

But it's worth it. She reminded herself of that frequently during these mental flip-flopping sessions. Even if she had to clench her teeth—and her vagina—to make herself send a sexy young guy away, *it was worth it.* Even if her vibrators were getting a workout lately because she couldn't help fantasizing about all the stuff she *really* wanted to do with Jordan, *it was worth it.*

Jordan had recently told her that sometimes if he was demonstrating the power of one of the tiny spy cameras he sold, he would point it at her store, enabling him to see her very clearly and close-up through the window. Now, she suffered the sudden urge to do something wild and crazy like lift her top over her breasts and flash him in true French Quarter style—just in case he was watching.

But if he was watching, that probably meant *customers* were watching, too—and besides possibly costing him a sale, he'd think she was the most barbaric, unsavory, tacky woman he'd ever met.

Oh, if only I could show you the real me, baby.

Easing back onto the tall stool behind her, she envisioned herself slowly, slowly easing her top up, taking her filmy bra with it, putting her breasts on display for him through some tiny camera three doors down. She imagined running her hands over them, slowly squeezing, massaging, twirling the taut nipples that now rubbed against the fabric of her bra every time she moved. She wanted to feel his eyes on her while she touched herself for him. Were there people on the street? No, not today—too rainy. But it didn't matter either way in a fantasy.

Lynda thought of Jordan watching, getting rock hard for her. She imagined him wanting—*needing*—what *she* needed. Rough, urgent sex.

In the fantasy, she suddenly saw him burst through the door of Spy Games and come striding across the street toward her like a man possessed. Their eyes would meet through the window as she continued smoothing her palms over her bared flesh.

He would barrel through the door, making the bell clang wildly, and she'd see the unmistakable lust in his gaze just before he leapt across the counter, too impatient to walk around.

There would be no words—only action.

Rough hands. Pushing up her skirt. Ripping off her panties.

A hot, hard cock. Plunging into her. Nailing her to the wall. *Oh yes.*

As Lynda tried to feel it, feel him filling her, slamming into her, taking her the way she so deeply wanted to be taken by him, she couldn't resist letting her fingers dip between her legs where they parted across the stool, the light fabric of her skirt falling in between. *Mmm, nice.*

But she wanted more, wanted to touch herself, flesh to flesh. Glancing out the window, she saw that the rain still fell, keeping St. Peter Street quiet and lonely but for a few passing cars. It was still dangerous as hell to go on with this—someone could walk in at any time just like Mr. Young and Wet a little while ago—but she didn't care. She'd been bottling up her desires for too long, and they needed to come out, even if it was a solo act.

Feeling incredibly daring and naughty, she reached one hand up under her long skirt, bringing it to rest between her legs, then pushed her fingertips beneath the elastic edge of her silk panties. A second later, she found her swollen clit, let out a gasp of pleasure, and began to rub in rhythmic circles to the image of Jordan's hands on her ass as he pounded into her in long, hard, relentless strokes. *Yes, yes.*

Her fingers grew wet as her legs instinctively parted farther. *Fuck me, Jordan.* How she longed to purr those words into her lover's ear. *Fuck me hard.*

But in the fantasy he couldn't have fucked her any harder than he already was—each stroke echoed through her whole body and her legs grew weak. Finally, she curled them around his thighs so that he supported her completely, bracing her back against the wall.

In time with his imagined strokes, Lynda continued to rub her clit, harder, harder. Her pelvis gyrated, lifting in short, hot motions to meet the pressure of her hand. She'd long since stopped caring if anyone saw her through the window or came in the door—she'd nearly forgotten where she was altogether. *Fuck me, Jordan. Fuck me.*

Seconds later—*oh yes, yes!*—she came, the orgasm roaring through her like a locomotive barreling right through the French Quarter, so intense that she cried out, then clamped her teeth down on her lower lip to ride out the last surges of pleasure.

Mmm, yes. That had been good. Surprisingly so, given the risk element. Which apparently demonstrated just how much she yearned for what she'd been envisioning. Ah, if only it were true.

She sighed just as the phone on the counter trilled, drawing her back to the real world—seldom as perfect as a fantasy. Struggling to catch her breath, she reached to pick it up. "Cajun Lady Antiques."

"Any progress with Mr. 007?" It was Liz, with whom Lynda had shared her woes over a recent lunch.

Still recovering from the climax, she tried to organize her thoughts, feeling Liz's timing was uncanny. "No. But then...I haven't actually tried to *make* progress. I think he'd be appalled."

Liz sounded regretful. "I'm so sorry, Lynda—I thought he'd be perfect for you. When I got the idea to fix you two up, I guess I wasn't thinking...about your wilder side."

"He *is* perfect for me. In most ways," she added. "And it's nothing to be sorry for, honey. I'm nuts about the guy. I just wish...you know."

Sadly, Liz had exactly what Lynda wished for. A fabulously hunky guy who adored her sweet side but who also knew how to get down and dirty with her behind closed doors. She supposed when Liz had suggested fixing her up with a friend of Jack's, she'd envisioned getting the same sort of man. Ironic that when Lynda had put Liz in touch with Jack, *she'd* been the one with the wild sex life and had wanted her friend to know the same pleasures. Oh, how the tables had turned.

"I still say you should just go for it," Liz said. "If he can't appreciate the real you, then screw him."

Lynda laughed. A couple of years ago, Liz would never have phrased it in that way—but her introduction to Jack had changed her whole life, made her so much more at ease with herself and the world. Lynda felt dangerously close to finding something just as transforming to *her* being, something life-altering and important and wonderful—with Jordan. But the differences in the way they approached sex were just enough to keep her from feeling *totally* connected to him. And she'd considered doing exactly what Liz had just suggested, yet... "I know you're right, but the thing is..."

"What?"

She sighed. She didn't like admitting this—it was *so* not her. "I don't want to mess this up. I don't want to lose him. Maybe things aren't *quite* right between us in bed—but things are good in every *other* way. And I'm not ready to risk that. I've never had a guy like him before, Liz, not in my whole thirty-five years. It's the way he treats me. And it's also the way I feel about him. Both are so...grand. I don't know how else to say it, because it's just...an extraordinary event in my life." She glanced toward the spy shop again, feeling tender and—just for a moment—not overly horny, thank God. It probably helped that she'd just come. "So if the sex is just good and not great, maybe that's okay. Because I'm not ready to give up what I have with him for something as...*temporary* as sex." She let out another sigh.

Liz sounded puzzled. "Sex is temporary?"

"Well...it's only one part of a relationship, right? And by the time we're seventy or eighty, hell, it probably won't matter at all."

She let out a short laugh and Liz did, too, but Lynda wasn't really amused by her own desperate attempts to make herself believe sex wasn't important to her. It *was* important, damn it.

Yet so was Jordan, so she'd just have to learn, once and for all, to be the type of refined lady who befitted a man of his nature. If she wanted him, she had no other choice.

She supposed that made it official.

The Sex Queen was dead.

Except maybe in her own mind.

* * * * *

Linda peered at her reflection in a cheval mirror in the apartment above her shop. Up until recently, she'd rented the place to a nice gay couple, but they'd chosen to leave the city after recent devastating storms. The same storms had made it a sensible time to have some renovations and repairs done on her house, so she was staying here for a month or so until they were done, at which point she'd put the apartment back up for rent. The mirror was a gorgeous antique she'd decided to "borrow" from the shop temporarily, both for practical purposes and to add a little character to the apartment while she was here.

She couldn't decide what she thought of the way she looked tonight, wearing a dress of dark lilac lace. It wasn't that the dress didn't look lovely — it did, and it complemented her green eyes and the long blonde hair currently pulled back into a chignon. But Lynda never wore lace — *never, never, never.* She might wear silk or satin, denim or spandex — hell, she wore everything from cotton to leather. And it so happened that leather was definitely her fabric of choice in the bedroom. But when it came to lace…well, she thought the feminine material lovely on more *demure* women, but it had never been for her.

Until now, that was — until *Jordan.* The guy loved the stuff. So far, he'd given her a pink lace teddy, a lacy bra and panty set in baby blue, another pair of peach lace panties with sequins and rhinestones sewn in — and now this lovely-but-not-really-Lynda dress.

She had to wear it, of course. It was probably more expensive than anything else in her closet, and when she'd opened the lavishly wrapped gift box, she'd been able to tell he'd taken great care picking it out. The truth was, he had wonderful taste — not surprising given how suave and stylish he was himself.

She had to wear it because — besides not wanting to hurt his feelings — she didn't really want to admit to him that she saw herself as being too rough and raw of a woman for lace. If Jordan thought she was a lace kind of girl…well, it was just like the sex — she didn't want to dispel his notions of her, didn't want to tip him off in any way that maybe she wasn't the perfect woman for him. If his perfect woman wore lace, she'd wear it.

You're being untrue to yourself.

Damn it, what was with all the little voices in her head today? This one she just blatantly chose to ignore. People could change. And besides wanting Jordan Ellis more than she wanted to breathe, she also wanted to be *worthy* of Jordan Ellis. She wanted to be his ideal lady, in every way.

Just then, a knock came on the door and—following a last-second impulse—Lynda tugged the dress's lace cups down a little, plumping up her cleavage. Hell, if she was going to wear lace, she'd at least wear it a little bit audaciously. Staring at the cami-type bodice in the mirror, she couldn't deny that he *had* chosen a rather *sexy* lace dress, and that even if it didn't exactly suit her, she still looked pretty damn good in it.

A few seconds later, she whisked open the door to find her lover standing before her, looking impeccably handsome in twill trousers and a tailored jacket, his shirt open at the throat. His dark eyes honed in on her as a predictably charming smile unfurled across his lightly stubbled face. "Hey, precious." She loved the endearment—it made her feel so very treasured. "You look good enough to eat."

She instinctively lowered her chin and flashed her sexiest look. "That can be arranged. Would you like me now or later?"

He let out a soft laugh. "I'll try to hold off until after dinner."

She smiled prettily. "I hope you don't get too full."

"Too full for a taste of *you*?" He gave his head a short, certain shake. "Not possible."

Lynda practically felt her breasts swelling within the snug confines of the lace as she accepted the small pink box he held out to her, wrapped with a matching satin ribbon.

"Something lovely for my lady," he said.

More lace—she'd bet the store on it.

Gently pulling at the ribbon, she let it fall to the floor between them as she lifted the box's lid. Inside pink tissue paper lay a baby doll nightie with lace cups, in a soft, spring yellow.

It was beautiful—for someone like Liz, maybe. But a baby doll nightie—for *her*? She held in her sigh. Why, oh why, couldn't it have been a slick black vinyl corset or a nice little flogger they could play with?

"It's lovely, just as you promised," she managed. She smiled up at him, thankful she'd always been a decent actress.

"For later," he told her. Then he reached in the box and plucked out the matching lace panties, tossing them toward one corner of the room. "Except we won't need these." He leaned closer, spoke lower. "Why hide that pretty pussy when I'll be ready to feast on it the second I see you in this?"

Lynda pulled in her breath at the naughty promise and felt utterly guilty for privately shunning his thoughtful, sexy gift. Jordan was by no means a prude—most women would consider him a fabulous lover, and she was incredibly fortunate to have him. She just wished she didn't have such *extreme* tastes.

And as she shut the door and walked carefully down the steps in her heels, with Jordan's strong hand steady at the small of her back, she thought she had a lot of nerve complaining about him, even to herself. After all, she had a hot, sexy man who was going to take her out to a fabulous dinner, then bring her back here and use his skilled tongue to lick her to orgasm.

She could wear a little lace for that. And hell—she could even live without the animal sex.

No, you can't.

Shit—it was that damn little voice again.

Shut up, she replied.

Chapter Two

80

Jordan couldn't get enough of the beautiful lady sitting across from him at Antoine's—she was as elegant as the classic old-world setting, yet a certain zing of excitement laced the edges of her personality and he couldn't help wanting to see more of it. Since the moment they'd met, the woman had possessed the ability to make him hard on sight. Even at this very minute, he had no idea what was keeping his cock from bursting free from behind his zipper—damn, it was almost painful.

Tonight she wore the lace dress he'd bought for her. Lynda was lovely no matter what she wore—but he found the vision of her in lace particularly stunning. He'd discovered it only after his first gift to her of a sexy lace teddy, but since then, he couldn't help lavishing still more of it on her.

Watching her eat shrimp wasn't helping his hard-on any. She had a way of almost sucking them into her luscious mouth that brought to mind the incredible blowjobs she delivered.

"Is it good?" he asked, unable to resist a teasing smile.

"Delicious," she assured him, and her playful eyes told him she knew exactly what he was thinking.

He said it anyway. "You have a great mouth."

She replied by slowly, sensually licking her lips. "It likes you, too."

"I've noticed," he said on a laugh, and realized he'd hardly touched the appetizer they were sharing—too caught up in staring at her.

Odd, he'd never felt so constantly turned on with a woman before. Oh sure, maybe as a horny teenager—but since then he'd mellowed, matured. He'd always enjoyed sex, but something about Lynda kept it constantly on his mind.

And it wasn't that he appreciated her only for sex. He loved her personality—she was funny, frank, and genuine, and she made him laugh. She was also just as flirtatious as she was intelligent, a combination he'd at first found surprising, but it had quickly enchanted him.

The only problem with Lynda, he'd decided, was that little bit of herself she was holding back. He couldn't help thinking she had a secret of some kind, that there was something about herself she didn't want him to know. It was almost as if she was on guard around him at times, too careful. Despite loving the sex they'd shared, he'd noticed it even in bed.

"Tell me something." He leaned slightly forward across the candlelit table, reaching to touch her hand where it played with the stem of her wineglass on the pristine white tablecloth. "Tell me…your wildest fantasy."

She looked taken aback, blinking. "Sexual?"

He gave a short nod. They'd had enough sex, grown intimate enough, that he felt comfortable asking her—now, he only hoped she would answer. Maybe if he could get her to open up, she'd start to trust him more and let him in on whatever it was she kept back.

She stayed quiet for a moment, took a drink of her wine. "I…I'm living it," she finally said, her tone staid, quiet. "With you. Every time you make love to me."

Hmm. Nice words. But he didn't believe them. Just like always, she was holding back.

"That's quite a compliment, precious. But are you sure there isn't…anything else? Some wild, crazy thing you're secretly curious about? You can tell me. Even if it's something you don't think you really want to do."

She blinked again, unerringly pretty, and bit her lip. He thought for a second she was going to give him a real answer, open the door to her heart and mind, let him inside. But then she said, "No. Just you. Between my legs. Touching me. And licking me. And then coming inside me."

Okay then. He still didn't think she was being honest, but it was hard to argue when the woman you were nuts about was telling you how masterful you were and making your impossibly hard cock even harder. "Eat up, precious," he said. "Then I'll take you home and we'll get back to living out your fantasy."

With that, he watched her suck another shrimp between those full lips and forgot all about her secrets for tonight.

* * * * *

Damn it. Why hadn't she told him? She'd never get an opportunity that perfect again—and yet, she just hadn't been able to reveal her darker desires. She kept flashing a sexy smile across the table as the waiter delivered their entrees, but inside she was kicking herself.

Well, you've made your bed, so now you can lie in it. And now, if it remains a nice-but-vanilla, nothing-out-of-the-ordinary bed you have no one to blame but yourself.

When Jordan's cell phone softly trilled, he reached quickly in his pocket to extract it. Glancing at the display, he said, "Excuse me for just a moment, precious. I need to take this."

Most men would have snatched the call up in a second without apology, and Lynda wouldn't have minded. But witnessing yet another example of Jordan's courteous respect made her let out a small, weirdly girlish sigh.

"I'm wining and dining my lady right now," he said into the phone with a quick wink in her direction, "so I'm afraid it's not a good time."

Lynda gave him a smile, then sliced into her lamb chop, still vaguely listening.

"Tonight?" he asked, then shook his handsome head, looking irritated. "No, I can't do it tonight."

Setting down her silverware, she reached across the table to touch his sleeve. "Whatever it is, it's all right—I don't mind," she whispered. This might be something business- or family-related, and as anxious as she was to get him naked, she didn't want to stand in the way of anything important.

He shook his head at the suggestion, but from the way the conversation continued, she could tell the person on the other end was insistent and that Jordan was working to stay polite.

"*Really,*" she said softly, drawing his attention. "If you need to do something, it's okay."

Finally, Jordan sighed and said into the phone, "Fine then, in an hour or so. But it'll have to be brief. See you then."

When he snapped the phone shut and slid it back into his pocket, Lynda tilted her head inquisitively. "Problem?"

"Just a customer—but a potentially important one. A local P.I. named Steven Waite recommended Spy Games to a friend of his in Baton Rouge. The friend is head of a large investigations firm, which could result in a sizable account—and it just so happens the friend is in town, for tonight only, and wants to meet me before doing business. I appreciate Steven's recommendation, but I wish I'd had a little warning about the meeting."

Lynda shook her head to let him know it was all right. "Honey, this isn't a problem at all. If you like, I'll just head back to the apartment after dinner and you can meet me there later. I'll put on my new yellow nightie." *And I won't even cringe when I look in the mirror. I'll just remember that it's going to get me gloriously eaten when you get there.*

But Jordan cast her a possessive, authoritative look that she liked. "No, precious—no way I'm sending you home without me. I'm meeting the guys at a bar called Michael's, so you can come along—and in order to keep it short, I can explain that we're on our way somewhere. Of course, I'll refrain from mentioning that the 'somewhere' is your bed," he concluded with a wink, then knit his brow lightly. "Have you heard of the place? He says it's near Bourbon and Conti, but it doesn't ring a bell."

Lynda pursed her lips, thinking. "Not for me, either." And she knew the French Quarter bar scene like the back of her hand. "Must be someplace new." The area was only a couple of blocks away, so it would be an easy walk into the Red Light District at night, a sensually charged atmosphere which Lynda always enjoyed.

In fact, as they continued eating, the idea appealed to her even more. She'd resisted the temptation of the club scene since she'd started seeing Jordan, but just strolling through the crowds of partiers that hung out on Bourbon Street at night sounded like enough to get her blood running a little hotter.

* * * * *

"Are you sure you don't mind this little delay?" Jordan asked, taking her hand as they exited the restaurant an hour and a bottle of wine later.

"Not at all," she replied, squeezing his fingers as they turned from Royal Street onto St. Louis. "I sometimes find Bourbon Street after dark a bit...invigorating." She laughed softly as she spoke and felt like a fake, since what she really found Bourbon Street after dark was more like *exciting, electrically charged* and *an invitation to sin* — an invitation which she usually accepted without a hint of hesitation.

Jordan grinned down at her teasingly. "Really now."

She shrugged playfully, unsure of the right response, but very certain she *shouldn't* tell him some of the more risqué activities she'd indulged in right on Bourbon Street. She'd lifted her top for beads more times than she could count. She'd once let a guy she was seeing pour wine down her bare breasts and lick it off. And during the debauchery of Mardi Gras a few years back, she'd let *two* hot guys she'd never met do the same with a slushy strawberry daiquiri. And those were just a *few* of the naughty things she'd done out on the street—which paled in comparison to the some of the forbidden fun she'd had behind the doors of bars and dance clubs.

Just remembering such events made her pussy tingle as they moved toward the party district—even as her heart burned with a mixture of worry and guilt over keeping it all from this man who clearly cared for her just as *she* was coming to care for *him*.

But she forgot her concerns when Bourbon Street beckoned. As they grew closer, the sounds of music—Zydeco, rock, bits of jazz—grew louder, filling her senses. And as they turned onto the legendary street of sin, neon glowed above doors thrown open to tempt passersby inside on a warm April night and people stood in the street drinking colorful concoctions or enormous glasses of beer, their necks draped with beads of purple, green and gold. Lynda remembered a time when beads were accessories worn only during Mardi Gras, but that had changed when word got out that it gave girls an excuse to flash their breasts any time of year.

Above the thoroughfare, people partied on wrought iron balconies—drinking, singing, letting out catcalls to the opposite sex. Without staring—normally, of course, Lynda *would have* stared, but Jordan's presence inhibited her—she caught glimpses of a guy and girl making out, grinding hotly together on one crowded balcony, and of a group of girls on another tossing beads to guys below, who were playfully lifting *their* shirts in a reverse of the racy custom. In return, one of the girls lifted her short skirt to show barely there panties of red that made the guys yip and yell.

Back down on the street, Lynda's attention was drawn to hawkers inviting people into strip clubs and peep shows. "Most beautiful girls on the strip!" one long-haired guy yelled. Another, across the street beneath a flashing neon promise of *Live Sex*, said, "They do it all in here—anything and everything—come see for yourself!"

Cheers from a group of nearby guys attracted her gaze to two pretty college-aged girls making out with each other, likely on a dare, but they kissed passionately, their necks draped heavily with beads they'd no doubt earned with their breasts.

"Sorry about this, precious," Jordan said, clearly embarrassed on her behalf.

Oh baby, I wish I could tell you how turned on I am right now, just from watching it all. Her cunt practically sizzled beneath her lilac lace and her own breasts ached to be touched.

Just tell him. Now. Just say it.

"No need to apologize," she assured him. "Being here…" *Gets me hot. Makes me wet. In fact, I want to rip your clothes off right now. I want to open your pants and suck your cock right here in front of all these people.* She sighed and tried again. "Being here is…kind of interesting."

Damn it.

Jordan chuckled warmly, smiling down on her. "That's one way to put it."

Apparently, it's the only way I can *put it. Since I just can't seem to be honest with you about everything so dirty and hungry inside me.*

Just then, a few doors past Conti Street, Michael's came into view. Only, under the name, red neon sported the words "Gentlemen's Club". The sight of a gorgeous redhead standing at the door in nothing but a see-through black bra and panties, along with two nicely-attired-but-scary-looking doormen, drove the point home—it was a new addition to Bourbon Street's many strip clubs.

Lynda's nipples rubbed provocatively against the lace cups of her dress as they neared the entrance. "Looks like this is the place."

"Hell," Jordan said, clearly disgusted. "I'm so sorry, precious—I had no idea it was a men's club."

"Of course not—there's no way you could have known."

Jordan hesitated, looking around, then pointed toward the big, bright, open-air souvenir shop next door, where t-shirts and beads hung on racks and feathered masks lined one wall. He sighed, clearly uneasy with the situation. "Maybe you'd like to browse around in there while I'm inside? I'll make it quick—five minutes tops."

Was he kidding? As it happened, Lynda had been in more than her fair share of strip joints and this looked like a perfectly nice one. Not that she could tell him that. But she still had no intention of waiting it out in t-shirt land. "No, I'll just go in with you."

He flashed a look of doubt. "I don't think you really want to do that, precious."

Oh God, now he was trying to protect her from naked women. She decided to—timidly—take a stand. "Why not?"

He tilted his head indulgently. "I just don't think you'd be comfortable. Things can get pretty wild in these places."

She took a deep breath and managed a tight, thin smile. "I'm a big girl, Jordan, I can handle it. And like you said, if *I'm* with you, it gives you a reason to leave quickly."

Not that she was sure she'd *want* to leave quickly. Going to a strip club together would be the kinkiest thing she'd done with Jordan and it sounded fun. But she knew *he'd* want to leave fast. Either way, she didn't want to end up stranded outside in case he had trouble getting away from his business associates.

He gazed down at her with those dark, sexy eyes, the mere look turning her wetter than she already was. "Well, I'm not sure you're going to like it in there—but you're right. If you're with me, it will make my getaway easier."

She teased him. "Don't worry, I'm not afraid of a few erotic dancers."

He smiled the smile that melted her. "Erotic dancers or not, the only thing *I* care about right now is getting you home and getting your panties off."

There it was again—*she* wanted to be wild and kinky, and all *he* wanted was her. It made wildness and kinkiness sound rather empty. And how could she possibly complain about a man so anxious to get to her aching pussy? She must be out of her mind.

"Well," she said, her voice coming out a little throaty as the warmth of his promise oozed down through her chest, "we'll just have to make this quick." Placing her hands on the lapels of his sports jacket, she leaned close, brushing her curves against his body, to whisper in his ear. "Then you can take me home and lick me. And after that, I can wrap my mouth around your perfect erection. And then we can do it *all night long.*"

As Jordan's mouth pressed steamily over hers, she let the ripple of lust vibrate down through her, soaking up every nuance. Only...she'd wanted to use different words. She'd wanted to say *cock* instead of *erection*. And she'd wanted to say they'd *fuck* all night long. Yet she'd edited herself. She simply didn't seem to possess the power to let him see the real her, even when she was oh-so tempted.

When the kiss ended, as they started toward the darkened door of Michael's Gentlemen's Club, she let out a sigh, irritated with herself for being such a goody-two-shoes. For heaven's sake, Jordan wouldn't mind if she said *cock*. Would he? *He* used such terms sometimes. And yet, doubts lingered. But if Jordan noticed her distress at all, he probably thought she was just steeling herself for the horrors within.

After one of the scary doormen took the ten dollar admission from Jordan—ladies entered for free—he led her, still hand in hand, into the shadowy bar. Red and purple lights swirled, giving the space an otherworldly glow, but once Lynda's eyes adjusted, she honed in on the catwalk-like stage. It sported three poles, each attended by a naked girl.

Well, naked in every way that counted anyway. One girl, a blonde, wore a pink cowboy hat, little white cowboy boots, and a thick white belt that hovered just above her thin thatch of light pubic hair. A brunette in high black boots had lowered a black shimmery camisole to her waist, baring large, high breasts. A nurse's cap perched on the head of another blonde. Below her shaven cunt she wore white fishnet thigh-highs with bows in the back and white, fuck-me platform heels. All three girls were worthy of the high-class strip joint, gyrating every shapely curve around their respective poles. Lynda couldn't help being riveted until she realized she and Jordan had stopped just inside the door, and she glanced up at Jordan to see why.

She was sure she'd find him scanning the dark room for his customer, but instead his gaze found the sexy strippers. The cowgirl released her pole to run her hands sensually over pert, medium breasts with uptilted nipples, long and taut. She pinched them lightly, licking her upper lip. Meanwhile, the nurse swiveled her pussy toward her pole in the rhythm of slow, potent sex.

As the brunette did an impressive spin, Lynda's *own* pussy wept with arousal and she tried to picture the look on Jordan's face if she requested a lap dance from one of the hot girls. Because even if *he* was caught up in watching them, too…well, that just meant he was a normal guy—it *didn't* mean he wanted his girlfriend to leap on the stage and join them.

"Sorry," he said when he caught her glance, then offered an endearingly sheepish smile.

"Nothing to apologize for. They're lovely," she added.

"Still, I can't believe I brought you here." He shook his head as if reprimanding himself.

"Get over it already," she said laughingly. "It's not a big deal. Now, do you see your friend?"

Jordan looked around and, a moment later—while Lynda watched the nurse stroke one long finger lightly over her cunt, eliciting a collective groan from at least half the men in the room—he announced, "Yeah, I see him." Taking her hand, he led her through the plush, dark surroundings where she noticed the occasional naked girl giving a lap dance to some lusty-eyed guy whose expression dripped sex.

"Jordan," called a man with a slight southern accent, pushing to his feet from a half-circle booth set against a wall. He shook Jordan's hand and Lynda couldn't help noticing that he was tall and blond, in his early thirties, and looked like just the type of guy she'd love to party with if Jordan wasn't in her life.

The guy went about introducing Jordan to two other men, both a little older, but pleasant-looking, indicating that one of them, Nate, was "my buddy from Baton Rouge".

"I'm sorry I didn't know you were going to be in town," Jordan said to Nate, his deep voice just barely audible above the thumping, sexy music, "or I'd have taken you out to dinner to talk business. As it is, I can only stay a minute as I'm on a date. Gentlemen, my lovely lady, Lynda Phelps."

Lynda smiled her hellos, making eye contact with each man, finally ending on Jordan's blond friend—Steven, if she remembered right. She found his gaze an appreciative one, with a tendency to drop to her chest, and she didn't mind. It only upped the temperature of her cunt, which had been growing hungrier with each passing moment since they'd arrived on Bourbon.

"Lovely indeed," Steven said.

"And a trouper, too," Jordan pointed out on a soft laugh. "Didn't even blink about coming in here with me."

"You know," Steven said, sounding like a more casual guy than her lover, "I wouldn't have forced the issue so much if I'd realized you were gonna bring your date here *with* you."

Clearly, he'd expected Jordan to dump her off for the evening before joining the guys. Which made her want to show them she could hold her own. "Don't worry—I can appreciate the appeal of a sexy girl." She glanced toward the stage where the three nude dancers still swayed in the motions of simulated sex.

"My kind of woman," Steven laughed, gaze still wandering downward to her cleavage.

"Too bad, because she's very taken." Jordan slid an arm around her waist and lowered a short kiss to her mouth, and even just that made her thighs tremble with need. "And we need to take off quickly, as I said, so shall we talk business, Nate?"

With that, Jordan stepped closer to the older man and Steven scooted over on the long, curving seat that faced the stage, offering Lynda a place next to him. She took it with a smile, then boldly turned her attention to the entertainment. She knew he watched her, noticing that she wasn't shy about enjoying the dancers, and that he liked it. Would *Jordan* notice, too? Or would he be too busy talking spy gadgets? And if he did notice, what would he think? Would he be appalled, as she'd always assumed, or aroused?

She feared the only thing making her this brave was the wine from dinner—apparently just now fully hitting her as she experienced that floaty, happy feeling a little intoxication could bring. She watched the nurse bend over, holding onto her pole, to get a spanking from the brunette, who now brandished a nice leather flogger much like Lynda had wished for earlier in the evening.

"So, you and Jordan been together long?" Steven asked, clearly trying to be friendly and make conversation.

"A couple of months."

"He's a great guy."

"Yes, he is," she agreed. "I can't wait to get him home and fuck his brains out."

Steven grinned, obviously surprised and amused—and Lynda covered her mouth as realization washed over her. "Oh God, did I just say that?" She shut her eyes. "Too much wine at dinner."

Steven simply laughed. "That's all right, sweetheart. But I'll say this—Jordan is a very lucky man."

She smiled at the compliment, and couldn't help flashing a slightly flirtatious smile. "Thank you." The ironic part, she thought, was that if Jordan was a little looser and she were a little braver, he'd be getting a *lot* luckier than Steven could probably even imagine.

Just then, the current song ended and the crowd gave a light applause, along with a healthy dose of whistles for the dancers, who soon exited the stage with a plethora of bills wedged into their boots and stockings—since none of them wore even g-strings to have the dollars tucked into. "Next," a voice announced over a microphone, "welcome to the stage the lovely and voluptuous Kayla!"

The men clapped again, a few cheering as a hot, tall blonde in a pair of sexy, silver, ultrahigh fuck-me shoes came dancing onto the stage in a sparkling silver evening gown that showed lots of round cleavage and slender, shapely leg. Long white gloves graced her arms and a white feather boa adorned her shoulders to complete the glamour girl look.

"Pretty," Lynda mused, watching as the stripper ran her gloved hands over her voluminous breasts in a way that made Lynda's whole body even warmer than it already was.

She felt Steven studying *her*, rather than the girl on the stage. "I mean it, about Jordan being lucky. You're a very cool chick."

She offered him another short grin, then returned her attention to Kayla in time to see her rotate her ass toward the crowd and teasingly unzip the back of her already-low dress, all the way down to rhinestone-studded thong undies and the rose tattoo just above. "Hot tattoo," Steven observed in his sexy southern accent.

"I have one on my ankle," Lynda replied, lifting her leg enough that he could see the delicate vine twining in a circle just above her right foot, "and I have a blood-red heart on my ass."

"Not gonna show me that one?" he teased.

"Tempting," she said with a grin, "but Jordan might have a heart attack."

They both giggled, then resumed watching the show. Soon enough, Kayla shimmied sensually out of her dress to reveal extremely large, gorgeous breasts with enticing pink peaks, along with the rest of that shimmering g-string. She tweaked her nipples and glided long fingers over her thighs and belly as she swayed with stripper expertise around one of the gleaming chrome poles.

"Damn, she's hot," Steven murmured under his breath, then tossed a quick, sheepish glance in Lynda's direction. "Oops, sorry."

She only laughed, reaching a soft, reassuring squeeze to his arm. "Don't be. She *is* hot."

Steven gave his head a speculative tilt, again concentrating on Lynda more than the stripper. "Tell me, just what do you think is so hot about her? From a lady's point of view. I wanna to hear what appeals to one sexy woman about another."

Lynda continued studying the voluptuous blonde on stage. "Well, the tattoo, of course, like you said, and—"

Just then, Jordan's masculine form blocked her view, causing her to peer up into that oh-so-handsome face.

"Ready to go?" he asked.

"In just a minute. Sit down." Since the half booth was full, she stood up to let him take a seat next to Steven on the end, then perched in his lap, facing his friend.

As she slid one arm around Jordan's broad shoulders, he said, "What's up?" and then leaned a little closer. "I thought we were in a hurry." He punctuated the comment with a sexy little wink.

She looked back and forth between the two men. "We are, but it would be rude to rush out in the middle of a conversation."

Jordan laughed. "Is this a private discussion, or can I join in?"

The wine was still making her bolder than usual, even with *him* now. "I was just discussing with Steven the attributes of the girl on stage," she shared, observing his reaction closely.

He looked surprised, but at the same time playfully interested. "Oh? And what do you think of her?"

Lynda looked back to Kayla, who now teasingly lowered one side of her g-string, then the other, without quite showing her pussy. Finally, in response to the cheering men—even Steven, next to her, let out a hearty, high-pitched whistle—she lowered the sparkling panties swiftly to her ankles, then kicked them off into the crowd. The g-string headed straight toward the booth where they sat until Steven jumped up and plucked it from midair to the approving yells from those around him, and Lynda found herself laughing and clapping at his little victory.

"Well?" Jordan asked. "What do you think?"

Lynda smiled back and forth between the two men. "She definitely has nice taste in panties," she began, eyeing the ones clutched in Steven's fist, because lace might be a bit too froufrou for Lynda, but rhinestones she could get into. "And that sexy tattoo is in just the right spot because her back and ass are flawless. Her breasts are gorgeous, as well, no denying that. My only criticism would be…"

Both men seemed to wait with bated breath. "Yeah?" Jordan said, looking duly aroused.

"Her hair could use some work."

Jordan's face lit with amusement as Steven chuckled. "I hate to break it to you, honey," Steven said, "but you're the only person in the room looking at her haircut."

"Maybe," Lynda shrugged. "But when a girl wants to be hot, she has to think about the whole package. Personally, I try not to neglect *any* part of my appearance."

"And I can promise you that she looks good all over," Jordan chimed in.

Steven's gaze had strayed to her chest once more. "She looks good in that dress, that's for damn sure."

"A gift from me," Jordan told him.

"Don't punch me in the mouth, buddy, but that dress does fine things for her tits."

Lynda feared the compliment would make them swell from the fabric as her pussy surged with still more moisture from all the erotic sights and conversation. Although she feared how Jordan might react.

But again, to her surprise, he looked unfazed, like a guy who was just going with the flow. "That's not an accident—I knew that when I bought it."

Geez, talk about *surprises*—that was a big one. The wine must have gotten to him, too. She was shocked not only to hear him admit that, but for them to be discussing her body so openly with another guy.

Their eyes met and her astonishment tripled when he said, right in front of Steven, "You're gonna be lucky if I can wait to get home before I rip the damn thing off you."

With that, he slid one palm to a spot high on her thigh, squeezing lightly, then leaned in to bestow a mind-numbingly hot kiss to her neck. She couldn't help arching for him as her cunt yearned for stimulation. She felt the lace stretch teasingly across her breasts, revealing a bit more of the curving flesh to both men's eyes, and now her pussy pulsed madly.

What the hell was happening here? Was she discovering a whole new Jordan?

Unable to resist, she spread her legs just slightly, dying for her man to cup her with his big, strong hand, or to just simply stroke his fingertips there. She longed for him to rub her burning pussy while Steven watched. Or maybe while *everyone* watched. A vision assaulted her—she and Jordan as the next act tonight at Michael's Gentlemen's Club, fucking right there in the booth while all the lusty men in the room cheered them on.

"I want you," she whispered seductively into Jordan's ear. "I want more of you than I've ever had before."

With that, she pulled back to look at him, and finally quit holding anything in, finally let him see the full measure of hot and dirty desire in her gaze. "Will you give it to me, baby?"

Chapter Three

ဢ

"Oh, I'll give it you, all right," Jordan promised her with uncharacteristic fervor. He barely knew what was happening to him, but he was almost to the point of losing control. He suffered an untamed arousal he didn't think he'd ever experienced before and it was difficult to stop himself from yanking down Lynda's lace and kissing her beautiful breasts right there in the club. He longed to have them in his mouth, longed to sink his cock into her hot, sweet cunt.

Damn, he hadn't been in a strip club in a while—only on a few occasions, actually, since college almost twenty years ago—but the sights on the stage were intoxicating. All those bare pussies and round breasts—his cock was about to explode. He'd been hard enough at dinner, just watching Lynda eat shrimp, and now his cock was downright painful, pressing firmly against her thigh. He whispered to her, unable to hide the heat that infused him. "Do you feel what I've got for you in my pants?"

Had Steven heard? He didn't know and didn't much care. That wasn't like him, but such powerful arousal overrode every other concern.

"Mmm, yes," she cooed. "You're big and hard for me, aren't you, baby?"

Had Steven heard *that*? He almost hoped so.

He nodded numbly, watching the girl on the stage run that feathery boa back and forth between her legs and enjoying the heated show—but at the same time knowing they had to get out of there, *now*. He had to get Lynda back to her apartment where he could get inside her sweet, luscious pussy. Nothing else mattered.

"We need to go," he said low, his hand snaking higher up her thigh, under her dress now, and taking the lace fabric with it. He could sense Steven watching, could feel the guy's eyes on his hand, and he knew he should stop for Lynda's sake, but he needed to touch her so desperately, needed to stroke that sweet, soft mound, feel the wetness through her panties.

If he wasn't mistaken, *she* looked excited, too. "Okay."

A good enough reason to pull his hand out from under her dress. In a few minutes, he'd shove the dress up, yank the top down, and have *all* of her.

"We're taking off, Steven."

His friend laughed. "That's a shame—this was getting good."

Trying to pull his mind back to business, just for a second, he stepped past Steven and shook Nate's hand. "I hope to hear from you soon."

"You can bet on it," Nate said, and as Jordan ushered Lynda to the door, he felt on top of the world. He'd just cultivated a promising business arrangement and would soon plunge his cock into the woman he was wild about. Did life get any better?

Well, life might be better if his damned hard-on didn't *hurt* so fucking bad.

But soon, baby, so soon, I'm gonna give you all the cock you can handle.

He held the words inside, though, for fear they'd sound too rough, forceful. He *felt* forceful, but he didn't want her to know that if he could possibly contain it. It wasn't like him, and it surely wasn't what Lynda wanted in a man.

Outside, the party still raged, drinking and laughter and music flowing from every door. On a balcony above a strip club across the street, girls in lingerie flung shiny strands of beads into the cheering crowd. But Jordan felt as if they were in a vacuum, like nothing else mattered but him and Lynda, getting her home, getting her naked.

They walked quickly through the crowd and he noticed other men ogling her. Normally, that might bother him, but tonight it filled him with caveman-like masculine pride. Damn, she did look good in that dress—even hotter than earlier now that the clingy skirt had ridden up her thighs a bit and the lace that held her breasts had gotten lowered a little in the club. Earlier, she had looked sexy and classy in it—but now the slight tugs in fabric made her look like a woman to be ravished.

As they made their way out of the party district, crowds thinned and the night grew darker around them. Her shop and apartment were only a few blocks away, but Jordan was beginning to wonder if he could make it. He simply didn't want to wait. He thought his poor, aching cock had been punished enough.

Still, he kept putting one foot swiftly in front of the other, willing the distance to pass faster and get them there. He squeezed her hand in his and yearned for more sensation—him touching her, her touching him. He felt like a bottle rocket in that last moment before it shoots and explodes—wholly combustible, ready to blow.

As they walked, he glanced down at her, at the high color in her cheeks, at the sexy stiletto heels that moved with just as much speed and purpose as his own strides. Then his gaze settled on her breasts, which bounced lightly with every fast step she took—and that was it. The last vestiges of control vanished.

"Damn it, I can't make it," he growled as reckless need roared through him.

She looked up, clearly startled. "What do you mean?"

Turning to brace his hands on her bare shoulders, he pushed until he'd pinned her against the nearest brick wall. He knew a few people traversed the sidewalk—just across the narrow street, and up ahead of them as well—but it didn't matter. Curling his fingers tight into her soft ass, he pressed his rampant erection to the juncture of her thighs and thrust his tongue into her mouth in a hard kiss. "Have to have you," he heard himself mutter through clenched teeth.

Below, he heard her shocked breath, felt her body tense. With only a few streetlights illuminating the air, he more sensed than saw the look of surprise in her beautiful eyes.

He should have stopped, but he didn't, *couldn't*. Looking hurriedly about, he spotted an open wrought iron gate just a few yards away, between two buildings, which surely led to a courtyard around back. Locking his grip around her elbows, he took backward steps, pulling her through the gate that teemed with wild, twisting vines.

Once within the narrow passageway, he pressed her body back against the brick with his own, then drew with both hands at the stretchy lace concealing her breasts. It came down with ease, baring the lovely mounds. He closed his hands over them in a firm massage, letting her hard, pointed nipples jut into his palms.

He kissed her again, with rough urgency, then sank his hungry mouth to the dark pink tip of one breast. She cried out softly as he suckled, drawing her nipple deeper, as deep as he could, and savoring the hard, beaded feel of it on his tongue, trapped there against the roof of his mouth. With his free hand, he molded her other breast, then pinched the peak between thumb and forefinger.

Next thing he knew, he'd abandoned her breasts to unzip his pants. His painful cock burst free and even just that was a relief. He shoved the lace dress up his sweet Lynda's hips, then reached for her hot pussy. Her slit was soaking wet through tiny, filmy-feeling panties that let her moisture leak readily onto his fingers. He couldn't resist lifting his hand to his mouth, sucking her juices off in one brisk move, before thrusting back between her legs to jerk the stretchy undies aside.

Up to now, he'd heard her labored breath, a quiet panting sound, felt the way her fingernails clawed into his back through his jacket or down his shirt in front. But when he reached for her ass, used one hand to lift one of her thighs over his hip, and plunged his aching shaft into her silky moisture, she let out a hot sob of pleasure. "Ah, *yeah,*" he groaned at finally being inside her, finally feeling her smooth, tight walls close around him, giving him a hot little cave to move in and out of.

He fucked her slow and hard at first, making her feel every powerful thrust, making her moan with each, watching the sweet agony on her beautiful face. He wanted to somehow be in her deeper than ever before, make her feel his cock even farther up inside her. "*More,*" he said through still-gritted teeth. "Need to give you *more.*"

With that, he pulled out and dragged her by the hand deeper into the passageway until, indeed, it opened into a courtyard. Quiet, dark—he reminded himself that these were homes and someone might be in them. But on the other hand, this was the French Quarter and he couldn't believe they were the only couple to ever indulge in an urgent fuck here before. They weren't really bothering anyone—so he wasn't going to stop now. Hell, he couldn't have stopped if he'd wanted to— that was how they'd ended up here in the first place.

His eyes fell on a wooden staircase lining the building's back wall at the edge of the small court. Tall bougainvillea grew over the outside of the banister, arcing upward. Without a word, he turned Lynda around, facing her away from him. Taking the cue, she leaned over at the waist, bracing her hands on the steps. Without delay, he grabbed her hips and rammed his damp erection back inside that sweet, perfect cunt. She cried out, but no lights came on and Jordan felt as good as alone with her.

He didn't fuck her slowly any longer—this time he went hard and fast, pummeling her with the full power of his stiff cock. "Tell me you feel it deeper," he demanded.

"I do, honey, I do," she whimpered.

"Tell me you love it deep."

"I love it deep! Oh God, I love it!"

Her hot acquiescence fueled him to pound into her harder, harder, never stopping, never holding back, giving her everything he could deliver. Her cries sounded at each hot stab of his shaft, bringing him closer and closer to explosion. Hell, it was a miracle he'd held out *this* long, all things considered, so he didn't try to wait. He let it build, felt his balls growing fuller—tighter—as they slammed into her, and then let it go. "I'm coming, baby—coming so fucking hard!"

It spilled out in hot rushes and he imagined his semen coating the pink inner walls of her pussy, somehow making her more his.

And then sanity returned.

Jesus God, what had he just done? What the hell had come over him?

Still inside her, he let his arms close around her waist as he leaned near, to hug her from behind. "I'm so sorry, precious. So, so sorry."

"What?" he heard her utter softly.

Extracting his erection, he helped her stand up and turn around. Damn it, he couldn't believe this. "I'm sorry," he said again, letting his arms fold back around her, using one hand to press her head to his chest, partly because he wanted to be close to her and partly because he didn't want to see the horror that surely shone in her eyes.

"For...what?"

Poor, sweet baby—she sounded disoriented.

"I'm so sorry I did this," he said above her, breathless. "I can't believe that I...that I...dragged you back here like some kind of freaking animal and practically...forced you." Shame rained down on him like ash from those earlier fireworks. A beautiful woman comes into his life and he treats her like *this*?

"You didn't force me, Jordan," she said, lifting her head. "I promise."

He ran one hand back through his hair, exasperated. "Well, I sure as hell didn't give you much of a choice. And I wouldn't blame you if you never wanted to see me again." He let out a sigh, at a loss for how to apologize enough.

As she raised her gaze to his, he peered down into eyes filled with more understanding than he deserved.

"This isn't me," he said, shaking his head. "This isn't the kind of guy I am at all." He ran another hand through his hair, feeling a little disoriented himself. "Damn, must be the wine or something."

"Yeah," she agreed, nodding, "it was potent."

"But still, damn it, I don't know what got into me. I didn't consider your feelings at all, and I feel like a piece of shit."

Still stunned by the whole event, Lynda reached up to stroke his arm, an effort to comfort him. "Baby, it's okay. I...didn't mind." She sucked in her breath. Okay, there, she'd said it. Kind of.

Only he didn't quite believe it—she could tell. He continued shaking his head. "That's sweet of you, precious— truly. But you're just saying that, trying to make me feel like less of an ass. You couldn't possibly have *wanted* something like that."

But I did. I loved it insanely and I want more, more, more.

Although it was hard to get such words out when *his* words implied there might be something wrong with her if she'd really enjoyed their fast and frantic little fuckfest. Clearly, he thought his actions deeply reprehensible.

And she'd *tried* to tell him how she really felt, damn it. Perhaps too feebly, yet maybe that was because she couldn't help sensing the repulsion he'd feel if he really *understood* what she yearned for.

In addition to her own selfish concerns, though, she just plain hated seeing her sweet lover so overwrought simply from having unplanned sex in an alleyway. God, what would he think if he found out she'd done this before, more than once? Hell, for all she knew, she'd probably done it in this very same alley.

"Can you ever forgive me?" He lifted a warm palm to cup her cheek.

"There's nothing to forgive," she said softly. Maybe she should have said more, tried again to tell him the truth, but her chief goal at the moment was simply to make him feel better, and this seemed the easiest way.

"You're too sweet to me."

"I disagree. You're easy to be sweet to."

He gave his head a rakish tilt. "Is there anything I can do to make this up to you?"

She let out a long sigh. *Please stop feeling so guilty, Jordan.* How could he feel so horribly over something she would probably now masturbate to the memory of?

But maybe part of this was *her* fault. She wished she'd managed to react as she normally would have while he'd been fucking her, but she hadn't. She'd simply been too shocked and overwhelmed to spew out the usual "more, baby, more"s. And she'd been trying not to scream too loudly only for the practical reason of not wanting to draw a crowd and ruin the fun.

I loved it. Just say that. But she couldn't. He'd think she was a total slut. Which wasn't a term she'd ever really been offended by, except when used as a blatant or nasty insult. But she didn't want Jordan to think of her that way. Now it was just too late for honesty.

So she finally replied with, "Well, yes, I can think of *one* thing you can do." Something that would take the focus off his guilt and put it back onto pleasure.

"Name it, precious."

"Take me home and give me the thorough licking I was promised."

A slow, heated grin formed on his face. "*That's* my punishment?"

"Torturous, I know."

"I'll take that kind of torture any day."

* * * * *

Lynda leaned up against the headboard, wearing nothing but the little yellow confection Jordan had given her earlier. Lacy cups held her breasts snugly, creating deep cleavage, and a yellow ribbon tied the nightie together just beneath. Pale chiffon wafted downward from there to her hips, parting in the center to bare her stomach. As Jordan had requested earlier, she didn't bother with the matching panties, so when she spread her legs across the sheets for Jordan's perusal, the move put her pussy on bold display.

"*Mmm*, my hot, precious baby," he said on a low moan. He stood naked at the foot of the bed, his majestic cock standing at thick and glorious attention.

A flash of memory rushed through her head—an hour earlier, him ramming all nine inches into her with spectacular force—and the jolting recollection made her hotter than she already was. She looked him in the eye, licked her upper lip, and knew instinctively that her pink folds glistened for him.

"You look so damn pretty."

Drawing his gaze from her eyes to her waiting cunt, Jordan crawled slowly toward her from the foot of the bed, the muscles in his shoulders and back shifting beneath his olive skin, sexy and smooth with every move he made.

His strong hands rose to massage her inner thighs, the sensation spiraling inward and forcing Lynda to let out a high-pitched sigh. Then he bent close, closer, to blow on her pussy. She shuddered softly, then watched as her man dragged the very tip of his tongue lightly over her clit.

"Oh," she gasped as the pleasure rippled upward.

Then he did it again, slightly firmer this time, with a little more tongue, and the pleasure pushed deeper, nearing her very core.

"Yes," she whispered. "Lick me, lover." Then, on impulse, she lifted her hands to her breasts and squeezed, only to realize she couldn't feel them very well through the thick cups. Damn lace.

But she bit back her frustration and instead reached downward, running her hands through Jordan's dark hair. She moved her fingernails gently over his scalp, knowing the area could be one of those unexpected erogenous zones, then listened to his responsive moan.

He sank fully into his work now, raking his wet tongue deeply through her furrows, clearly trying to taste her very essence and make her feel his ministrations as thoroughly as possible. She relished watching him lavish such affections on her, liked seeing her wetness around his lips and on the tip of his sexy nose when he looked up at her. The sweet, hot joy echoed through her body and had her spreading her legs even wider, wider, as she suffered the impossible urge to somehow open herself to him even more.

Mmm, she couldn't help thinking that maybe a little lace was okay if it got her *this*, and as he ate at her with unconcealed enthusiasm that rocked her very soul, the memory of the alley gave her hope for her man's darker, more animalistic side.

Well, a little, anyway. If he hadn't freaked out about it so much.

And yet, once more, as Jordan's skilled tongue pressed deep now, gaining entry into her wet passageway, she was forced to ask herself, what was so boring about *this*? His head between her legs, delivering pure, searing pleasure? *Nothing.* No one could call such an eager tongue on such a sexy and sophisticated man boring.

Except that…

She wanted it *all*!

She wanted *this—and* the alley.

Maybe she didn't mind lace—if there was sometimes leather.

She longed for lovemaking—but also for hot and dirty fucking.

She hated realizing that, even now, even as she soaked up pleasure from him—but it only drove home how very true it was and how deep her needs ran.

Yet, thankfully, when Jordan's attention turned back to her swollen and oh-so-sensitive clit, Lynda stopped thinking. Each delightful stroke of his tongue radiated pure fire that blazed through her, all the way to the tips of her toes.

She watched him again, getting caught up in the unrefined heat of sex. She said, "Yes, baby, lick me. Harder, harder." And as his hands curled beneath her, cupping her ass, as he tilted and lifted her to his hungry mouth, she remembered he thought this was punishment, and heard herself saying, "Such a bad boy you are. Lick me, you bad boy. Lick me." Damn, but it would have been a fine time to have a little riding crop in her hand, to flick his bare ass while he worked at her.

She pressed her palms to his head, held him to her pussy, moved against him, working toward the climax she suddenly needed so fucking bad.

Control.

That's what Lynda liked in sex.

To feel control over her lover.

Or to have her lover feel control over *her*.

At this particular moment, she was the dominatrix, punishing her naughty boy, making him do her bidding, towering over him and forcing him to lick her until she came. God, yes. Just watching her hands, holding him there, at her mercy, made her pump against his mouth harder and harder…

Until the orgasm exploded through her like a fireball shooting through the night sky. She heard herself screaming, hot sobs of pleasure, as the climax racked her body with uncontrollable spasms. *Yes. Oh yes.*

When Jordan raised his head, she yearned to tell him everything. *I just came so hard because you gave me the feeling I was controlling you, making you give me what I wanted. And I loved our fuck earlier in the alley because I gave you the control then, let myself be taken by you.*

A psychologist, she feared, might well have a field day with such sexual needs. But Lynda didn't care. She only knew what made her feel good. And she only wished she could share it all with Jordan without fear of his rebuff.

Moving up over her body, Jordan pushed his cock into her moisture, sinking deep. "Oh *yeah,*" she said on a deep moan. She'd always loved that glorious moment of entry, but with Jordan, it was even better.

He lowered a warm kiss to her mouth and she tasted herself on him.

"Mmm, I taste good," she teased, smiling up at him as he began to thrust slow inside her welcoming cunt.

His dark eyes sparkled. "That's hot as hell."

So it turned him on that she liked the taste of her own pussy. *Oh, lover, if you only knew…* And just like earlier, in the alley, she couldn't help thinking maybe there was hope for him yet.

"I love you, Lynda," he said, his voice soft and deep.

She gulped. He'd never said it before. No one had — not since Charlie, and that had been in another lifetime.

She'd fantasized about this — fantasized that someone like Jordan might really fall in love with her. And she knew in that perfect moment that she loved him, too. Hell, she *had* to love the guy to be willing to deny herself the harder pleasures she was accustomed to, and to try to make herself into a new sort of person for him. "I love you, too, honey," she said.

"Yeah?" he whispered. His soft, surprised grin was shockingly boyish and utterly endearing, and she wrapped her arms around his neck to pull him down for another hot kiss.

"A lot," she whispered.

"Oh, precious," he replied. "Me, too. Me, too."

And then he increased his thrusts, taking them deeper, harder, making her sob with joy, and she drank it up, all the sweetness, all this fresh, new, amazing love. "I'm coming, baby," he said then, his voice husky. "I'm coming!"

And in those pristine moments as he filled her with the evidence of this new love, she truly didn't care about what the sex was or what it wasn't. She only knew she was committed to this man now, completely, and that she would never let anything as trivial as a lack of leather—or an overabundance of lace—part them.

* * * * *

They lay in bed, cuddling after another long round of sex, and Lynda found herself feeling uncharacteristically girlish and dreamy. She'd been right—she did want the whole hearts-and-flowers, lifelong companion thing. Not that Jordan had mentioned anything that equated to "lifelong", but "I love you" was as close as Lynda had come to such a thing in a very long time.

Jordan raked caressing fingertips across her bare stomach. "You know you can tell me anything—share anything with me—right?"

She looked up at him, wondering why he'd say such a thing. "Of course," she lied. "Why?"

"Because…sometimes I feel like there's something you're not telling me, some part of you I can't quite see. And I want us to be totally open with one another, precious, not have any secrets."

This was her opening, *again*—no doubt about it.

But she couldn't bear to risk marring the perfection she felt in this moment.

It was her own fault and she knew it, yet she was now officially *serious* about transforming into the sort of woman who didn't need anything kinky to feel satisfied. She'd thought she was serious before, but love made a big difference on the satisfaction scale—it made up for a lot.

"You've got all of me, Jordan." And she really meant it. Because the rest was getting tossed out the window, right this minute. Kink was *not* a necessary part of a relationship.

"You're sure?" he asked, nuzzling closer. She still wore her yellow lace-and-chiffon negligee and had decided she was even starting to like it. After all, Jordan *loved* it—he kept telling her how pretty she looked in it. And even if it had kept her breasts feeling a little neglected, her pussy hadn't suffered at all. *Trade-off, trade-off, trade-off*, she reminded herself. It was all a trade-off, and that was okay.

"Absolutely," she promised, then leaned in for another kiss. To her surprise, she could still taste remnants of her juices on his lips. "And if you want to know what's on my mind right now, it's how incredibly you licked me tonight."

A hint of wicked pride entered his gaze. "Your pussy is inspiring."

They laughed softly together—and Lynda got an idea. She wanted her pussy to inspire her lover even more, and she thought she knew exactly how to accomplish that. Right now, her mound was covered with pale brown hair, well-trimmed but not shaven. She usually kept it bare, but she hadn't shaved it since she'd met Jordan—afraid he'd be shocked or think it too naughty, too much of a sign that she was a wild woman.

"You know what I bet would make eating me even nicer for you?"

"I can't imagine," he chuckled. "What's that, precious?"

"Well," she began, tentatively, even shyly, "when we were in the strip club, I noticed how most of the dancers were smooth down there, no hair. And watching you lick me, well…I wondered if maybe that would make it better for you."

When she gathered the courage to meet his gaze, he looked thoroughly excited. "I'd never ask you to do that for me, baby, but…yeah, it probably *would* be nice. Although, that seems like a dangerous place to shave," he added.

Little did he know that she was an expert at such hair removal, with years of practice. "Well, maybe I'll get brave enough to give it a try," she offered. "We'll see."

Not that this meant she was still trying to ease Jordan into *her* brand of fucking.

No, she was going to *love* all the lace he gave her. She was going to love their sex, no matter how vanilla. And most importantly, she was going to love *him*.

If she could find little things to excite them both a bit more — like a denuded cunt — all the better. But she was in love and committed to being content, and even happy, with the same kind of sex *most* people had, once and for all.

Chapter Four

∞

"It's been good talking to you. I'll get back to you soon." Jordan hung up the phone, pleased that the man he'd met at the strip club the other night wanted a quote on a sizable order of merchandise and sounded like he planned on doing business. Then he set about keying the order into the computer.

Yet as he typed in item numbers and quantities, his mind drifted to the same place it always drifted lately, to Lynda.

He'd spoken words of love to only a few special women in his thirty-eight years, and she was the first in a very long while. And though he'd always enjoyed his bachelor status, he was starting to think that maybe, just maybe, the time was coming to share his life with a woman in that all-important way—that maybe he wanted to get married.

So he loved this woman, yet...he found himself wanting to do awful things with her. Like that rough sex in the alley. He still didn't know where that had come from. And he still suffered some guilt for getting so intimate with her in that strip club in front of Steven. Admittedly, he'd been turned on by the lovely erotic dancers. And Lynda had looked beyond incredible in that pretty lace dress. But that still didn't explain what had come over him. He'd never wanted a woman with such urgency before, and he continued feeling like a brute for it, so it had to stop.

In addition to that, he remained plagued with wondering what she was holding back from him. Even through all they'd shared the other night and how understanding she'd been, and later how passionate, he'd still sensed her holding something inside, not being completely forthcoming with him—even when she'd denied it. Was it just in his head?

Well, he knew one thing that *wasn't* in his head—his hard-on. The damn thing remained a near-constant in his life, always keeping him on edge because it never went away for long. Now, he felt his cock growing, rising, over the memory of fucking her in the alley. He didn't want to salivate over the recollection, but he'd clearly enjoyed what they'd done— which he just plain didn't understand.

Only now, when he fantasized about it, he found himself imagining that he pushed up her dress to find a smooth, bare pussy—which had started with her offer to shave for him. He'd kind of thought only strippers and porn stars did that— but the idea definitely appealed, and was adding to his arousal problems.

Just then, the door opened and Steven walked in. "Hey, bud, my binocs in yet?"

Jordan nodded. "Just came this morning." Steven had ordered a set of super-high-powered binoculars last week.

As Jordan reached under the counter to get them, he added, "Heard from Nate this morning, too. Thanks again for the recommendation and introduction."

Steven let out a slight laugh. "You weren't the only one who was glad you changed your mind and stopped by. I have to admit, I thoroughly enjoyed meeting your girl, and Nate and his friend thought she was a real looker, too. She's very hot, man, and also very cool."

Jordan smiled at the description. "Yeah, she's pretty amazing, isn't she?"

"You ever want to share, just let me know," Steven added with a wink.

But Jordan was shaking his head before Steven even finished talking. "Not gonna happen."

Yet after Steven had paid for his binoculars and exited the store, leaving Jordan in quiet surroundings again, a new fantasy entered his head, unbidden. He envisioned Lynda back in Michael's with him — back in her tight lace dress — fucking him while all the other guys watched in awe. He saw them sitting in a plush chair placed up on the stage, her straddling him, the dress at her hips. He saw her thrusting her gorgeous breasts at his mouth, the lace pulled down just as it had been in the alley, as she rode him, grinding hard.

Before Jordan knew it, he found himself leaving the front counter, heading into his office. Taking a seat at his desk, he unzipped his pants and let his erection burst free. As usual, a relief — but he needed more. He took his thick cock in his fist and began to pump. Behind his closed eyes, he imagined Lynda's pussy squeezed him instead of his hand, imagined her beautiful face lost in passion, imagined her breasts bouncing before his eyes until she came, screaming and moaning, as the men surrounding them yelled their raucous approval. And then *Jordan* came — on his desk and pants. Shit. Not even time to reach for a tissue. And a fine example of the insanity the woman wrought in him.

Damn it, what was happening to him? Why did he want things with her he'd never wanted with anyone else? And why did it have to happen with a woman who he'd fallen in love with, a woman he'd never want to offend or hurt or risk in any way.

He looked down at his still-erect cock and said, "You picked a fine time to start liking kinky shit."

* * * * *

It was Monday morning and Jordan had just spent an invigorating weekend with Lynda.

On Saturday, they'd had breakfast together at L'Madeleine's on Jackson Square, then walked along the Mississippi, hand in hand, watching barges and fishing boats and soaking up a sunny day. They'd listened to a little jazz in an open air cafe near the French Market while sipping on hurricanes, then rented a movie and headed back to her apartment to watch it over pizza. They'd made love for an hour before falling asleep.

On Sunday, they'd driven the short distance to Metairie, where Jordan had introduced her to his parents and younger sister, Pam, along with Pam's husband Chad and their two kids, a niece and nephew of twelve and ten who Jordan loved to spoil rotten. Lynda had been nervous, he could tell, but had finally relaxed over dinner in his parents' dining room and later told him how much she liked them. They'd liked her, too—it had been obvious. His family was slightly well-to-do but not stodgy, and he suspected his mother appreciated in Lynda that same genuine quality that so attracted him to her, as well.

That evening they'd had dinner back in the Quarter—casual Italian at a place on Decatur, then headed back to her place again. He didn't sleep over last night, but it had been hard to drag himself home to his house out on St. Charles in the Garden District after more incredible sex. She'd sucked his cock so well that he'd felt himself falling in love with her more every hot second, and he'd returned the favor, having discovered that licking Lynda's pussy was his favorite thing to do with his mouth these days. If he were forced to make a choice between Lynda's cunt and food, he'd happily starve.

Now he stood behind the counter, caught up on his work and a little bored. Business was good, but Monday mornings were typically slow.

So, of course, his thoughts turned to his sweet lover.

And then his eyes, too.

He'd told her that he had, on occasion, demonstrated a few of the tiny spy cameras he sold by honing in on her at Cajun Lady, which set diagonally up the street from Spy Games. Customers seemed to find it amusing when he'd say, "Let's spy on my girlfriend for a minute, see what she's up to." Today, no customers, but a new camera-in-sunglasses gadget that he hadn't yet tried out.

Removing the glasses from a display shelf behind him, he slid them on and peered out the window toward Lynda's shop. Then he touched the nearly invisible zoom feature above the left lens, holding the miniscule button in until the camera narrowed tightly on her door. A slight shift to the left and there she was—his lady stood behind the counter talking to a young woman with bouncy auburn hair, a pretty face and ample breasts held in a low-cut camisole. A customer, he supposed.

Lynda smiled as she spoke, then reached across the counter, lifting her hand gently to the girl's chest to touch a large pendant hanging there. Lynda was into jewelry—always admiring it, especially anything antique. She slid her fingers beneath the pendant, cupping it to look more closely—and he suffered the first hint of a hard-on.

Shit. Why? What was so erotic about *that*?

But then he figured it out. Another girl. There was nothing sexual about the move, but something about watching Lynda touch another girl, even that innocently, was enough to spark arousal.

Because his passion for her was growing more intense with each passing day.

Sure, he'd kept it mostly under control this weekend, but that didn't mean he hadn't had a barrage of dirty thoughts about her running like a film strip through his head. He continued having the raging urge to do things with Lynda that he'd never done before.

At first, when this had started, he'd thought she simply inspired powerful fantasies, but the longer it went on, the more he couldn't deny it—this was about more than fantasizing. This was about truly wanting to indulge in hedonistic acts he'd never before had any real interest in. His lack of control with Lynda after leaving the strip club had proven that, beyond a doubt. And he didn't know what to do about it.

"Morning."

Jordan took off the spy glasses to see Ginger Larkins, his second-in-command at Spy Games, walking in the door. When he'd first hired Ginger six years earlier, she'd only minded the store on weekends, but before long she'd wound up fixing the computers, keeping the books, you name it—and now he'd be lost without her. "Hey, Gin. Good weekend?"

"Two dates," she replied with a confident shrug. The tall, shapely brunette exuded a cool confidence he'd noticed the first time he'd met her, at the tender age of twenty-five. Now, at thirty-one, she was even more attractive, and more self-assured as well. Her raven hair hung in a straight, blunt cut to her shoulders, and a sizable tattoo—something like a swirling spider web—stretched from her neck down onto one shoulder. She wore lots of rings, all different in design, claiming each was either a gift from—or just reminded her of—a particular lover.

"With?" he asked of the dates.

"On Friday, a guy who plays blues guitar sometimes at Tipitina's. On Saturday, a girl who bartends at The Funky Pirate." Ginger had announced she was bisexual a few years ago and since then, men and women had seemed completely interchangeable to her. Although she'd told Jordan she eventually expected to settle down with one person, for now, she enjoyed what she called "ultimate sexual freedom".

"How'd they go?"

"Guitar player, thumbs down," she said. "I thought he'd swallow my face when he kissed me. Bartender, though…maybe." She shrugged again. "Kissed much better anyway. All over."

Soon after meeting, he and Ginger had ended up in bed together one night after too much to drink, and that one encounter had somehow started a friendship in addition to their working relationship. But ever since Ginger had swung into her alternative lifestyle, Jordan had felt as if he didn't know her very well anymore, as if it distanced them—he supposed he just couldn't relate to her any longer. Thus her easily shared sex tales seldom affected him much one way or the other.

Today, unexpectedly, however, he found his dick growing hard at the vision of Ginger kissing another girl, and he couldn't help but wonder—was something inside him suddenly changing? Or was this all about Lynda? He feared his untamable passion for her was now keeping him in such a constant state of arousal that it took less than ever to turn him on.

As Ginger shed her stylish black leather jacket, heading to the back room to hang it up, Jordan let his mind wander.

To girls kissing.

And then more. Touching each other's breasts, licking each other...everywhere.

He'd seen it in the porn movies he occasionally ordered on pay-per-view if he was feeling a little horny, not dating anybody, and wanted some help getting himself off. Hell, he'd even seen a little bit of it on Bourbon Street. He understood well enough that most guys got into it—when he was younger, he'd enjoyed the notion, too. But it had never made him as hot as it was making him in this very moment.

Girls kissing.

He imagined it again.

Ginger kissing her bartender girlfriend.

Then...*Lynda*. Kissing her customer in the low-cut top.

He wondered...

Would she ever?

Could she want to?

Of course not.

This was Lynda, the woman he was seriously considering proposing to soon. She was sexy as hell and exciting in bed, but…nothing about her had ever really said "untraditional" to him.

Yet then an idea entered his head. Was it just a fantasy? Or…one more thing, one more burning urge, that he longed to make into a reality?

Glancing toward the back room, he shook his head at his own insane thoughts. Was he *seriously* considering this? *Seriously?*

No, no way. He couldn't do it. It was over the top, especially given that they'd never even discussed such a thing. It would be a huge violation of trust and she'd hate him forever.

Unless…he made it completely clear that it was okay if she didn't want to do it, that he was just putting it out there as an idea, a possibility.

It would be risky even then, though.

And it was probably stupid to even contemplate such a wild thought.

But he couldn't seem to control those damnable reckless urges for her that had begun plaguing him the last week or so, and the fantasy in his head had him *so* hard and *so* very hungry for her.

He weighed the factors and found a few things already in his favor. Lynda loved sex—that was clear—their sex life was great. And *he* loved the way she looked in lacy lingerie, so another little bit of it could only up the heat. And she hadn't seemed to mind watching the strippers on that steamy night last week—she'd even seemed somewhat interested, kind of flirtatious about it.

This was a lot different than watching a stripper, of course—a *hell* of a lot different. And he should probably be hung by his balls for even contemplating this. He loved the woman—and he couldn't quite believe he was going to risk upsetting her by doing something she'd probably find shocking and offensive.

But his cock disagreed.

And his cock seemed to have a mind of its own lately, especially when it came to his sweet Lynda.

And...well, hadn't they agreed they'd be open and honest with each other? Even if he still feared she was holding something back, that didn't mean *he* should hold back, right?

Of course, no matter how he tried to justify it, it remained an insane thing to do. Unthinkable. Unconscionable.

And he almost *knew* he'd end up regretting it.

But when the visions in his head grew more and more detailed with each passing second, it was just too hot and beautiful for him to push down.

His heart in his throat, he looked up at Ginger when she came back through the doorway. "Hey, Gin, I have a proposition for you."

Chapter Five

ϾϽ

"I don't know if I can go on like this," Lynda told Liz over beignets at the Café du Monde on Wednesday afternoon. They sat in the shade of the famous green-and-white awning, eating pastries and drinking café au laits. "I thought I could, but now I'm not sure."

"I *knew* pretending to be something you weren't was a mistake," Liz said, using one hand to shove a lock of hair behind her ear and the other to lift a bite of the sugary confection to her mouth.

Lynda pursed her lips. "*You* pretended to be something you weren't when you met Jack," she couldn't resist reminding her. In fact, she'd loaned Liz a racy dress just for the occasion.

"Yeah, but the act didn't hold up long, if you recall."

Lynda sighed wistfully. "No, just long enough for Jack to see a few glimpses of your inner vixen and decide he needed to show you everything you were missing." If only Jordan could be so bold and sexually creative as the tales she'd heard from Liz about her sizzling courtship with Jack. "The problem is, with Jordan, I'm going in the wrong direction—covering *up* my inner vixen. And I thought I could do it, thought I had convinced myself that regular sex is enough, but today I'm feeling all hot and horny and as if regular sex could *never* fulfill me."

"Then you have to tell him."

"Do you know what I want?" she asked, ignoring Liz's reply as she got on a roll. "I want a man who loves me *and* who wants me to be just as wild and dirty as I naturally am.

But I just don't think I can have both of those things—at least not with Jordan."

Across from her, Liz lowered her beignet to her plate, looking disgusted. "Well, if you don't tell him what you want, *of course* you can't. But for all you know, he'll *love* finding out you're such an adventurous woman!"

"I can't tell him," Lynda said morosely.

As a horse and carriage clopped by a few yards away on Decatur, Liz flashed a look of disapproval. "And just why not?"

"I've tried—sort of—and I can't seem to get it out. Even when I have the perfect opportunity. And I think it's because…well, I can't bear to mar the way he thinks of me. No man has ever thought I was so perfect or been so proud to take me places and introduce me to people. No man has ever looked at me like I'm so flawless. And no matter how I try, I just can't risk messing that up."

Liz appeared confused now, not to mention aghast— understandably, Lynda supposed. "So you're saying you're willing to lose him or break up with him, as opposed to trying to save the relationship by telling him about the real you?"

Numbly, Lynda nodded. She knew it sounded stupid, but she'd been thinking it over and it was the conclusion she'd drawn. "Liz, I just don't *get* guys like Jordan. I get guys like *Charlie*." She'd told Liz all the horror stories about her ex. "All through high school and after, right up until I got married, the only guys who were really crazy about me were…well, the ones who turned out to be lowlife losers, and I would have seen it from the beginning if I'd looked, because the signs were always there.

"After Charlie, of course, I quit paying attention. Sex just became a social thing and I made that clear to any guy I hooked up with, so I quit even *thinking* about whether the guys were good ones or bad, as long as they had a nice cock and knew how to use it.

"Even lately, after I started realizing I might want more from a guy than just sex, I never really expected a man like Jordan to enter my life, or to think I was worthy of him. He's just too wonderful. And if I can't have him the way I want him... Well, if we split up, I'd just prefer that he remember me the way he *thinks* of me, not the way I really am. And if I tell him the truth, I'm almost sure we'll split up, so why mar his image of me?"

Liz let out a derisive sigh. "Look, I understand why you don't want to mar his perfect vision—but this is *not* the Lynda I know and love. The Lynda *I* know is honest and forthright and doesn't care if anyone doesn't like it. She's bold and outgoing and gets what she wants. And mostly, the Lynda I know is *happy*. You haven't seemed like *any* of those things lately, and I think if you're honest with Jordan, no matter what happens, you'll at least get *you* back. Know what I mean?"

Linda let out a long, tired breath. She did know what Liz meant. In fact, she missed her old self—this new, refined Lynda was for the birds. "I guess," she finally admitted, "but part of the problem here is that I'm in love with him. That really complicates things. There's a lot more at risk by being honest. God, I never thought I'd be choosing between a man I love and...some guy in a bar who'll wear a mask and tie me up and make me call him daddy."

Liz laughed, and so did Lynda, glad she'd injected a little levity into the conversation. Yet Liz still spoke dryly when she said, "What I can't believe is that there's actually any contest. I mean, are you listening to yourself? Seriously considering breaking things off with Jordan just so you can go have wild sex with other people? Without giving him a chance to be wild first? If I didn't know better, I'd say you just need a good orgasm."

"That's the problem. I need *more* than orgasms. I need *sex toys*. I need a little *force*. I need *the forbidden*."

Liz sounded thoroughly exasperated with her now. "And you might be able to have all that stuff — with Jordan — if you'd just suggest it to him and see what he says."

Lynda shoved the last bite of a nearly forgotten beignet in her mouth, at a loss for an answer. "Here's what it boils down to. I want to go through life knowing that one person, just one person, who I really care for, thinks I'm perfect. Apparently, I value that so much that I'm just not willing to risk losing it, even if I lose everything else just to keep it. I know that sounds crazy, but is wanting him to think I'm perfect such a horrible thing?"

* * * * *

Lynda had just changed into a pair of jogging pants and settled on the sofa to watch a little TV on Wednesday evening when the doorbell rang. She looked up, surprised. The only people who really knew she was staying at the apartment right now were Jordan and Liz, and neither was the type to stop by without calling first.

Unless, of course, Jordan wanted to surprise her or something. She hoped not. She was just as in love with him as she'd been a few days ago, but the sobering realization she'd shared with Liz today had her wanting to keep to herself and think all this through.

Everything Liz had said made sense — why give him up without at least seeing if he'd be open to some kinkier sex? — but that damn perfect vision he had of her remained so important to her, *too* important. She didn't think she could go on playing prim and proper Lynda who wears lace and likes the missionary position. Yet she'd never been the delicate kind of woman a man *cherished* — and she didn't want to stop being that, at least in Jordan's memory.

Clicking off the TV with the remote, she rose to open the door, shocked to find Jordan's coworker, Ginger, on the other side. She'd had a few friendly conversations with Ginger at Jordan's shop, but she couldn't imagine what the attractive brunette was doing on her doorstep. As usual, Ginger looked fabulous in a pair of embroidered jeans, a clingy low-cut sweater that accentuated her breasts, and a fitted leather jacket. "Ginger — hi. This is a surprise."

"I know," Ginger replied with a confident half-smile. "I've been sent on a mission."

Lynda blinked. "A mission?" Only then did it fully register that Ginger held a pristine white box with a pink ribbon tied around it. When she held it out, Lynda said, "This is from Jordan?"

The other woman gave a short nod as she handed the gift off to Lynda. "May I come in? He wanted me to wait while you open it."

Lynda backed up a bit, allowing Ginger into the apartment, but she had no idea what was going on and felt a bit disoriented. The big, pretty bow on the box had Jordan written all over it, but the method of delivery was out of character and confusing.

When she looked up, Ginger had headed toward the living room that overlooked St. Peter Street and taken a seat on the couch as comfortably as if she lived there. Still off balance, Lynda sat down in the adjacent easy chair, lowering the white box to her lap. "Um, not that I don't enjoy your company, Ginger, but is there any particular reason Jordan didn't deliver this himself?"

Ginger smiled slightly, as if anticipating the question. "He said he just wanted to try doing things a little differently as a way to spice things up. He said to tell you to trust him and you'll see where this is leading very soon."

Hmm. Spicing things up sounded good — even if not very Jordan-like. But she couldn't imagine what he was planning or what Ginger delivering a gift could possibly have to do with it. "Okay," she said, sounding a bit tentative, even to her own ears.

Yet Ginger, always confident, appeared unfazed by Lynda's uncertainty. "Go ahead. Open it."

"All right." But this was getting weirder by the moment. What the hell was Jordan planning? Although...as odd as it seemed, she couldn't deny the little frisson of anticipation now running like an electrical current along her skin.

She pulled on the pink ribbon, untying it and letting it fall free around the package. Then she removed the lid to find, not surprisingly, some item made of lace resting in a nest of pink tissue paper. And—argh—not only was it lace, it was *white* lace. How much more virginal could you get?

She tried not to cringe, tried not to let the sight ruin the building anticipation.

After a quick glance toward Ginger, she pulled out the lingerie to discover it was a merry widow. Which, as luck would have it, was one of her *favorite* pieces of naughty apparel, so that excited her a little. It would haven been better if it had been constructed of black leather, or even red or black lace—but she knew it would hug her body snugly and make her look sexy for Jordan, albeit a little too saintly for her liking. She spied white stockings with lace tops still nestled in the pink paper.

"Jordan says you have some white strappy heels he likes. He thought they'd look hot with this."

Lynda lifted her eyes back to her visitor. If she hadn't been so sexually experienced, she might have felt a little weird discussing lingerie from her lover with someone she'd only just started getting to know—but fortunately, she was accustomed to talking about such things with ease. "I know the ones he means." And another current of electricity hummed through her then—only because Jordan had never suggested sexy shoes with lingerie before. Another baby step in the right direction.

"You should try it on," Ginger said in that even-toned way of hers as she motioned toward the lace in Lynda's hands. She didn't smile and it was hard to read her face.

"Now? Why?"

Ginger gave her head a slight tilt, and as her expression took on a mischievous quality, her green eyes sparkled. "Jordan wanted me to make sure it fits."

Lynda lowered her chin, trying to understand. "Are you…reporting back to him when you leave here or something? Is he waiting for you somewhere? Or waiting for *me* somewhere?"

The striking girl's hesitation was deliberate, teasing, until she finally said, "Maybe." Clearly a non-answer. For the first time, Ginger cast a small, playful smile. "Remember, Jordan said to trust him. And right now, that means trusting *me*."

Lynda had no idea what to think. Where on earth was this headed?

But if Jordan wanted her to trust him, and trust Ginger, well…she *was* in love with the guy, so she was willing to go with it, at least for now.

Without another word to her visitor, Lynda tucked the merry widow into the box and carried the whole thing down the small hallway to the bedroom.

Standing before the cheval mirror, she slowly stripped out of her clothes. A glance in the glass revealed her bare pussy. After discussing it with Jordan, she'd decided to rid herself of pubic hair. That had been before she'd had a change of heart and concluded that she couldn't keep on like this. But now, she remembered, Jordan *had* seemed at least mildly interested in the idea of her shaving it. Another baby step, maybe, that she'd failed to recognize at the time?

Peering in the mirror head on, she ran the tip of her middle finger through her slit, wondering what Jordan's response to her naked cunt would be. Then she ran her palms lightly up her stomach and onto her breasts, lifting them and teasing the nipples just a bit until they hardened. It didn't take much, though, because she was already aroused. She didn't understand his plan, but the longer it went on, the more excited she was that he simply *had* a plan!

Sitting down on the bed, she rolled the stockings slowly up her legs, then slipped on the barely there thong which, she noticed, possessed little snaps on each side of the front panel for easy removal. *Nice touch*, she thought, and hoped this meant Jordan wanted to rip them off her.

Next, she squeezed into the merry widow itself, pleased that the scalloped edges of the underwire cups just barely covered her nipples and succeeded in making her breasts look larger than their medium size. The lace was sheer, too—and as Lynda spied her flesh through it in the mirror, as well as the pink of her nipples, she suddenly realized that maybe lace wasn't all that bad if it could show off this much of her body.

After attaching the satin garters to the stockings, she grabbed the white strappy heels from her closet and slipped them on, then glanced back in the mirror. She couldn't deny that the stretchy lace felt good shifting against her skin when she moved and that it hugged her breasts deliciously. The lace at the tops of the stockings delivered the same subtle sensation on her upper thighs, making her pussy a little moister.

But besides what she felt in that moment, she also couldn't turn away from what she saw. She looked…beautiful. Not virginal—and not as wholly naughty as some of her old bedroom attire made her appear. But somewhere in between. An angel of sin. A bride of lust.

And for the first time, she truly understood what Jordan saw when he looked at her in lace. She wasn't just *trying* to feel it, or hoping to convince herself lace was okay—she really, truly *felt* it.

And in that shocking moment, she realized she had no desire for leather, or vinyl, or anything rougher. She sincerely loved her body in Jordan's lace.

Maybe *she* was taking baby steps now, too. And maybe, if she got really lucky, she and Jordan could both keep taking these baby steps until they finally met somewhere in the middle. Maybe this was all going to be okay if she just *let* it be.

"Um, Ginger, it fits," she said loudly, suddenly remembering her guest in the other room. "It fits just fine," she added, more softly to herself.

"Show me," Ginger called back.

Show her? Lynda blinked at her own reflection in the mirror. Had she just heard that right? Was Jordan's little messenger coming on to her?

The truth was, pre-Jordan, Ginger was exactly the sort of woman who would have caught Lynda's eye and had her thinking lecherous girl-girl thoughts. But she'd been so busy trying to be "the good Lynda" that it hadn't crossed her mind beyond having noticed that Ginger had a great body with to-die-for breasts.

And if she didn't have Jordan right now, she'd *happily* show Ginger her sexy new ensemble. But she *did* have Jordan. And she was focusing on baby steps right now — baby steps for both of them. Fucking Ginger would hardly be a baby step.

"Show you?" she finally yelled back. She'd considered going into the I'm-flattered-but-have-to-decline type answer, but perhaps it wasn't safe to assume this was a come-on just yet.

"Jordan wants you to."

Lynda's pussy warmed as heat climbed her cheeks. Jordan *wanted* her to?

This was suddenly getting interesting. "He does?" she asked.

"Remember," Ginger said, her voice going a bit silky, "he wants me to *make sure* it fits."

Intrigued, aroused, curious and just generally sucked in now, Lynda left the bedroom, listening to the click of her heels on the hardwood floor. When she emerged into the living room, Ginger stood before her wearing only a revealing pale lavender bra and panty set, along with the same black high-heeled sandals she'd arrived in. The lingerie was constructed of lace, with a few tiny beads and sequins sprinkled over it, and despite Ginger's unerring confidence and the almost-harsh-looking tattoo adorning her neck, the lace not only softened her, but looked sexy as sin. Yes indeed, Lynda was understanding the appeal of lace more and more.

Ginger said nothing at first, and neither did Lynda. But her pussy pulsed with the same rhythm of her heartbeat as she waited to see what came next.

Her sexy visitor crossed the floor to where she stood and gently placed her palms on Lynda's hips, the very touch scintillating. She slid splayed hands up over Lynda's waist, stomach, ever-so slowly, until finally she cupped the outer curves of Lynda's lace-covered breasts. Curling her fingers inward in a soft, sensual squeeze, she raked her thumbs over both beaded nipples through the fabric.

Lynda pulled in her breath at the shock of pleasure, and Ginger's voice came out husky. "You were right. It fits."

But Lynda still didn't understand. Why had Jordan sent her? What did *he* get out of this? Unless he was coming over, too? "Is Jordan coming?"

Ginger responded with a wicked little grin. "Oh, not just yet, probably. But if we get each other off, I'm sure he will."

Lynda blinked, confused. "What?"

"He's watching us." Ginger's smile widened. "He's watching us right now through a tiny secret camera he left here the other day. He wants to see you do another woman, Lynda. And I volunteered for the job."

Chapter Six

ဢ

Lynda couldn't have been more stunned. Had she heard Ginger correctly? It hardly made sense. *Jordan* had snuck a spy camera into her apartment? *Jordan* wanted her to fool around with another girl? While he *watched*?

She found herself looking around the room. "Where? Where is it?"

"He didn't say specifically—just somewhere in that corner." Ginger pointed across the room next to the old mantel. A few houseplants left behind by her old tenants sprinkled the area and seemed likely culprits, as did the magazine rack next to the TV. Lynda stared in that direction, knowing that—unbelievably, amazingly—she was looking at Jordan.

Without warning, Ginger took her hands and Lynda raised her gaze to the other woman's. "Listen to me, though. He wanted me to make it very clear that if you're not into this, it's okay. Just tell me and I'll go away and Jordan will spend the rest of his life making it up to you. That's what he said. He's crazy about you, Lynda, and wanted to surprise you with this because he thought you both might enjoy it—but if you don't want to experiment, he doesn't want you to, either. All right?"

Lynda switched her gaze back toward the corner, focusing on the houseplants—imagining she was staring directly into Jordan's dark, sexy eyes. It was taking her a long moment to truly wrap her mind around this, to truly understand what was happening—but slowly, surely, she was getting it.

She was getting that her dreams were coming true.

Jordan wanted more, just like she did!

And he'd found an exciting, innovative and thrillingly naughty way to get it!

Her pussy spasmed at the thought of what she was about to do—in front of her lover, *because* of her lover, *for* her lover—and knowing that he watched every wicked move she made was going to make the hot encounter that much sweeter.

She only hoped he was able to see the fire in her eyes through his camera when she said to him, "I'm into it, baby," then looked back up at Ginger to repeat the words. "I'm into it."

Her acquiescence seemed to infuse the air with heat. High color rose to Ginger's alabaster cheeks and Lynda felt her nipples pucker tighter against the lace that barely concealed them.

With another short glance toward Jordan's camera, Lynda stepped closer to the other woman, slowly reaching out, letting her hands find Ginger's slender hips. Ginger moved nearer, too, until their breasts brushed together, sending tendrils of fresh desire spiraling downward through Lynda's body. She hissed in her breath at the tender, feminine contact, knowing her passion grew from much more than simply touching the other woman—knowing it came from feeling Jordan's eyes upon her, and from knowing he wanted this. It seemed like no less than a miracle and filled her with a hot joy unlike any she'd ever known.

Ginger's hands rose to Lynda's shoulders as she leaned in for a delicate kiss. Lynda hadn't experienced such soft, supple lips in a while, but again, it was Jordan's presence—even if distant—that brought her pleasure. Another kiss, this one with a bit of tongue, and Lynda found herself arching her breasts against Ginger's larger ones.

Ginger's hands dropped back to Lynda's chest for a slow massage that had her leaning her head back and moaning, and she instinctually followed suit, letting her palms graze over

Ginger's soft skin until she was cupping the outer edges of Ginger's round, lace-covered mounds, stroking her thumbs across the beaded nipples jutting through.

The gentle touches added power to their kisses, and Lynda thought, *Watch me, Jordan, my love. Watch me.* It still seemed like a dream that he could desire this the same way she did. Her cunt felt swollen and achy within the tiny thong panties and she knew they were already soaked.

When Ginger's fingertips closed over the lace that concealed Lynda's breasts, her nails scraping teasingly over the sensitive flesh, Lynda let out a soft moan of anticipation. "Oh yes," she whispered as Ginger pulled down the cups, just enough that Lynda's nipples were freed, perched atop the lightly molded fabric.

Ginger rolled the turgid pink peaks between her fingertips, turning Lynda's breath thready. The kisses had stopped because Ginger wanted to look, clearly wanted to watch herself play with Lynda's breasts. A sensual smile had snuck onto the other woman's face, her eyes seeming glued to Lynda's pointed nipples. "Kiss them," Lynda heard herself breathe without quite planning it.

Ginger's eyes shot up to hers, filled with heated glee to discover Lynda was going to be bolder than Jordan had likely told her to expect. Lynda was glad to have pleased her, but didn't want to wait, so she thrust her breasts forward insistently, causing a soft giggle to erupt from Ginger's throat.

Ginger's tongue played slowly about one nipple, making Lynda's cunt weep with sheer pleasure. She ran her hands through the other woman's raven hair, letting her fingers become tangled at the nape as Ginger licked teasingly around the distended nub. Finally, Ginger closed her lips around it to suckle and the sensation shot straight to Lynda's pussy.

Soon Ginger moved to the other breast, delivering the same heavenly ministrations and leaving Lynda crazed with desire. So crazed that she found herself pushing Ginger toward the sofa until they both fell onto it, Ginger on her back, Lynda on top.

Reaching for Ginger's shoulders, Lynda drew both lavender bra straps down Ginger's silky arms just enough to reveal her ample breasts, as sublime as Lynda had suspected. She moaned at the sight and Ginger offered a naughty little grin upon seeing that Lynda was so taken by them. Lynda's palms closed around the plump mounds of flesh, thrilled to finally have them in her grasp, even though her hands couldn't begin to contain them.

Ginger's long nipples blushed a dark, deep mauve, and drew Lynda's tongue without delay. As she licked the enticingly hard peaks, she instinctively found herself grinding against Ginger's pelvis, their legs interlocking, and again she thought, *Watch me, Jordan. Watch me lick her breasts. Watch me rub against her.*

As Lynda sucked and massaged those voluptuous breasts, Ginger let out low moans that increased Lynda's pleasure. Her own breath grew labored as the tension between them rose, and the only thing missing was Jordan—she found herself wishing he was there with them, watching them even closer, joining in so that she could touch and suck him, too. Still, just knowing his eyes focused on her every move fueled her passion and she imagined him unzipping his pants, pulling out his big cock and stroking it while he watched.

The two women continued moving together until Lynda finally stopped sucking Ginger's breasts in lieu of wiggling her way up Ginger's shapely body a little, just enough to rub their bared chests together. Ah yes, the sweet sensation of hard nipples colliding, teasing one another—the hot and naughty joy of feeling Ginger's dark pearled tips jutting into her softest flesh. Both women breathed heavily, the rhythmic sounds almost creating a sort of music in the quiet air. Of course, from outside, Lynda could make out the distant echo of a lone saxophone, could hear the occasional sound of a honking horn or laughter on the street, but here in the apartment above her shop, the only sounds that mattered were those of sex.

As Ginger's hands closed over Lynda's ass, pressing their pussies closer, Lynda feared she might implode. "God, yes," she heard herself murmur. Although they might have achieved more direct friction from keeping their legs intertwined, Lynda found herself shifting, wanting to rub her cunt directly over Ginger's.

"Mmm," Ginger purred at the change in contact. She slid her legs together so that Lynda could straddle her, move on her. "Yes, rub your pussy on mine, baby," she whispered.

Lynda liked the invitation—it made her cunt even heavier, and a twinge of pleasure arced through her nipples where they raked over Ginger's voluptuous mounds. She rubbed her crotch against Ginger harder, harder, wishing again that Jordan were there as she soaked up every nuance of delight, her garters stretching tight across her ass and her stocking-covered legs moving silkily against Ginger's bare thighs.

* * * * *

Jordan sat in his office, just across the street from Lynda's place, watching in wonder as she so enthusiastically enjoyed his little surprise for her. Part of him couldn't believe it—he'd thought, at best, she'd be nervous and tentative, and *really*, he'd thought she'd be horrified by the suggestion and the blatant way he'd chosen to present it. But she *hadn't* been horrified—or tentative—and a bigger part of him was simply glued to his computer screen, amazed at her.

In one hand, he held his super-hard erection, pumping lightly. With the other, he worked the mouse, which was hooked up to allow him to zoom in or move the camera around if necessary. Right now, he had the lens honed in tightly on the two girls' beautiful breasts, sliding back and forth against one another so energetically that he could almost feel the friction from here. The orbs of flesh looked sumptuous and pretty, still surrounded by the lace that had once covered them but now circled beneath like delicate frames.

He pulled back then, wanting to see more of them. Lynda rode Ginger's pelvis the same as if Ginger had a cock, gyrating atop her cunt just as she did on his shaft when she was working toward orgasm.

Then she sat up, arching her back as she continued writhing on Ginger, now boldly massaging both of Ginger's big, lovely breasts in those dainty feminine hands. "Damn, precious," he heard himself mutter. How could this be Lynda? *His* Lynda. But at the moment, his shock was overridden by the hottest, dirtiest lust he'd ever experienced, so the whys and the hows could come later. The present was all about pleasure. Pleasure he was tired of just witnessing and now wanted to be a part of.

He could have watched the two gorgeous girls go at it all day, but he supposed he'd forgotten to factor in just how strong an effect it would have on him, and he was in need of some stimulation, too. He worked his cock in his hand, of course, but why settle for that when there were two beautiful, tantalizing women just a few doors down. It excited him even further to imagine pleasuring Lynda as she went on pleasuring Ginger. He hadn't planned that—really hadn't thought far enough ahead on this at all—but the idea of Lynda being with both of them at once was nearly enough to push him over the edge.

He started to release his cock, save his orgasm—yet then it dawned on him that he'd have another hard-on in a heartbeat just observing these two, so why not let it all go. Watching Lynda continue her passionate kneading of Ginger's round globes, he pulled on his shaft harder, faster. *Yes, precious, rub your beautiful cunt against hers.* Ginger's hands rose to capture Lynda's breasts, as well, pushing them upward. Both ladies moaned and purred their pleasure and Jordan got lost in the sights and sounds.

81

"What a *bad* girl," Ginger said in a deep, naughty tone — and something about the sentiment, simple as it was, sent Jordan toppling headlong into a brutal climax. His come shot violently, but at least this time he had tissues ready — he caught his juices in one hand and continued stroking his cock with the other until the hot, swallowing pulses finally ceased.

And as he came back to earth, he instinctively knew why that one little utterance was enough to make him explode — because the deeper into this he got, the more he realized he *liked* having a bad girl. And he wasn't going to miss another second of her badness.

Flipping off the camera, he zipped his pants, rushed out the front door of Spy Games — hurriedly locking up behind himself — then sprinted toward his incredibly hot lady.

* * * * *

Ginger took turns suckling Lynda's needy breasts as Lynda rubbed her pussy in rhythmic circles over Ginger's. She didn't think she could come this way — the connection wasn't quite right, not allowing enough stimulation to her clit — but it still felt good. She let out a groan as Ginger pulled hard on her with lips and tongue, then she arched deeper into the other woman's mouth. *Oh, Jordan, why don't you come? I want you here!*

As if in answer to her silent plea, the door burst open and she looked up to see her gorgeous, sexy man — his eyes filled with a heat darker than any she'd witnessed there before. Thank God she hadn't locked the door after Ginger had arrived.

She didn't mean to abandon Ginger, but the look in his eyes beckoned her, drew her to him. She got to her feet and ran to where he stood, breathing hard. She lifted her hands to his stubbled cheeks as his grip locked on her hips. "You are astounding," he said.

Odd, the compliment made her feel girlish, almost shy. She peered up at him from beneath lowered lids, utterly pleased at his words, and said, "Am I?"

"Are you ever, baby," he replied with dark, naughty chuckle. "I had no idea you could be so…"

She smiled when he trailed off. "I had no idea you would *want* me to be *so*."

He leaned his forehead against hers. "You take my breath away."

"I want you," she purred up at him. "I want to make you feel things you've never felt before." And with that, she dropped to her knees and began to work at his belt buckle, then the zipper on his khakis, more anxious to get to his cock than she'd ever been. Above her, he hurriedly ripped at the buttons on his shirt, casting it aside just as she yanked his briefs down over his oh-so-majestic shaft. Not quite at its full length just yet, it was well on its way and as arousing as always.

"I just came," he said, breath still labored, "watching you over at the store. But I knew you'd get me hard again on sight."

Ginger seemed to admire his shaft, too. "God, I forgot how hung you are." Not that it was hanging.

Then Lynda realized what Ginger had just said and glanced up at her lover. She didn't mind if they'd had a fling, but she was curious. "One night, a long time ago," he said, reading her mind and running his hand through her hair as she gently stroked his length.

"Mmm," she replied. Was that a sliver of jealousy running through her veins? Not really, she decided. Okay, maybe a pinch, but maybe the fact that the two had been together once upon a time made this easier, too.

Ready to quit thinking and resume acting, Lynda boldly swirled her tongue around the tip of Jordan's cock as she gazed sensually up at him. She left behind a trail of wetness and felt him growing in her hand to his full length and width. He felt so powerful, so strong, wrapped in her fist. And she wanted him inside her, but first, just as she'd said, she wanted to make him feel good.

So she sank her lips over him, listening to his groan, feeling the gentle massage of his fingers in her hair—and she took him deep, deep, as deep as she could, until well more than half of his long cock was inside, touching her throat. She knew he thought her particularly skilled at this art, and tonight she wanted to perform especially well. After holding him captive for a moment, she released him from the depths of her mouth to slide her lips up and down on him, enjoying the vigorous moves, and changing up the rhythm—fast and furious to slower and more lingering, and then back again.

She loved feeling his hot gaze on her, and Ginger's as well—and though she mostly watched Jordan's shaft or his face, she finally glanced to the sofa to find Ginger lying with her legs spread, knees bent, her fingers in her panties, stroking her pussy while she studied Lynda at work.

"Come help me," Lynda said softly on impulse.

Ginger looked tempted yet hesitant. "Really? Are you sure?" Apparently, Jordan and Ginger hadn't planned anything beyond him just watching the two women.

Lynda simply nodded. Because she wanted to make him feel as good as humanly possible, and she figured two mouths were better than one. She also assumed Jordan had never been with two women before, and suddenly she had the power to give him that, to give him every man's fantasy.

As Ginger slowly rose to make her way over, Lynda looked up at Jordan to witness the sheer awe in his eyes. Good, he wasn't going to decline—he was going to accept her return gift, going to let this liaison go farther, deeper, into the decadent sort of sex Lynda craved.

Ginger knelt next to her on the hardwood floor and their gazes met across Jordan's magnificent erection. Ginger licked her lips, wetting them, and Lynda's pussy rippled with fresh desire. Reaching up, Lynda placed her hand behind Ginger's head and drew her inward, as if for a kiss, but instead both girls' lips met the cock standing upright between them, passionately kissing it. Jordan moaned and a glance upward revealed his head dropped back, eyes shut. Mmm, yes—she wanted him thoroughly overwhelmed by pleasure.

The two women continued kissing his length, their mouths sometimes meeting each other's, as well. Lynda cupped Ginger's nape and Ginger's hand rose to caress one of Lynda's breasts. Soon enough Jordan was watching them again, letting his hands stroke through both women's hair.

"Suck him," Lynda said, adrift in passion and following her instincts.

Ginger's eyes lit with fire as she lowered her mouth over the tip of Jordan's shaft and Lynda's breasts and pussy both ached hotly at the sight. Reaching beneath, she switched back and forth between caressing his balls and playing with Ginger's breasts.

When Ginger backed off, Lynda took her place, pulling him in, letting that perfect cock fill her entire mouth as she shut her eyes and lost herself in the hot task. She saw that below her, Ginger was licking and sucking Jordan's balls, and the combination of pleasures set him to moaning loudly. "God, yeah, oh yeah," he managed to get out. "I can't fucking believe…oh yeah…"

She felt his gaze and loved taking him to this new place, and even if there *had* been some tiny twinge of jealousy, it was well worth it to please her man so deeply. Both girls continued taking turns on him and Lynda discovered she liked watching Ginger run her lips and up and down the slick shaft almost as much as she enjoyed doing it herself.

Finally, Jordan said, "Stop. No more." His hand curled into Ginger's dark mane so that she'd free him, and his cock popped from her mouth to stand proudly between the two again.

His pants and underwear had long since dropped to his thighs, so Lynda slid one palm up his groin alongside his erection. "Why, baby?" Her mouth suffered that pleasant, stretched sensation left after sucking cock a long while, but she still hungered for more.

He gave her a look of warning and spoke between heavy breaths. "Can't take any more. And don't want to come again yet. And…"

"And what?" She peered expectantly up at him, appreciating the view of his broad chest and muscled stomach.

"And I want to lick your pussy so bad I can already taste it."

Lynda could have sworn her nipples hardened into tighter buds as her cunt grew still wetter.

"Mmm," Ginger purred, looking dreamy-eyed and ready for more, "now that you mention it, I want to lick her, too."

Lynda bit her lip, glancing back and forth between her two lovers, her gaze finally ending up on Jordan. "Can you share, baby?"

A wicked gleam twinkled in his eyes. "I'd *love* to share, precious."

And Lynda knew her impossibly hot dream-come-true was only just beginning.

Chapter Seven

❦

As the other two watched, Lynda rose to her feet and walked slowly back toward the sofa, hoping they were enjoying the view of her ass in the tiny thong between the white garters that still rubbed so deliciously against her with every move. Turning around to take a seat, she leisurely parted her thighs wide and ran the tip of her middle finger over the center of her panties. The touch trailed like a line of fire, her cunt swollen against the lace. She hissed in her breath, loving the two sets of eyes upon her.

Next, she found the little snaps at the front of the thong and dramatically popped them loose. Using both hands, she whipped the thong off, stripper style, and flung it across the room.

Jordan gasped at the sight of her shaven pussy—this was the first time he'd seen it.

"God, baby, you're beautiful," he said, voice deep and raspy.

She licked her upper lip and *felt* her bareness there, where she'd left only a small triangle of hair above her clit. She also felt how very pink and open she was, excited from everything that had already taken place. Her entire pelvic region was weighted with anticipation, ready to seek a hot release, so she wasted no time, saying, "Lick me."

Jordan stepped out of his pants, leaving himself gorgeously naked, and he and Ginger moved toward her, both kneeling between her spread legs. Both of them made a thorough visual study of her cunt, Ginger murmuring, "So pink and slick."

"And so fucking smooth," Jordan added. He lifted his hand and gently dragged the tips of two fingers down the soft, bare flesh to both sides of her parted slit.

Lynda shuddered. "Don't make me wait. Eat me now."

Jordan and Ginger looked at each other, as if not sure quite how to proceed, until finally Jordan said, "Ladies first," and watched as Ginger gently bent to flick the tip of her tongue over Lynda's protruding clitoris.

"Oh!" she said at the tiny shock of delight. "Mmm."

Clearly encouraged, Ginger sank her mouth more fully onto Lynda's pussy, licking up her center and letting her lips close over her clit to pull lightly. "God, yeah," Lynda said, and as Ginger came back for more—*oh yes, baby, lick me good*—Jordan brought his warm palm to rest high on Lynda's thigh, pressing as if to spread her wider. With his other hand, he reached down below Ginger's face, using his thumb and forefinger to hold Lynda's cunt open.

Ginger's long tongue licked a deep path through Lynda's pink flesh, making her wetter and wetter with every stroke, each lick ending on her sensitive clit, now engorged and prominent. Lynda moaned at each pass Ginger made, watching the erotic sight along with Jordan, who now massaged Lynda's inner thigh with one hand and caressed Ginger's ass and the small of her back with the other. "God, that's so hot," he breathed. "Lick her, honey. Lick that pretty pussy."

Lynda moved against Ginger's mouth, lifting to meet each swipe of her tongue. She bit her lower lip, lost in the sensation.

She sobbed with excitement when Jordan brought his hand back to insert two masculine fingers into her opening beneath where Ginger licked. "Oh yes, fuck me, lover," she whispered, and pushed harder against them both.

And then, finally, Jordan bent his head to join Ginger. While she swept her tongue over Lynda's clit, he lapped at her below, down in the softest, dampest part of her, just above where his fingers still thrust.

Lynda had been the recipient of a lot of oral sex in her life, but this was the first time she'd ever had two tongues on her at once. She'd never experienced anything quite so delicious and all-consuming—her whole pussy, from top to bottom being lavished with wet tongues and plunging fingers. She heard herself practically mewling from the pleasure—not only what she felt but what she saw. The sight of Jordan sharing her with a hot girl, the sight of two heads down there working to get as much of her pussy as they could, was more exciting than whips and leather had ever been.

"God, don't stop, don't stop," she begged, because she knew she'd come soon. She'd been trying to hold back, trying to stretch out the dirty joy of it, but it was too much now, taking her over, and she was losing control. She pumped at both mouths harder. She cried out louder. She reached down, curling her hands about their heads, holding them firmly in place so that they couldn't stop now if they wanted to. "Lick me! Yes, lick me! Lick my pussy!"

She yelled her demands, clenching her teeth as her body drove madly forward—finally plunging into ecstasy. "God, yes! *Yes!*" she cried as the hard waves of heat shook her, rolled through her, twisting her very soul with the intensity of an orgasm the likes of which she'd never before experienced. She rode it out, bucking at her lovers' obliging tongues, soaking up every bit of joy for all it was worth, still sobbing, sobbing…until finally the sensation waned to leave her spent and utterly well-pleasured.

"Oh…" she said, amazed. Then, on impulse, she reached down to take Ginger's face in her hands, kissing her, tasting herself on the other woman's lips—and then she kissed Jordan, pressing her tongue into his mouth, tasting the remnants of his ministrations, as well, as she grazed her fingertips along his stubbled cheeks. When she pulled back to look at him, there were no words—nothing could adequately explain all she felt at this moment. Nothing except…

"I love you," she whispered heatedly.

His hands found her face, too. "Ah, precious, *I* love *you*."

More lingering kisses—lips, tongues—and Lynda's fist wrapped around Jordan's cock. He let out a groan as she ran her fingers across the tip, then lifted them to her mouth to suck off the pre-come.

Her arms wound back around his neck as his hands slid up over the lace covering her torso to cup her bared breasts. "I haven't had a chance to tell you how beautifully sexy and naughty you look in this," he murmured, glancing down at her ensemble.

She gave her head a thoughtful tilt and spoke the truth in her heart. "I *feel* sexy in it for you, lover. More than ever before."

He growled his approval, then kissed her again—and keeping their faces close, Lynda said, "Are you ready for more of your little game, baby? Do you want to watch me eat Ginger's pussy?"

His eyes opened wide, as if he hadn't even imagined that would happen, but then said, "*Oh* yeah," on a heavy breath. "Oh *yeah*, I want to watch you eat her."

She giggled lightly at his enthusiasm, then turned seductive eyes on Ginger, who still knelt patiently at Jordan's side. "You, on the couch," Lynda said, half teasing, half serious.

A familiar little smile of acquiescence formed on Ginger's face. "My pleasure," she replied, climbing up onto the sofa next to where Lynda still sat.

Lynda boldly took the lead, reaching up to caress Ginger's breast, tweaking the pointed nipple lightly before swiftly sliding her hand down onto the front of those pretty lavender panties. Ginger sighed her delight and Lynda couldn't help noticing that Ginger's cunt felt swollen through the lace, too.

"Help me get these off," Lynda said softly to Jordan.

Replying with only a heated smile, he moved to Ginger's other side and as she lifted her ass, together they peeled the stretchy lace thong to her thighs, over her knees, and finally over the sexy heels she still wore.

Ginger bit her lip and spread her legs to reveal an entirely bare pussy, gaping with dark pink flesh, a similar color to her nipples. The sight was so erotic that Lynda went weak. Jordan still knelt on the floor, his cock jutting upward near Ginger's thigh, and Lynda felt torn between wanting to suck it and wanting to lick the hot pussy before her. Kneeling between Ginger's slender, sexy legs, Lynda couldn't resist bending over her thigh to give Jordan a quick little suck that made him gasp before she turned her attention to Ginger.

First, she lifted her hands to those delectable breasts and leaned in to drop one light, moist kiss onto each mauve nipple. Then she proceeded straight down to that waiting cunt. Bracing her hands stop Ginger's thighs, she dragged the tip of her tongue from bottom to top, ending with a swirling motion around her clit. "Oh yeah, baby," Ginger moaned. "Do that again."

Lynda obliged. Once, twice. She hadn't been with a girl in a while and found herself relishing that salty, delightfully forbidden taste in her mouth—forbidden because it came from another woman, and the very thought excited her. It was so much stronger than when she caught hints of her own taste, passed through a kiss. Fueled by it, she locked her lips around Ginger's clit to suck on it, listening as the other girl began to sob softly.

But Lynda needed more. Jordan. She still loved having his hot gaze on her, but his cock was so close, and she hungered for it so much. Still torn between pussy and cock, she decided she had to have both. Still suckling on Ginger's swollen clit, she reached out and grabbed onto Jordan's enormous shaft. Mmm, so good, even just in her hand.

She pulled him by it, drawing his big erection up over Ginger's bare hip until Jordan's body was flush against Ginger where she'd sunk down on the couch. Lynda lay his cock across Ginger's lower abdomen, so that it stretched across her belly, right above her slit. Both Jordan and Ginger breathed heavily now, watching, obviously wondering what Lynda had in mind. But she'd simply needed his big, hot tool closer, so that she could indulge in both lovely playthings.

Positioning her head sideways, she dipped to scoop Jordan's cock into her mouth, sucking him as she pressed her breast into Ginger's cunt, raking it so that the hard, pointed nipple would gently abrade her inner flesh. Both of her lovers moaned hotly until Lynda backed off to rake her tongue up through Ginger's slit again while pulling on Jordan with her hand.

She moved back and forth between cock and pussy that way, licking one while she stroked the other with hand or breast, and though she never lifted her gaze to Jordan's, she could feel his continued and mounting awe. Once, she rose to let Jordan lick Ginger's feminine juices from her breast. It felt incredible to finally be her true sexual self with him, to finally be holding nothing back, finally giving pleasure exactly as her body inspired her to without worry over what he would think.

Over time, though, her body needed more, and now it was her own pussy that longed for attention. She looked up from suckling Ginger's clit to Jordan. "Fuck me, baby," she begged. "Fuck me while I lick her."

A low groan left him as he pulled his wet cock off Ginger's stomach and moved to Lynda's rear. Still on her knees, she parted her legs and arched her ass toward him as his hands firmly gripped her hips. "Oh yeah, baby, give it to me," she begged.

He entered her with a hard drive that made her cry out. Oh yes, this was *perfect*! Her man's long shaft inside her, filling her up, as she licked Ginger's widened slit. Sex encased her — it was all around her, the biggest part of her, swallowing her whole. Jordan delivered hot hard strokes into her hungry passage, making her lap even more energetically at Ginger's sweet pink cunt, so wet with their combined juices.

All three of them moaned and groaned together, creating a dirty little symphony as Jordan thrust at her from one end, Ginger from the other. And then, like wet, gooey icing on an already delicious cake, Jordan bent over her, sliding one hand around her hip to sink his big fingers into her pussy. Oh yes. She'd come not long ago, but God knew she needed her clit rubbed. She moved against his hand, which meant she also moved harder against his cock. She locked back onto Ginger's hot clit and sucked, sucked, sucked, with each hard plunge Jordan delivered behind her.

They were all getting close, she knew. But there was no way they'd come together. Hell, it was hard enough to get *two* people on the same exact orgasmic path — *three* would be impossible.

But that was okay — she didn't care who came when — she knew she'd be happy to finish off Ginger no matter what happened, and she knew Jordan would be happy to rub her to climax even if he exploded inside her first.

"God, oh God," Ginger said above her, her voice wrenched.

Lynda kept suckling, hard, as Jordan's fingers rubbed in her moisture, bringing her closer with every passing second. He fucked her harder, too, and was beginning to groan.

"Oh God, yeah — now!" Ginger cried out and Lynda slowed her sucking to meet Ginger's rhythmic orgasmic thrusts against her mouth — and *she* toppled, too, moaning against Ginger's clit as the hot waves of pleasure took her, roaring through her, all the way out to the tips of her fingers and toes.

"Fuck yes!" Jordan yelled through gritted teeth, and slammed into her with powerful strokes that meant he was coming as well.

All three of them rode it out together, their amazing triple orgasm, pumping and thrusting and moaning for all they were worth.

When they'd all finally stilled, the room went quiet, and for the first time ever during such a liaison, Lynda wondered—what now? Because *what now* didn't usually *matter*—but this time it did. Would Jordan have regrets? Think of her differently? Suddenly be filled with repulsion?

When he eased out of her, she missed his presence in her body immediately. Turning to look at him, she said, "I love you, and this was the most amazing sex I've ever had." It wasn't a lie. Experiencing what she liked to think of as her "extremes" with someone she loved was brand new, and it made it better than ever, transformed the entire encounter into something overwhelmingly intense and special to her.

Her heartbeat slowed a bit when she saw love still gleaming in his eyes. "I love you, too, precious. So very much." It dripped from his voice and shone is his expression, and she knew everything was okay.

Better than okay, actually—because she had everything she wanted now. Jordan—and the hot, hedonistic sex she relished.

"So, you two are the real thing, huh?"

They both turned to Ginger, who remained resting on the couch in a post-climactic lull. She wore a peculiar smile, as if maybe she hadn't quite believed you could combine love and lust this way—until now.

"Definitely," Lynda replied, casting Jordan a look brimming with all the warmth she felt for him.

Ginger reached for her panties and put them on, then walked to the easy chair where she'd lain her clothes over one arm. Jordan and Lynda fell easily onto the sofa in the spot she'd vacated, in a loose but sweet embrace. After Ginger dressed, she bent to give each of them a light kiss on the mouth. "This was fun. Thanks for inviting me, Jordan." Then she switched her gaze to Lynda. "And thank *you* for being so welcoming."

With that, she grabbed up her purse and walked out the door, leaving them alone.

Silence fell over the room like a blanket as Jordan peered deeply into Lynda's eyes. "So, you don't hate me?" he asked with a suddenly sheepish grin.

She lifted one hand to cup his strong jaw. "Hate you, baby? No, this is…this is…" There was no reason to hold anything back now. "This is my dream come true, Jordan. Everything about it."

He raised his eyebrows. "You've fantasized about doing something like this?"

Gently, she shook her head. "Not exactly."

And he looked confused. "Then…"

Time to come completely clean. "Before I met you, I…actually *did* things like this. A lot. Because life is short and sex is amazing and I wanted all of it I could get." She was on one of her rolls now, so she decided to just keep going. "And so ever since we met, I've *longed* to do something this wild with you. The whole time we've been together, I've wanted to let you see this side of me. I've wanted to show you how bad I can be. And now…well, you don't know how happy it made me to discover tonight that you want the same thing. And now we can have it all! Leather and whips! Handcuffs and vibrators!" She was laughing, still amazed by it all.

Next to her, though, Jordan ran his hand through his hair, looking taken aback. The realization stilled her laughter.

Shit, she should have known. She'd spewed too much at once. She'd been too honest. "You're upset to find out about my sex life before we met," she said.

95

"No," he replied quietly, shaking his head. "Surprised, but not upset. Although, seeing you tonight, I guess I *shouldn't* be surprised. Because you were incredible."

"Then...what's wrong?"

He lifted his gaze to hers. "I guess I'm just wondering...why you didn't tell me. Because we've had a lot of sex, Lynda, and we've talked a lot about it." He let out a breath of what sounded like disgust. "And I *knew* you were holding something back, and I tried to get you to tell me. Remember, I asked you about your sexual fantasies and I said you could tell me anything? But still, you didn't."

Lynda sighed, bit her lower lip. "I was afraid. Afraid you'd hate me. Afraid I'd lose you."

"Lynda, we're not a couple of college kids. Of course we've both had lovers. And maybe you've done things I haven't—but I don't know what I've *ever* done that would make you think I'd break up with you over something in your past."

She swallowed nervously. This wasn't going well. "I didn't want to tell you because...I didn't want it to be only in my past. I wanted to do things like that, things like what we just did tonight, with you—*now*. And when you took me in that alley, I loved it. I wanted more. I wanted to experience every kind of sex with you." Her voice had grown breathy with passion, and fear.

Only he was shaking his head now, looking angry. "And yet you didn't tell me that. I tried to get you to open up, I tried to let you know I was open-minded. You arouse me more than any lover I've ever had, driven me to do things I've never done before—and you *know* that, yet you *still* wouldn't tell me what you wanted, what I could do to make you happy."

She let out a another long, heavy sigh. "I'm sorry, baby. But...you figured it out on your own, and you gave me this sizzling gift tonight, and it was *wonderful*. I love you so much!"

Wrapping her arms around his neck, she kissed him, trying to make this all right, but he seemed wooden.

"What's wrong?" she asked, confused.

"I feel like an idiot, *that's* what's wrong. Here I think I'm pleasing you, pleasuring you, all this time, only to find out it wasn't enough."

"It *was* enough, Jordan—I promise, it *was*." Only, in truth, there *were* moments when it *hadn't* been enough, and only now did she realize how unfair it had been not to tell him the things she wanted, not to give him the opportunity to deliver them.

"And I guess I'm hurt that no matter how much attention I lavished on you, no matter what I did or what I said, you didn't trust our love enough to be honest. Which kind of makes me feel like I was the only one of us really *in* this relationship, the only one of us stupid enough to fall in love."

Lynda was aghast. "Oh my God, Jordan—that's not true! I love you *so* much! And I'm *so* sorry I wasn't honest. I was just afraid."

He let out a sigh. "Well, now *I'm* afraid. Afraid this relationship isn't what I thought it was."

* * * * *

The next couple of days were torture for Lynda. She kept reliving the horrible moment when she'd realized Jordan was angry. So angry that he'd soon gotten up, put on his clothes, and departed. He hadn't stormed out or anything—that wasn't Jordan's style—but he'd simply continued seeming hurt, upset, adrift. And none of her repeated apologies or pleas had made any difference.

They'd left things painfully uncertain.

"Are we…are we over?" she'd asked, still stunned by the change in his demeanor.

He'd let out a tired sigh. "I'm not sure, Lynda. I'm just not sure. I...don't know if I can be with a woman who doesn't trust me."

They'd been over that already by then, of course, so she didn't bother telling him—again—that she *did* trust him. Because the truth was—she *hadn't*. She hadn't trusted him to love her no matter what.

And now that she'd had two days to mull it over, she felt his pain. She knew Jordan didn't fall in love easily—she didn't either. She knew their relationship had recently started sailing into serious waters, and that such a change in course was rare for both of them. And now they were both hurting for it—her because she hadn't been brave enough and truly *hadn't* trusted their love enough, and him because she'd hurt him, probably made him sorry he'd ever allowed himself to get that close to her.

She looked out the window of The Cajun Lady toward Spy Games, but didn't see any movement. She knew he was right across the street from her, same as he had been for the last two days, yet they hadn't seen each other, and neither had picked up the phone. Lynda had hoped he would call, but he hadn't. She'd hoped he would forgive.

Yet as Friday afternoon turned to Friday evening, she wasn't sure she could survive the weekend like this. Because one thing had become shockingly clear. She *did* love the man. *Great* sex or *no* sex—she no longer cared.

Well, that was a lie—she cared, but this was about so much more than sex. This was about a man she truly *did* trust now, with anything and everything, and she wanted to make a life with him. Maybe forever.

Flipping the *Open* sign to *Closed*, she stepped outside, locked up the shop, then headed up the exterior stairs to the apartment, suddenly on a mission. A mission to get her man back.

As soon as she gave him time to close up and drive home, she was going to get in her car and head out to St. Charles Avenue herself, to his house, not far from her own. But first, she went to the chest of drawers in her bedroom and dug out the yellow baby doll nightie with the lace cups and matching panties. Because there was one more thing that had become very clear—she really did feel lovely in lace now, after the other night. And she was going to show him just how deeply he moved her.

Chapter Eight

๑

Jordan stood in Liz and Jack's apartment, kind of glad Jack wasn't home.

"So, be honest," he said to Liz. "Can I pull this off?"

"Uh, *yeah*," she said as if it were a silly question. He wore black leather pants, a fitted black t-shirt, and a black leather jacket. "Don't tell Jack I said this, but Jordan, you look *hot*."

He grinned, getting a little of his confidence back. "Yeah?"

She nodded.

The truth was, he hadn't the first idea what he was doing, but he knew he had to get Lynda back and make up for acting like a jerk the other night. He also had to show her that he was the man she needed him to be, a man who could keep her satisfied in every way.

As luck had it, he'd bumped into Liz on Royal Street on Thursday and had ended up telling her that he and Lynda were having problems. Before he knew it, they'd decided to grab a drink at Pat O'Brien's, where he'd opened up to her about why—and she'd helped him see the light, made him understand that Lynda loved him so much that she simply hadn't wanted to risk losing him. She'd also explained Lynda's desire not to mar his vision of her, no matter what it cost, which had touched a place deep inside him. Before it was over, he'd felt like a heel for walking out on her.

By that evening, he'd had a chance to mull over the things Lynda had mentioned liking in bed. Whips. Handcuffs. Items he didn't know much about, but he was willing to learn, so he'd called Jack to go out for a drink with him. An hour later at Lafitte's, he'd asked his friend's advice on exactly how a straitlaced guy like him could go about showing Lynda he could give her what she wanted.

"Uh, the three-way was definitely a good start," Jack had laughed with his Cajun drawl. Jordan had filled him in on that particular event as they'd talked.

"Maybe, but...I'm not sure I'll be into the multiple partner thing on a regular basis."

Jack had nodded knowingly. "I hear ya, *ami*. Liz and I played that fun little game once upon a time ourselves, and even though we had a night or two we'll never forget, after that, I just wanted to play one-on-one."

That captured Jordan's feelings exactly. He found himself not really wanting to share Lynda, yet still confident he could satisfy her—he just needed to be pointed in the right direction. After talking to Jack, he'd picked up a few accessories he thought his precious lady would enjoy now that he was starting to understand her tastes a little better. And today he'd bought this outfit because he just didn't think his usual carefully pressed khakis were gonna cut it tonight.

"Wish me luck," he said to Liz as he headed toward the door.

She gave him a conspiratorial smile. "Go get her, Jordan."

* * * * *

Lynda had just slipped on the strappy white heels she knew Jordan liked and was tying her trench coat shut when someone banged on the apartment door. Who the hell could it be, right when she was on her way to seduce her man back into her arms?

Marching over, she checked the peephole and—oh my God!—found Jordan.

Stunned, she opened the door to see him standing before her dressed in black leather from head to toe. Whoa. Who *was* this masked man? And if he looked this good in leather, why hadn't he worn it before now?

He looked her up and down, too. "Going out?"

She nodded, still a little numbed by his appearance. "Going to see *you*."

"We're staying here," he said so forcefully her pussy trembled.

Her reply came soft, with continued shock. "Okay."

"Tonight you're going to do exactly what I say."

She simply stared in awe.

"Do you understand me, slave?"

Her mouth dropped open. She was beginning to think she did understand. And that she liked it. *A lot.* "Um, yes. Master," she added for good measure.

"Show me what's under your coat," he demanded, his voice still much rougher than usual.

She hurriedly untied the sash, spreading the coat open to reveal the yellow negligee underneath—and could have sworn he had to bite back a grin when he saw it.

Only as he stepped inside did she notice the large black shopping bag he toted. She considered asking what was inside, but then decided she'd rather be surprised. She gave her lower lip a sensual little bite, realizing she was going to have a better night than she'd even hoped for.

"Take it off," he told her, pulling at the coat's sleeve. "The panties, too. I want to see your pussy, and it better be smooth."

The commanding tone to his voice already had her cunt practically dripping. "It is, master. I shaved it especially for you."

"Hurry up," he snapped, and she obeyed, anxious to do exactly what he demanded of her. She dropped the coat to the floor, then pushed down the yellow lace panties while he watched, stepping free of them.

He eyed her bare slit intently, making her even wetter, then stepped up close to pin her against the wall. His middle finger sank deep into her folds, making her whole body flinch at the impact, as he said, "I'm gonna fuck you so damn hard."

She quivered with excitement at the threat, but decided to play the damsel in distress. "I'm afraid, master. I'm afraid of your big, hard cock."

"You'd *better* be afraid, slave. I'm gonna ram my rod into you so deep," he said through clenched teeth, his face close to hers, "that you'll beg for mercy."

Mmm, she couldn't wait.

"But first, you're gonna suck my cock."

Oh, yummy! But she only said, "Please don't make me, master. It's so thick and long and scary."

"You'll suck it if I say you suck it, slave!"

Ooooh—she loved him like this! He had every nerve-ending in her body standing on end, her breasts achy and her mouth ready.

Next, he grabbed her wrist and pulled her to the sofa, lowering his bag there. Then he sat down, shoving her to her knees on the floor, between his legs. "Release my cock," he commanded.

Entranced by him now, Lynda thoroughly enjoyed unzipping those sexy leather pants—and he'd left off underwear, so his erection burst free. Both of them shuddered softly at the sight.

"Now suck it," he said, and Lynda forgot to act scared—instead licking her lips.

She went down on him, taking him deep, pleased when his fingers threaded immediately through her hair, urging her just a little farther. She took another inch, loving how very full her mouth felt and that he was making her do it.

"Yeah, slave, suck it hard," he said, softer but still commanding, and she worked hard to pleasure him, so thrilled to have her man back, and in leather, too!

She closed her eyes, sank into the joy of sucking him, and thought she couldn't be any happier—until something snapped against her bare ass.

Stunned, she released him from her lips and looked up to see a lovely black leather flogger in his hand, much like one she already owned. "Oh my," she purred in naughty delight. She wouldn't have believed he had it in him—but thank God he did!

"Did I say you could stop, slave?"

"No, master, I'm sorry," she said merrily, then lowered her lips back over his long, lovely tool, and flinched with pleasure when the strips of leather bit into her flesh once more. The sensation spread all through her nether regions and down her thighs, and by the time she recovered from it completely, he used it on her again, harder this time—*delightfully* harder. She flinched again and sucked with more enthusiasm.

"Enough," he said. "Stop!"

She yanked her head up, letting his erection fall wet against his belly where his t-shirt had ridden up. She watched, still on her knees, as he rid himself of the jacket and shirt, and she thought he looked like the perfect Adonis in nothing but those open black pants and black boots.

"You are perfect, master," she told him.

Their gazes met, filled with heat and mutual appreciation. "So are you," he whispered, sounding more like his usual self, and she felt the compliment more than any he'd ever given her. She was perfect. Even after the difficulties and misunderstandings they'd just come through, and the mistakes she'd made—he still thought she was perfect.

She wondered if maybe the naughty game was over, but then he said, "Stand up and walk to the window."

The wide, multi-paned glass overlooked St. Peter Street and was lined by an old radiator that had long ago quit working. Her heels clicked across the floor until she stopped and peered out on the dusky night.

The next thing she knew, Jordan was hooking a handcuff around one of her wrists! And not the wimpy furry kind, either, but a hard circle of cold steel that would bite deliciously into her skin.

"Oh, you bad, bad man, you," she said, but knew she sounded more excited than frightened. Keeping her facing the window, Jordan slipped the other cuff through part of the radiator, then snapped it around Lynda's free wrist.

"Now," he said, leaning close so that his hot cock pressed into the crack of her ass and his voice came low in her ear, "I'm going to fuck your hungry little pussy until you scream."

Another shudder of anticipation snaked through her as she arched her ass toward him, bracing her hands on the radiator.

His hands pressed to her bare hips, under the chiffon nightie, and he slammed all nine inches of his hard shaft into her. She cried out at the rough intrusion—loving how *taken* she felt. "Oh, master!" she sobbed.

"Your pussy's so tight," he murmured.

"With *that* monster cock in it, of course it is!"

This time he didn't manage to hold in his chuckle, but it faded quickly as he said, "You better hold on tight, baby, because I'm about to fuck your brains out."

And then he pounded into her—hard, hard, hard—brutal and relentless strokes that had her sobbing and then screaming at each as they ripped through her with the rough pleasure she craved. Her whole body felt fucked—each stroke sent sensation blaring out from her cunt through her ass, her legs, her arms. He didn't stop, plunging deeper and deeper, ramming his powerful cock in without ever breaking his harsh rhythm, until Lynda went weak, wondering how much more she could take.

She screamed, "Yes! Yes! Yes!" but soon couldn't even form words. She gripped the radiator tight, felt the pleasant slice of the cuffs into her wrists as her body was jostled so delightfully hard, and thought—finally, *finally*, her man was giving her the hot, dirty fucking she relished.

And just when she was sure neither of them could go on much longer, Jordan anchored one arm around her waist and used his other hand to rub her pussy in front. "Oh, oh yes!" she whimpered, growing even weaker from his powerful strokes, but still they came, propelling her clit against his big fingers in just the right way—and it took only a few amazing seconds before she was screaming out her orgasm. "Oh God, baby, oh God! I love you, Jordan! I love you so much!"

"Oh fuck, here I come, too," he breathed in her ear, and finished in three long, rough strokes that nearly lifted her from the ground.

* * * * *

Five minutes later, they lay nuzzling on the sofa naked, kissing, touching, smiling at each other. "Forgive me for being an ass?" he asked.

She grinned. "If this is how you make up, you can be an ass every day."

He laughed, then promised her, "This isn't just making up, precious. This is how things are going to be from now on."

"You're the master and I'm the slave?"

He shrugged. "Or the other way around, if you like. I'm new at this, so you may have to give me a little guidance along the way. But I plan to do *lots* of kinky things with you." He motioned vaguely toward the shopping bag that had gotten shoved onto the floor.

And only then did it dawn on her that it was an awfully big bag for just a flogger and a pair of handcuffs. Leaning over, she pulled at one edge of the paper and glanced down inside to see a lovely array of dildos, anal beads, a blindfold, and more.

When she looked back to her lover, slightly astonished at his thoroughness, he said, "Those are for later," with a wink.

"I can't wait, baby," she purred, nuzzling against him. Then she lifted her head, gazed into his eyes, and said, "Thank you."

"For?"

"Your willingness to please me."

A slow smile spread across his face. "*You've* been very willing to please *me*, precious. And pleasing *you* pleases *me*, too. In fact, I'm starting to get into this."

"Mmm, good."

"One thing, though. Any chance I could try keeping you satisfied without company? You know I loved watching you fool around with Ginger, but...I think I can give you what you need all on my own if you'll let me try."

A reasonable request, she thought. And since she'd discovered, surprisingly, that she was a little jealous of Ginger when the three of them had been together, she said, "I think you can, too. So do your damnedest."

They laughed lightly, but then Jordan turned suddenly serious. "Would it be a weird time for me to propose to you?"

Lynda's back went rigid and she blinked. Had she heard him right? Was it possible? Her perfect, debonair man, who also now wanted to play kinky sex games with her, wanted to marry her? It seemed too amazing to be true! "Um—no. Now would be a *perfect* time for you to do that."

With that, he zipped his pants, got up, and dropped to one knee. He reached in the pocket of his leather jacket, which had gotten discarded on one arm of the sofa, and drew out a small gray velvet box. "About some things," he said, "afraid I'm still traditional."

"That's okay," she said quickly, biting her lower lip. She hadn't realized it until this moment, but maybe she was, too.

He opened the box to reveal a gorgeous sapphire ring, marquis cut, surrounding by tiny diamonds. "My grandmother's," he said. "If you like it, it's your engagement ring."

She smiled into his eyes. He knew she loved antique jewelry, and she couldn't imagine anything more ideal to bond them together. "I'm so honored, Jordan. It's beautiful."

He slipped the ring on her finger and said, "Will you marry me, precious?"

"Oh, honey, will I ever!" she replied, making them both laugh.

They shared a long, slow kiss, but when it was done, Jordan said, "Now I'm finished being traditional. Let's get back to these sex toys."

"Mmm, sounds good," she said. And with a glance toward the window and the French Quarter beyond, Lynda thought to herself, *The Sex Queen of New Orleans rides again.* And she was more than ready to charge full speed ahead with her perfect, forever lover.

CARTER'S CUFFS

෨

Trademarks Acknowledgement

so

The author acknowledges the trademarked status and trademark owners of the following wordmarks mentioned in this work of fiction:

Bellagio: Bellagio, LLC

Big Mac: McDonald's Corp.

Caesars Palace: Caesars World, Inc.

Coke: The Coca-Cola Company

D.A.R.E.: D.A.R.E. America Corp.

Flamingo: Harrah's Operating Company

Ford: Ford Motor Company

Mandalay Bay: Mandalay Resort Group

McDonald's: McDonald's Corp.

The Mirage: Mirage Resorts, Inc.

Nissan Sentra: Nissan Jidosha Kabushiki Kaisha Ta Nissan Motor Co.

Porsche: Dr. Ing. h. c. F. Porsche AG Corp.

Chapter One

Ꙙ

"Hey, Sparks. Lookin' good tonight."

Erin Sparks glanced up from the parking lot toward a second-floor balcony to find her sexy-as-sin neighbor, Carter Brooks, giving her a wink. He leaned forward in his patio chair, his arms resting on the railing, his chin perched lazily atop loose fists.

Her pussy spasmed slightly.

Was it because he looked so damn good sitting there with his dark, messy hair and cutoffs, that naughty twinkle in his eye?

Or because of the way *she* looked right now?

She wore a tiny black skirt that barely covered her ass, a tight red halter top that hugged what it didn't reveal of her breasts, and red stripper heels. Her dark hair, which she usually wore straight, fell in voluminous waves around her face and over her shoulders. Her eyes were done smoky with thick eyeliner and mascara, and she'd painted her lips the same color as her top and shoes. She'd just been transferred to the vice squad a month ago and given that she was used to wearing a simple beige police uniform, it was hard not to *feel* how she was dressed right now.

"I'm on my way to work," she explained, holding in her smile. She had no intention of flirting with Carter, no matter how either *one* of them looked.

"Damn. If this is how lady cops dress for work, I might have to start breaking some laws."

His slow, teasing grin melted all through her, and her own snuck out—against her will. "This isn't our usual look, you know."

"It should be," he told her. "You'd have the bad guys chasing *you*."

"Well, tonight, hopefully they will. Not chase me," she added, a little nervous around him. "But…you know." They'd discussed her new assignment before—working north of the Vegas Strip, hanging outside a seedy old-time bar while her partner Danny sat nearby in an unmarked car. Two other plainclothes cops would be nearby, too, all waiting to move in for a bust.

"*Proposition* you," Carter replied.

She nodded, and for some reason her breasts tingled just hearing Carter use the word *proposition* and knowing they were talking about sex.

"I'm still confused by this," he said then, his expression less teasing and more puzzled. "There are naked chicks parading around on stages all over this town, and signs on every cab and billboard offering female company—but the Vegas P.D. is on a mission to stamp out prostitution?"

She only shrugged. She saw the weirdness in that, too. People came to Las Vegas seeking forbidden pleasures they couldn't get at home, and the city catered to their fantasies—in every way but one. In the *state* of Nevada, prostitution *was* legal, but in Las Vegas city limits, no. "I don't make the laws," she pointed out.

Carter laughed quietly as he gave her another unguarded once-over. "No, you just walk around making it impossible for guys to obey them."

Another twinge in her panties told her it was time to go. Besides, she didn't need to let the rest of their neighbors in the condo complex see her parading around looking like, well…like a whore. Even if the way Carter looked at her right now made her feel ready and willing to do her pretend job with him, instead of her real one. She reached for her car door and ignored the urge to give him another smile.

"What if *I* propositioned you, Sparks?"

She turned back toward him, raising her eyebrows. "With money? Afraid I'd have to haul your ass to jail." Despite herself, she grinned. She liked him. It was hard *not* to flirt, even if it was in her best interests to hold back.

"I wasn't planning on offering you money."

She lowered her chin. "What then?"

He grinned, easy and confident. "Just me, babe. Just me."

She threw her head back in a trill of laughter, pretending her panties weren't becoming more soaked by the second, then finally opened the car door. It was well past time to leave — before she climbed up onto that balcony and attacked him. "See you later, Carter."

"Have a good night, Erin. And hey, go easy on the bad guys. You *gotta* feel sorry for 'em, 'cause you're *extremely* hard to resist, honey."

She'd seldom been as aware of her own body as when she was finally driving away from him. Jeez, that man *did* something to her. Even though she barely knew him.

He lived two doors down from her place, but they'd only exchanged a few pleasantries in the hall until Diana and Marc, whose condo sat between theirs, had invited her to a dinner party — where she'd ended up seated next to Carter.

One mere look into those eyes had left her wanting. Even just brushing her arm against his at the table had been electrifying in a way she could scarcely explain to herself. He simply *moved* her. Deeply. Sexually.

Diana had told her Carter was a great guy, but not overly outgoing — and Erin thought it an apt description from her observations at the dinner. Yet with *her*, he'd whispered little jokes and flirted mercilessly the whole evening. He'd asked her out twice since then, but each time she'd turned him down, claiming her job kept her too busy and that she didn't want to see anyone right now.

"Aw, come on, Sparks," he'd said after her last refusal, his green gaze sparkling in the sun as he flashed a playful smile. "Throw a guy a bone."

He'd been outside at the time, running an electric edger along a walkway near the condo pool. He worked in construction, building the large hotel-casinos that sprang up one after another on Las Vegas Boulevard, but he also did some maintenance at the condos. Wearing a t-shirt with the sleeves ripped out, long cargo shorts tattered on the edges, and a pair of dirty work boots with the laces undone, he *shouldn't* have been sexy. But he *had* been. Big, messy, rugged, sweaty — and brutally, almost *painfully* sexy.

Turning him down had been agonizing — but she'd stuck to her guns. "Sorry, Carter," she'd said, trying to sound casual and carefree as she whisked toward her car — that day wearing her beige police uniform, her hair pulled back into a low ponytail. "No bones to spare."

But in reality, she wanted to *jump* his bones. She wanted to release her inhibitions and do things with him she'd never even thought about before.

She had no idea why she felt such a strong pull toward him. Could it be because of what Diana had told her over too many margaritas one night not too long after the dinner party — that early in her relationship with Marc, they'd shared a spectacular three-way with Carter? Did knowing he was that wild and that comfortable with himself and his sexuality increase her arousal for him? Or was it simpler than that? Was it his eyes? His body? His dark, tousled hair and the dark stubble on his chin? Was this just chemistry — the most powerful chemistry she'd ever experienced with a guy?

As she drove toward the downtown bureau to meet Danny, she let out a sigh. The fact was, it didn't really matter *why* she felt such heady attraction to Carter — she still couldn't act on it.

* * * * *

A little while later, she sat in the passenger seat of an old Nissan Sentra—light blue with a dented fender—that blended in on any city street. No one would suspect the guy behind the wheel was a plainclothes cop. Next to her, Danny maneuvered the car toward the Desert Oasis, which had probably been in its heyday about the time Frank and Sammy and the rest of the Rat Pack had been appearing nightly at the Sands.

"Explain this to me again," Danny said. Hispanic and a bit older than her, in his mid-thirties, Danny was happily married with kids. They'd grown close, as police partners often did, so it wasn't unusual for her to share personal matters with him. "You won't go out with the guy because you like him too much? Help me out here, Sparks—that doesn't make any sense."

She scowled at him from beneath her heavily made-up eyes. "You know how I feel about getting into a serious relationship."

Danny only gave his head a tired shake, which annoyed the hell out of her. "Well, don't come crying to me when you end up old and alone."

"I won't. Because as long as I'm a cop, *that's* what my life is about." Erin's father had been a Las Vegas cop, too. He'd died in the line of duty when Erin was fifteen—exactly half her life ago—shot during a response to a domestic violence call.

It had happened when her mother was ill—battling breast cancer—and the whole family had been stressed. Now her mother had long since beaten the cancer, but at the time it had torn her father apart. He'd tried to put on a strong face for both Erin and her mom, but Erin had seen how he'd suffered. And she'd also known that, because of it, he hadn't been focused on his work—he'd made a couple of mistakes on the job. She'd heard him talking on the phone about it to a friend when he didn't realize she was listening.

No one had ever said it, but Erin knew his worry over her mother had contributed to his death. He simply hadn't been at the top of his game. And a cop on the streets *had* to be at the top of his or her game — that simple.

Still, she'd admired her father immensely. She'd always understood from early childhood that he risked his life every day — but that he saw each and every moment up until then as a chance to help people in trouble. So Erin had followed in her father's footsteps without a shred of doubt that she wanted to live the same way — contributing something, doing a job that mattered. And even if standing on Las Vegas Boulevard shaking her ass at potential "johns" didn't exactly feel like a worthwhile contribution, she knew it was. Just as her previous patrol work had been, and just as the work she'd done with kids — taking the D.A.R.E. program into schools — had been worthwhile, too.

And if she kept at it long enough and did enough good work, someday she'd be promoted to detective and get to solve more serious crimes. After her father's violent death, it had become her passion in life not only to help others, but to help people find answers — families of murder victims and those suffering other kinds of loss. When and if she made detective, she hoped to make an even bigger difference.

So the work mattered. But the work required, for her at least, never letting herself become vulnerable, staying in control of herself and her emotions at all times.

So sure, she dated casually on occasion — and it met certain needs, for companionship, sex. But she would never let herself become so attached to someone that it would make her needy. She was a strong, tough cop, but she knew that inside her still lurked an emotional little girl. Falling in love with somebody, letting herself sink that deep into her heart, into her *feelings*, would only weaken her as a police officer. And a Las Vegas cop simply couldn't afford to risk losing her edge.

"You're a serious control freak," Danny told her as he pulled to the curb half a block from the bar. She spotted their backups already in position. Carl was reading the newspaper in an ancient brown Ford station wagon, and Bobby was dressed raggedly, pretending to be asleep on a bench across the street.

"But the difference between me and most control freaks," Erin pointed out, "is that I'm not trying to control anything but myself, my life. So it doesn't hurt anybody."

"Nope, nobody but you," he agreed. "Here you want to go out with this guy, but you won't. That's crazy, Erin."

She shrugged but felt a bit desolate. Normally, her "no relationships" way of life worked fine. She hadn't had a serious boyfriend since she'd joined the Las Vegas Metropolitan Police Department at the age of twenty-four. Six years later, she was content with her existence, liked living alone with her cat Columbo, and if she needed someone to lean on, she had her friends, her mom, or Danny. But damn it, something about this attraction to Carter was harder to fight— and making her feel lonely for the first time since she'd given up "attachments" to the opposite sex. "Maybe," she conceded to Danny. "But you know about my dad."

"I know your *theory* about your dad. And I know the guy had a fuller life than *you*, because his job was only one part of it. Just like me, he had a family he loved. And I'm betting when all was said and done, if you'd asked him which meant more to him—the family or the badge—he'd have chosen you and your mom without even blinking."

Erin sighed. She loved Danny, but she hated when he lectured her. Then again, she'd brought this up herself so it was her own fault. "I'm hitting the street," she said, ready to end the conversation.

"We got your back, babe, but be careful out there."

She nodded, then exited the car and once more felt the full measure of how she was dressed, how much of her body was on display as she sashayed up the lightly littered sidewalk toward the streetlamp she would lean against, licking her lips when guys slowed down to stare and maybe consider making her an offer.

Darkness had just fallen over Sin City and Erin's cunt still ached for attention. She'd thought talking with Danny had distracted her from her arousal, but now that she was by herself again, more able to think, more able to feel, she couldn't believe how turned on she remained after her conversation with Carter an hour ago. Glancing down, she wasn't surprised to see her nipples erect and jutting through her tight top. God, she hoped Danny hadn't noticed. They rubbed against the thin fabric when she shifted from one foot to the other and she found herself wishing she could touch herself.

For the first time, it occurred to her that maybe this assignment was the wrong one for a girl who didn't get a lot of action between the sheets. It had been six months since she'd last gotten laid — by a nice guy she'd met at the Mandalay Bay blackjack tables during a girl's night out. A nice guy, but she'd known immediately there was no risk of her heart getting involved, so it had been safe to have a short affair with him — four dates, three of them ending in his bed. Now lust for Carter Brooks hammered at her, and every sensitive part of her body was encased by snug fabric that created an utterly delicious and agonizing friction with each move she made. And sure, she had a vibrator and she knew how to use it, but it just wasn't the same as a real man.

Just then, a slow-moving sedan beeped, making her look up. Inside were four guys around her age who had bachelor party written all over them. They waved, and she winked, as sexy as she could, then sensually licked her upper lip. The guys appeared transfixed — but then passed on by, and she was glad. Each time she made a vice bust it saddened her on some level — wondering if the guy was married and cheating, or just so lonely and desperate that he was willing to pay for it. Of course, in this town, she knew hiring a hooker was sometimes about the thrill of it, the forbidden allure, but sex *that* casual, *that* meaningless, just didn't turn her on no matter how she looked at it.

Unless…Carter had been in that car. If she were really a hooker, and Carter wanted to pay for her services…well, she didn't like to admit it, but *that* would turn her on. Completely.

She sighed, imagining him pulling up to the curb, asking her how much—telling her she was worth any amount, priceless. She envisioned her breasts in his large, work-roughened hands, how she would arch them deeper into his palms, wanting him to push the fabric aside so that they'd be flesh to flesh—her bared breasts, his warm touch.

Oh God, if her pussy had been hot before, now it was on fire. And the sad truth was, she suddenly didn't know how she was going to stand here all night, feeling sexual, looking sexual, acting sexual, without *being* sexual.

Glancing toward Danny, she hiked a thumb over her shoulder toward the bar. The signal meant she had to use the restroom and was going in. He hated that, because it was dangerous for her to be out of sight, especially in a dive like this, masquerading as a streetwalker—so she tried to avoid it. But this, right now, wasn't really about going to the bathroom, and it wasn't something she could avoid. It was a need that had come on fast and furious.

Pushing through the door, she felt the eyes fall on her—men of all ages glancing up from the bar or from the pool table in the corner, all devouring her with their hungry stares. She ignored the whistle that echoed over the loud rock music and—God help her—enjoyed the attention, enjoyed being wanted in such a dirty way. She could have sworn her nipples got harder and her cunt flooded heavier with each step she took through the shadowy room. Her thighs ached, and her pussy felt huge, swollen with excitement.

When finally she reached the door marked Ladies, she wasted no time going in, locking it tight, then turning to lean back against it. Finally, privacy. She didn't hesitate to lift her hands to the roundness of her breasts, squeezing, molding. And pretending. That they were Carter's hands.

She shut her eyes, imagining he was there with her, all tall and broad and commanding. She wondered how big his cock was, and imagined it pressing rock-hard at the front of her mound. Trying like hell to be quiet—she was wearing a wire and didn't want the guys on the street to know she was doing anything besides peeing—she sighed as she dipped one hand under the sinfully short skirt and between her legs.

She'd worn a thin, red mesh thong—no one would see it, of course, but if she was going to dress the part, she was going to go all the way. Now she was glad for the choice, because it was cool and light and clingy and let her feel her own touch better than if she'd selected cotton.

Oh God, she was wet—just as wet as she'd suspected. She ran three fingers deep through the furrow of her cunt. She'd been right about how swollen she was—her pussy felt enormous, and she released a small moan. *Shit, be quiet.* Reaching down to the sink next to the door, she turned on the faucet so the sound would cover any other noises she couldn't hold in.

Next, she stroked her middle fingertip over her clit. Not gently, but hard and rhythmic, as her body dictated. She spread her legs as wide as she could, still leaning against the door. Her other hand still massaged one breast. The guys outside were totally forgotten, that quickly. *Touch me, Carter, touch me.*

She'd never done anything like this before—never masturbated outside her own home. She'd never needed to. But her lust for Carter was clearly driving her to new highs—or lows, depending on how she looked at it. Either way, it was overwhelming.

Needing freer access to her clit, she found herself lifting one red platform shoe up on the old porcelain sink. Then she rubbed harder through the red mesh. *God, yes. Touch me, baby.*

That's when she caught sight of herself in the old pockmarked mirror.

Jesus, she made an obscene vision. And under normal circumstances, that might have bothered her, but right now it only added to her wild arousal. Carter wasn't the only one who could go to sexual extremes.

What would he think if he could see her like this—touching herself, thinking of him? She bit her lip, knowing the answer instinctively. He would *love* it. She didn't know him well, but she already understood him on a sexual level, and she *knew* he would go instantly hard if he could see her now.

Feeling even bolder and more hedonistic, Erin pulled her mesh thong aside until she saw her pussy in the mirror—pink and open and glistening wetly. Oh Lord. She didn't hesitate to stroke her fingers through the moisture, thinking, *God, Carter, I want you.* She wanted him in any way she could have him—watching her, touching her, she didn't even care. She just needed to connect with him in some carnal fashion.

She whimpered softly as she refocused her touches on her clit, rubbing in deep circles at first and then moving her first two fingers over it more frantically, frenetically, more like a vibrator would. God. Oh God.

She looked in the mirror, at her body on display—her pussy revealed—but she imagined that it was her man watching her as she edged closer, closer, to blessed release. What she saw she pretended *he* saw. He watched her work her own pussy. He saw how badly she needed to come. He saw what a dirty, dirty girl she could be.

And then it happened—the orgasm rocking her almost violently. She had to let go of her breast to grip the sink and keep from falling down. *Yes, yes, yes!*

Oh God.

She couldn't remember ever coming so very hard.

And she was in the bathroom of a seedy bar. By herself. On the job.

Sheesh. Not exactly her usual way of getting off.

Letting out a deep, calming breath, Erin put her clothes back in place and washed her hands in the already streaming water. How long had that taken? Two minutes? Ten? She had no idea how long she'd been inside. God, she hoped Danny or one of the other two guys didn't come storming in thinking something bad had happened.

With that in mind, she hurried from the bathroom, this time ignoring the stares of the patrons as she made her way back out into the warm Vegas night. She found Danny still sitting in the car and waved. Seeing his sigh of relief, she was sorry she'd worried him. And thankful he apparently had no idea *why* she'd worried him.

Taking her spot back by the lamppost, Erin's thoughts returned to Carter. More specifically, to what Carter had just made her do.

The fact was, it *had* been dangerous to go into that bar by herself without really needing to. Stupid, in fact.

This is what happens when you don't stay focused, when you lose your edge. It was a minor mistake, but a mistake just the same. A feeling of cold dread washed over her as she thought of her dad.

Clearly, she was going to have to do something to fix this situation, get back in control of herself.

"Woohoo!" The catcall came from a passing limo—more bachelor party boys—but they drove on by.

Yet even now, their attention made her breasts feel heavy, still needy—or needy *again*. Already? She was already aroused after just coming? This was getting ridiculous.

I'm gonna have to have sex with Carter.

She didn't see any way around it, any other way to slake her needs.

And yet...she wasn't ready to surrender to him *completely*. Far from it.

Letting herself fall for the guy — which she already knew could happen very easily — would be just as bad as her present situation, just as dangerous.

So maybe she could find a way to make it seem…totally impersonal, just like naughty fun, nothing more.

It shouldn't be difficult. After all, his come-ons were all about sex. And given what she knew about that three-way he'd had with Diana and Marc, he was obviously into wild, no-strings-attached bed sports. In fact, for all she knew, that was all *he* wanted, too — just sex.

What if…

What if…she orchestrated her own dirty little ménage a trois? What if…she took precautions, safeguards, to ensure she'd be in complete control of the whole event? What if she even devised a way to make sure she could make a clean getaway afterward, so that he'd know this was just about fucking and not about seeing each other or dating or getting emotionally involved?

She released a small sigh, then looked up as a late model Porsche slowly trolled the boulevard, approaching the Desert Oasis.

Maybe she could do it, she thought, her pussy tingling softly once more. Maybe she could arrange one wild, no-holds-barred night of hedonistic sex with Carter — and they'd both be satisfied once and for all.

Just then, the silver Porsche eased to the curb. The electric window descended smoothly and a handsome, older man in an expensive-looking suit leaned across the passenger seat. "How much for an hour, honey? And I want it all."

"*All*? Sweetie, you gotta be more specific." She had to make him indicate it was definitely sex they were negotiating.

"A blowjob and a fuck. Nothing too kinky," he added with a wink.

"Three hundred," she said. She normally pretended to work cheaper given that she wasn't exactly painting herself as a high-class call girl here, but she knew this guy could afford it and it might seem suspicious if she didn't demand a decent amount.

"Get in."

"Do we have a deal?" She had to get him to agree before she could make a bust. She knew to go by the book or this rich guy's lawyer might be able to weasel him out of it.

"Sure, honey," he replied. "Now come on, I don't have all night."

That was it. Car doors opened, and the "bum" across the street jumped to his feet, all of them closing in quickly, reaching for their badges. Erin whipped her own from the waistband of her skirt, flipping it open. "Sure you do. I'm afraid you're under arrest."

Chapter Two

&

"Something for the birthday boy," a pretty voice said, and Carter looked up to see a blonde waitress making her way through the crowd to place a big piece of chocolate cake in front of him, complete with a burning candle. "Make a wish," she said.

I wish the real fun would start, he thought glumly, then blew out the damn candle.

His group of friends, along with the waitress, clapped softly, and Diana sat down next to him, sliding her arm around his shoulder. "What'd you wish for?"

He gave her a sarcastic grin. "That I'll get something better than a piece of cake for my birthday."

"There's more coming," she promised, eyes gleaming knowingly.

"You'd better hope there is."

Diana had arranged the get-together for his thirty-third birthday, promising him a "very special surprise". So far they'd had dinner at Stefano's on Fremont Street, then headed to the strip, where they'd done some light gambling at The Flamingo and The Mirage. Now they'd moved on to a Caesars Palace nightclub, Cleopatra's Barge. Shaped like a large boat, patrons had to cross a small, roped bridge to get inside. All perfectly fine activities — but Diana had made his "very special surprise" sound distinctly dirty, in a good way.

So at the very least he was expecting a stripper — but it was getting late and he was beginning to worry that Diana's historic penchant for naughty fun was changing. First, she and Marc had thrown that completely sedate dinner party last

125

month, and now this—a night on the strip with nothing risqué in the mix?

"You're getting way too tame since you two got married," he told her, but she only smiled—flashing an expression that didn't look tame at all.

"Just because I'm only my nasty little self with Marc now doesn't mean I've forgotten how to have fun." As usual, Diana was dressed to kill in a short, sexy cocktail dress, her silky brown hair cascading down her back and over her shoulders. The look in her eye almost made Carter believe her, but...

"Then where's my Nurse Goodbody? And why didn't we go to a strip club?"

"Whoa—down, boy," she said with a laugh. "Since when are you so...on the prowl?"

Admittedly, this wasn't his usual demeanor. He lusted for women and loved sex as much as the next guy, and the night he'd spent with Diana and Marc when Diana had first come to town was the most intense erotic experience he'd ever had—but he didn't usually sit around begging for sex and Diana knew him well enough to know it.

"It's Erin," he said without weighing his words. He hadn't even admitted that to himself before right now, but he understood, in an instant, that it was his unrequited attraction to Erin making him so damn horny.

"Erin, huh?" she said with a cute little grin. He trusted Diana and had confided to her how drawn he'd been to their neighbor ever since the dinner party.

He shook his head. "I can't get her off my mind. I don't know what it is—but I've got it bad. And she's just not interested. So I get the torture of watching her head off to work wearing her skimpy hooker clothes, but none of the rewards." The truth was, he wasn't used to women turning him down, so Erin's rejection had come as a blow in multiple ways.

"Poor baby," Diana said, sounding sincere but still smiling. She lifted a kiss to his forehead. "Don't worry — before the night is over, you'll feel *all* better."

He was so horny that his cock perked to life just from the promise, and from the feel of Diana's soft, feminine arm around his shoulder.

"Hey, sweetheart, they're playing our song!"

Carter looked up to see his buddy Marc, plainly intoxicated as he drew Diana to her feet. "Sorry to steal her away, dude," he said, "but I want to dance with my woman."

Carter just laughed, because only alcohol could make Marc dance, and he had a feeling *any* song would be *their* song right now.

But as Diana slipped her hand into Marc's, Carter suffered a pang of jealousy. Not about Diana, but about how damn happy they were. He'd never met two people better suited for each other, and since Diana had come into Marc's life, Marc seemed at once more energized yet content, always wearing a smile.

And given that Carter had turned thirty-three today, the idea of settling down didn't sound bad to him. The truth was, he'd trade twenty Nurse Goodbodies for a nice, settled life with the right woman. He couldn't help envying what his friends had.

That's when he realized *all* his friends had taken to the dance floor. Maybe he was the only one not yet drunk enough. With that thought in mind, he took a swig from his beer bottle and sank his fork into his cake. *Happy-fucking-birthday to me.*

"Hey, Carter — come dance!"

Glancing up, he found Lena, a redhead, and Holly, a blonde — both girlfriends of Diana's whom he'd gotten to know socially. He'd made out with Holly last Fourth of July after they'd all watched the fireworks together at Desert Breeze Park, but it hadn't gone any further. She was cute and a lot of fun, but a little silly for his taste. Not that he needed a genius, but…hell, he guessed he *was* looking for a girlfriend, someone he really wanted to spend time with, in *and* out of bed.

Yet as Carter found himself letting Lena and Holly draw him up out of his chair toward the dance floor, he decided that maybe tonight things *would* go somewhere with Holly. Or maybe Lena, who Diana'd met in her spinning class and had predictably great legs, which she was showing off in a short leather skirt. Yep, maybe he'd just get out on the dance floor, drink his beer, have some fun and see what happened.

And that plan might actually have worked if he hadn't been thinking so damn much about Erin and her naughty hooker outfit.

Where was a cop when you needed one?

* * * * *

Twenty minutes later, Carter was almost having a good time. Beer helped—and he'd just finished another. Something by Shakira blasted over the speakers, and though it wasn't his usual taste in music, he still swayed back and forth, the middle part of a sandwich formed with Holly in front and Lena in back. He still wished Erin was there, that it was *her* breasts rubbing so suggestively against his chest, but he was trying to make the best of it.

Diana and Marc danced next to them, and when Diana caught his eye, she leaned over to yell in his ear over the music, "Happy birthday, baby!"

And that was when it hit him. Holly and Lena. The sandwich. That was Diana's birthday surprise for him.

Shit. He couldn't help being disappointed.

On the other hand, though, what was he expecting? And who was he to complain? They might not be Erin, but Diana wasn't a miracle worker. And just a little while ago, he'd been hoping for a naughty Nurse Goodbody—and two ready-and-willing girls could be a lot more fun than a five-minute dance from a stripper.

"Hey, what's going on?" someone suddenly murmured behind him.

"Cops!" Holly gasped just then.

And Carter forgot all about his birthday present as he turned to see two officers making their way through the crowd onto the dance floor. Both of them women, he realized. "Sir, I'm afraid you'll have to come with us," said the blonde, fair-complexioned one.

He was just about to grasp that she was talking to *him* — when he recognized the other. "Erin?" he asked, taken aback.

She didn't answer — just peered up at him, her brown eyes wide and luminous, her dark hair tucked up under her hat. "What the—" he began, but the other policewoman cut him off.

"Hands behind your back, sir." The blonde cop was physically turning him around, reaching for his wrists.

And he was confused as hell. "What *is* this? What are you doing?" By now, everyone around them had stopped dancing and stood waiting to see what would happen.

"We're placing you under arrest," Erin said, her voice bolder than he'd heard it before. *Must be her cop voice,* he thought — but why the hell was she using it on *him,* and did she just say he was under freaking *arrest*?

"*What*?" He looked Erin in the eye.

"You have the right to remain silent. Anything you say can and will be used against you in a court of law." Erin continued with the Miranda rights and he heard the click of handcuffs around his wrists just as he felt the cool steel binding his hands behind his back.

As the two women began to usher him off the floor, Shakira still shrieking in the background, Carter couldn't think straight. Erin was arresting him? What had he done wrong? What law had he broken?

He looked up at Diana to see her mouth the words: *Don't worry—it'll be all right.* And Marc—*Marc* was fucking *laughing*! Given the beer Carter had consumed throughout the evening and the fact that he was good and drunk now, the whole thing felt impossible and surreal.

He stayed quiet, trying to wrap his intoxicated mind around it, until they'd woven through the crowd in the club and exited across the wooden bridge into a wide hall that connected two casinos. His "police escorts" turned him to the right, toward the main casino and registration desk. People stared.

"What's going on?" he asked, the club's music fading behind him. "What the hell am I being charged with?"

"Drunk and disorderly conduct," the blonde answered. They each had him by one arm, but given their hats, it was hard to see their eyes when he looked down at them now.

"When?" he asked, dumbfounded. "When the hell was I drunk and disorderly?"

An old couple passing by them scowled, apparently thinking he was a difficult prisoner.

"I think it's fair to say you're drunk right now," Erin said.

Erin. His sweet, sexy neighbor. He still couldn't believe this.

"And growing more disorderly by the second," added the blonde.

They brought him to a halt at a bank of lavish elevators and Erin pushed the up button. It didn't even hit him how weird that was until the doors opened and they led him inside. When a young family started to follow, the blonde held up her hand to stop them. "Police business, folks. We're making an apprehension here. Sorry." And the doors closed behind them.

"Where are we going? Since when does Caesars Palace have a police station?"

"Special outpost," Erin answered.

Special outpost? "Get real," he snapped.

"Oh this is very real, sir," the blonde said. "And we'll thank you to calm down and watch your tone."

Carter had never felt so bewildered in his life. And as the elevator opened a moment later and the two lady cops led him into a plush hallway, it occurred to him that he could easily overpower them and get away. But how far could he get with his hands behind his back? And now that he thought about it, Erin had mentioned knowing karate—and they *did* both have holsters at their hips.

"I don't understand," he said simply, at a loss as they guided him down the hallway lined with doors. "What is this about, Erin?" Again, he tried to look at her, but her hat shaded her face from his gaze.

This time no one answered, but the blonde cop drew a card key from her pocket and slipped it in the lock on the door they'd just halted in front of. When the little entry light flashed green, she pushed it open and they led him inside to a standard guestroom. King-size bed with a cherry headboard, large matching TV cabinet, table and chairs, and a small sofa near the window.

Guiding him to one side of the bed, they pushed him down until he was sitting on it. He'd quit asking questions since no one was giving him any real answers, and just waited to see what would happen next.

He couldn't have been more stunned when Erin walked toward the window, then turned back to face him, whipping her hat from her head to say, "Happy birthday, Carter," her voice turning silky, sexy.

He squinted. "Huh?"

She smiled bashfully, biting her lower lip, and now those big brown eyes looked...completely inviting. Especially when she reached for the top button on her uniform and gave a hard yank with both hands, opening her shirt to the waist.

"Oh," he said, blood rushing to his cock as all the puzzle pieces started falling into place. Man, he'd been stupid. And slow. He could only blame it on the beer. And her abject refusals when he'd asked her out. "You're not arresting me."

She shook her head, but it was suddenly hard to keep his eyes there because they kept dropping to what he could see of her bra—a lacy mix of lavender and blue—and the beautiful curves of her ample cleavage. "No," she said softly. "We're *seducing* you."

He shifted his glance to the blonde, who'd just tossed her own hat aside to send sexy, wavy tresses falling just past her shoulders, and who was, he'd just realized, a gorgeous girl. Then he looked back to Erin. "*We?*"

Lowering her chin provocatively, she gave a short but deliberate nod.

"Oh," he said again, and his cock got a lot harder, fast.

"This is Melanie," Erin said.

He looked back to the blonde once more. "Hi, Melanie."

"Nice to meet you, Carter," she replied with a suggestive smile. "Now just lie back, relax and let us do all the work."

Uh-huh, yeah, he could do that. He couldn't quite believe this was happening—that Erin was about to have her way with him and that she'd actually brought a friend along to help—but he wasn't going to argue.

Following Melanie's instructions, he eased back on the bed—only to find his hands trapped behind him. Damn, he'd gotten so excited that he'd actually forgotten about the handcuffs. He sat back up. "Uh, about these cuffs, could we, uh…"

"Yeah, about those cuffs," Erin said, then came to the bed, slid a small key from her holster, and a second later, one wrist came free. He instantly drew his arms around to his sides, ready to reach for her and get this party started—but just as quickly, her small fists closed over his hands, lifting them over his head as she urged him to his back again. Gazing up at the large, beautiful breasts curving from the bra beneath her open shirt, he let himself follow her lead, okay with the idea of surrender now. And only when he felt the cuff come back around his wrist with a snap did he look over his head to see she'd chained him to one of the tall cherry bedposts.

"Oh," he said. More fun with handcuffs. He'd never played that way before, and immediately realized he wasn't all that comfortable being confined. But on the other hand, he could be open-minded, and it was easy enough to go with the flow. Hell, his cock strained behind his zipper, so he must not mind being restrained *too* much. And if Erin and her friend wanted to have a three-way with him, he wasn't gonna nitpick over the details. Nope, he was gonna do exactly what Melanie had said—lie back, relax and enjoy.

Every nerve ending in Erin's body prickled with the reality of what she'd put into play here. She'd never really seduced a man before, and she'd *certainly* never taken part in a threesome, so she was a little nervous. But now that the plan had actually worked, now that they had him in the room and the seduction had begun, she was equally as turned on, her pussy warm with anticipation.

The idea had hit her a week ago, that night at the Desert Oasis when she'd been so dangerously aroused because of Carter. And Melanie was the perfect partner. New to the force, she and Erin had become fast friends and Melanie had happily shared her many sexual exploits since coming to town. She'd moved to Sin City from Peoria, Illinois, seeking some excitement while she was still young enough to enjoy it, she'd told Erin. When Erin had shyly shared her idea for Carter's birthday present, Melanie had agreed, without even having seen him.

But now it was hitting her what she'd started. She'd never so much as kissed Carter, let alone fucked him, and she'd never seen her friend naked and having sex, either—and she was about to get a big dose of both.

So she had to push her nerves aside and concentrate on how hot he looked, cuffed to the bed—where she could control this whole encounter. And on how her whole body was aching with the most reckless desire she'd ever experienced. Melanie had promised to follow her lead, and now...she had to *take* that lead.

Just pretend you're working. Get into your hooker mindset.

Don't feel anything for this guy, because you can't.

Feel only sex. Sex, sex, sex.

Feel it. Be it. Be his perfect seductress, for this one night only.

Blow his fucking mind.

With those thoughts fueling her, and Carter's eyes possessing her, she met his gaze, ran her palms slowly up over her lace-bound breasts, and slipped her shirt off her shoulders, letting it fall behind her.

Then she turned to Melanie and curled one finger toward her, beckoning her closer. When Melanie stood directly in front of her, Erin took a deep breath then reached between her friend's breasts to begin unbuttoning *her* shirt.

She hadn't contemplated how strange it would feel to undress another woman—they'd simply decided they would help each other, thinking it would arouse him—but a tingling sensation rippled up her arms and down into her chest as she parted Melanie's uniform to reveal a push-up bra of peach lace. Melanie's breasts were not as large as her own, but as they swelled from the cups, Erin suffered the shocking desire to see what they looked like without the bra.

Meeting Melanie's gaze only briefly, Erin pushed her friend's shirt off—then watched as Melanie reached for Erin's belt buckle.

Erin's stomach contracted with arousal. She looked down at Melanie's feminine, French-manicured fingers as she carefully removed Erin's holster, setting it aside, then unzipped her pants, her touch just barely skimming Erin's mound.

Erin pulled in her breath, then glanced to Carter, whose eyes were riveted on both bodies. "That's so nice, girls," he said, his voice deep, hungry.

That's when his eyes met hers, just for half a second, before she looked away. No eye contact—she couldn't handle that; it made her feel too connected to him. She could look at Melanie, or she could look at his body, or she could even look at her own—but she couldn't meet Carter's gaze while they fucked him.

"Keep going," he said, and as Erin responded by undoing Melanie's holster, she realized she'd just followed his command—which troubled her a little. *She* wanted control here—*full* control.

Which meant that she had to *take* it. Really *take* it. Really show him that she was the one calling the shots, running this seduction, and that they would do things *her* way.

She reached once more down to Melanie's waistband, this time unzipping her friend's pants, her skin tingling madly upon realizing where her hands were, stimulated by the mere fact that they were unclothing each other.

Both pairs of pants dropped to the carpet in a rush. Under hers, Erin wore a lace thong that matched her bra. Melanie's boy-cut lace panties hugged her round ass and coordinated with her bra as well.

"Mmm…" Carter moaned at the sight of them, and as both girls stepped smoothly out of their pants and kicked off socks and shoes, Erin couldn't help thinking it seemed more exciting to reveal the lace beneath their plain, utilitarian cop's uniforms than if they'd both been wearing dresses and heels. It was like stripping away their tough exterior to reveal the femininity hiding inside. She wondered if Carter felt that, too—felt them becoming softer, more womanly for him with each move they made.

They still stood facing each other when Melanie let her palms glide up Erin's arms to tenderly brace her shoulders, then leaned in to gently kiss her.

Erin couldn't have been more stunned by the soft meeting of lips—but given that Carter was watching, and that this was supposed to be sex in its most illicit form, her cunt pulsed. She tried to hide her surprise as she took in Melanie's soft, sexy smile.

Stay in control by taking control.

Her body's response to her friend's kiss spurred Erin to resume being the bold one, so she reached up to slide her thumbs beneath Melanie's bra straps, sensually drawing them from her shoulders.

The peach lace cups drooped to reveal pale, medium-sized breasts, the pink nipples upturned. Erin pulled in her breath, so close to them, her curiosity fulfilled—they were undeniably pretty.

So with a quick glance at Carter, who looked consumed with lust and strangely erotic—even fully dressed—because of the way he was cuffed to the bed, she decided not to stop there. Sliding her hands to the inviting curves of Melanie's waist, she began to push down her peach panties. Melanie wriggled her hips lightly to help, and her breasts jiggled, too. More hot blood shot to Erin's pussy, her arousal growing as any remaining nervousness faded, and she felt herself headed to that point of no return, the one she'd reached that night outside the bar.

As she eased the boy-cut panties over Melanie's ass, she glanced down and caught sight of her friend's cunt—shaved completely bare. She softly pulled in her breath, not having expected to see Melanie's slit so very on display. She herself kept her pussy well-trimmed, but it had never occurred to her to "take it all off", so to speak.

She lifted her gaze to find Melanie casting her a sensual little grin—which was when it dawned on her that both her companions had seen her studying Melanie's mound. The knowledge aroused her, and she whispered to Melanie, "Me now." It was Mel's turn to undress *her*.

"Turn around," Melanie said softly. "Face Carter." And, stepping free from the peach lace, she situated herself behind Erin—which left Erin nothing to look at besides the sexy man on the bed. Again, she met his eyes briefly, accidentally, but then shifted her focus to the large bulge at the front of his jeans. Yes, that was a much better place for her gaze. And it made her breasts heave with wanting more of him—very, very soon.

Melanie's hands eased slowly around from behind to splay over Erin's bare stomach, then moved upward, upward, just barely skimming her breasts before settling back on her shoulders.

Lord, she was *too* excited. Merely from Melanie's touches. And Carter's presence. She couldn't wait much longer to go further, get more—of him and the big, hard cock hiding behind that zipper. She kept her gaze there, wanting, wanting—and avoiding his handsome face.

She expected Melanie to lower *her* bra straps now, so it caught her off guard when her friend instead curled her fingers into the lace cups and pulled them down, letting Erin's breasts tumble out.

She gasped at the sensation of them spilling free, and Carter moaned.

Melanie rubbed against her from behind, ever so softly— she could feel the tips of Melanie's breasts at her back, Melanie's hips at her ass. A deep sigh escaped her at the intimate contact.

"That's so hot," Carter growled from the bed.

Oh *yeah*, it was hot—burning Erin up from the inside out. Touches from Melanie were something she'd never considered, even after they'd concocted this plan. But now she wanted them, craved them. Because Carter *couldn't* touch her. But he could *watch* her be touched—and to her surprise, at the moment that felt like the next best thing.

Melanie's palms splayed back across Erin's stomach, gently caressing, and when Melanie's kiss came on her shoulder, she instinctively tilted her head so the gentle female ministrations could move up her neck, delivering scintillating tingles that echoed all through her. She watched Carter's face the whole time—saw the heat in his warm green eyes, the way his darkly stubbled jaw had gone slack.

Which is when she realized she was breaking her own rule again, looking at him.

So she drew her gaze away once more and instead peered down—at her bared breasts, on display for him, at Melanie's long, tapered fingers stretching across her torso. When the fingertips of one hand barely grazed the top of her panties, her cunt throbbed and she drew in a rough breath.

"Are you ready for more?" she asked Carter, her voice deep with passion. God knew *she* was. And though it would have been strangely easy to let Melanie keep touching her in still other naughty ways, that last shot of heat to her pussy had reminded her that wasn't what she'd come here for. She'd come here to have *him*.

"Oh, *baby*," he rasped. "I'm ready for whatever you want to give me."

So with a sensual lick across her upper lip, she moved toward the bed, Melanie following. Because he was cuffed to the corner post, his body lay angled across the mattress, making it easy to situate themselves on either side of him.

Erin didn't hesitate to run her hands over his firm chest through his long-sleeved shirt as Melanie began to unbutton it, starting at the bottom. She'd feared maybe she'd turn shy at this point—given that she'd never touched him before—but she didn't. Because she *had* to have him—simply *had* to. Melanie's feminine touches had been unexpectedly scintillating, but she needed male flesh. *Now.* Beneath her fingers, between her thighs.

"Kiss me," Carter demanded then, looking up at her.

Whoa. The words caught her off guard. She narrowed her eyes and balked slightly, instinctively, even as she continued to meet his gaze.

"Damn it, I can't touch you," he said, clearly frustrated. "At least kiss me."

Oh hell.

She certainly *wanted* to kiss him.

His sparkling eyes and lush mouth both beckoned to her.

And kisses were far more intimate than she'd intended to get here, but...the cold, hard fact was that she simply couldn't resist.

With a huge sigh that stretched all through her, she lifted her hands to his face, the rough stubble of his jaw. Then she bent to kiss him full on the mouth, pressing her tongue between his lips until he met it with his own. The kiss traveled like electricity down the length of her body, making her bared breasts feel heavier as they raked the fabric of his shirt, making her thighs ache maddeningly.

That one mere kiss left her breathless, her heart beating wildly, her palms sweating—but she somehow found the strength to reel herself back in, both body and mind, and *not* to look into his eyes anymore.

Instead, she let her mouth trail downward, to Carter's neck, where she drank in the musky, manly scent of him, then to the broad, tanned chest Melanie had just bared by pushing his shirt open. She sank sensual kisses over thin, dark curls, his taut skin warm beneath her lips, then moved farther, farther, following the thin line of hair that led down into his jeans.

Melanie had beaten her to that particular area, though— she knelt at his side, working diligently at his leather belt, and Erin watched impatiently as her friend finally unbuckled it and lowered his zipper.

And—oh! *Oh my.* She pulled in her breath at how big he was, even just through the white cotton of his underwear. She felt the sight in her cunt.

Instinctively, she reached out to touch his erection, running the flat of her palm over the thick, stiff column. *So hard. Perfect and hard.* A tingle scurried up her arm and down through the rest of her body.

He moaned in response to her touch. But she *still* didn't look at him, his face—she couldn't.

This is only sex. Nothing more. Stay in control. Of him. Of Melanie. And most of all, of yourself.

A brief pang of regret over that decision darted through her, a longing for something passionate and *normal*, the need to gaze unabashedly into his eyes and kiss him all night if that's what she felt like doing. But when Melanie pulled down Carter's underwear, lifting the elastic waistband over the head of his cock, all Erin felt was *hunger*.

"Oh…" she murmured deeply. Yeah, he was big, all right. Big and hot, the full length of his shaft arcing up over his lower abdomen to his navel, an inviting dot of moisture resting at his tip.

At this moment, she no longer cared about looking into his eyes. She only wanted what jutted so prominently from between his legs. She wrapped her hand firmly around his cock and bent to lick the wetness from the rounded head.

As a strangled sort of groan left him, she felt the sound *everywhere*.

"So huge," Melanie purred above her.

"And beautiful," Erin heard herself add without planning, still holding him in her fist.

"Suck me," he said. Confident. And even a little demanding.

But she loved his voice. And she even loved his command, this particular one anyway. So hot, so sure. She didn't even think about not obeying, since she'd been preparing to indulge in that particular activity anyway.

She ran her tongue energetically around the tip of his erection, letting the action wet her lips—and then she sank down, taking him into her mouth, as deep as she could.

"Oh God, Jesus," he groaned behind her. She'd positioned herself so that she faced away from him.

Lord, he filled her mouth so well, and she edged deeper, deeper onto him, until his cock touched the back of her throat. She didn't know why she was trying so hard to take more and more of him, but she supposed it was just another form of fucking, and she wanted as much of him inside her *this way* as she would want when she finally took him into her cunt.

Eventually, she began to move her mouth up and down on him in a hot, even rhythm that had him pumping ever so slightly, softly thrusting between her lips. She heard her own breath, coming heavy, labored, and she loved the sensation of him fucking her mouth.

And—oh God, only when Melanie's dainty hand came up under hers, cupping Carter's balls, did she remember she was supposed to be sharing him! In fact, for a few minutes, she'd sort of forgotten this was a threesome instead of a duo.

She raised her gaze to Melanie, who hovered near, watching her every move, and was struck with how raw and erotic it was that she had Carter's shaft in her mouth even as she made eye contact with her friend. The odd sensation urged her to revert to the original plan—to share.

Releasing Carter's erection, she said to Melanie, "Help me. Help me with his cock."

Both Melanie and Carter moaned in response as Erin held him by the base, offering his erection up to her friend. Melanie looked happy to be invited, her eyes darkening and her full lips curving into a naughty smile.

Oh Lord—watching Melanie drag her tongue languorously up his length made Erin's pussy surge. And it made *her* want to lick him that way, too, so she joined in— Melanie licking one side of his majestic cock and Erin the other.

"Aw, damn," Carter said, sounding breathless. "So good, girls. So fucking good. You look so hot doing that."

His stirring words reminded her that she'd turned her head just enough that he could see her face. But she *wanted* him to see her suddenly — wanted him to see exactly what she was doing to him and just how naughty she could be.

So she followed her instincts.

Still running her tongue up his hard cock, she met his gaze — even held it.

Gently letting her eyes shut after a long, intense moment, she delivered hot, openmouthed kisses to one side of his long shaft.

She then eased her mouth around it, stretching, stretching, until her lips also met Melanie's, until they were kissing each other even as they kissed his hard-on.

The only sound was that of heavy breathing — all three of them. Melanie's hand wove into Erin's hair, and her own snaked beneath them to fondle Carter's balls. "Yeah, oh yeah," he groaned between clenched teeth. "So pretty, girls. So hot."

Backing away from Melanie, Erin kept right on following her urges and went down on Carter again, letting the hard heat of him fill her mouth, again feeling the pleasant stretch of her lips as they widened to encompass him, and this time she didn't look away — no, this time she wanted him to see her, so she looked him directly in the eye.

His moans echoed sharp, deep, his gaze almost anguished with what she knew was actually pleasure. She moved on him vigorously, and when her mouth tired, she eased off and again offered his erection to her companion.

Under any other circumstances, she'd have likely felt jealous watching Melanie eagerly sink her mouth onto Carter's shaft, but it was exciting to be sharing him, to be indulging in a ménage a trois. To watch her friend suck him so vigorously after she'd just done the same only added to the nearly overwhelming arousal pumping through her veins. Her entire body felt hotwired, every limb sensitive and pulsating with lust. "Yes," she heard herself murmur, watching Melanie —

even reaching to hold back her friend's hair so she and Carter could see better. "Yes, suck him."

Given her state of arousal, just speaking such words upped her own level of need. The sound of her voice, the frankness of the command, the feel of lips made swollen and sore from the same activity.

It was then that Melanie's hands closed full and bold around Erin's bared breasts, still framed and held high by her bra. "Oh…" she sighed, surprised, aroused. *Any* hands, any sensation right now, felt like heaven. She automatically arched them harder into her friend's soft palms.

Melanie massaged her in the same hot rhythm she used to slide her mouth up and down Carter's length. Her eyes were closed—she appeared lost in passion, and Erin felt nearly as lost to it herself.

That's when her glance fell back on his. She'd never experienced anything more intense than his gaze on her in that moment. *While my friend kneads my breasts.* It was strange. Wild. Utterly amazing.

His voice was barely audible when he spoke, low and intent, teeth still clenched. "I want to fuck you so damn bad."

Not Melanie. *Her*, he meant *her*.

And Melanie seemed not to hear or to care, still working over Carter's cock just as enthusiastically as she did Erin's sensitive breasts. Erin trembled. She wanted him to fuck her, too. She wanted him in her so deep. She wanted to wear him out.

But she didn't respond, because she could barely think, and then Melanie began to pull her, gently, *by* her breasts. She pulled Erin's full mounds closer, closer, until—dear God—she wrapped them around Carter's stone-hard shaft. A startled sob of pleasure escaped her, and Carter moaned, too.

Melanie continued to suck him—but just the head now as she rhythmically pressed Erin's breasts around him. Melanie's lips left Erin's flesh wet with each sensual descent she made.

And Carter thrust more vigorously than he had up to now, each drive delivered with a low, fierce growl. The three of them moved that way, the air filling with moans and groans, and Erin wondered if there was anyone in the rooms next door, if their neighbors could hear them, and she actually hoped they could.

"Aw God, stop," Carter said without warning, sounding pained. "You have to stop or I'll come."

Erin sighed, her whole body feeling the loss when she backed away. She'd had no idea her breasts could conduct that much heat through her whole body. When Melanie released him, his wet cock plopped to his belly, and her eyes looked wild with regret for having to let him go. They all paused in place, catching their breath, coming down from the passion.

"You know, you can let me loose now," Carter said. "I won't try to escape or anything."

But no way—Erin liked him right where she had him.

So she simply shook her head.

He'd probably think she was into bondage or something, but she didn't care. She was already having enough trouble staying in full control of what was happening here. At the very least, she had to keep him cuffed to the bed so she could keep calling the shots.

"I want to *fuck* you," he said again, sounding angry now. "I want to fuck you *both*, all damn night. And I can't even fucking *reach* you this way."

But she *couldn't* let him fuck her. As much as she wanted to. Because that sounded like…like he would *take* her. Like she would have no choice but to surrender her body, and maybe more. And as tempting as that sounded in some ways, she *had* to be the one in control. She had to. There was no other way.

"Relax, baby," she said, trying to soothe him. "Relax…and *we'll* fuck *you*."

Chapter Three

❧

"Get a condom," Erin instructed Melanie. She'd put three in her uniform pocket, and as Melanie departed the bed, she told her exactly where to find them. She and Carter both watched Melanie scurry naked across the carpet—at some point Erin hadn't noticed, her friend had shed her bra completely, and now her pert breasts bounced with her movements.

Erin's eyes dropped to *Carter's* body then, and she was discovering more and more that she liked the vision of him bound—even better now that his shirt was open and his pants down. Perversely perhaps, she liked the idea of him being her captive. And she instinctually ran her hand up his erection, rubbing, caressing, while they waited for Melanie's return.

A low moan left him, fueling her.

"Damn it, I want to touch you," he said then, sounding more exasperated than mad this time. He yanked at the cuffs, as if that would do any good. His voice softened then, just slightly, and she *felt* his need. "I want to touch you *everywhere*, baby. I want to run my hands over those big, beautiful breasts and all those luscious curves. I want to feel how wet your pussy must be by now."

It got wetter, just from that. And felt swollen beyond belief.

"*We're* doing the touching here," she informed him, still molding his cock in her hand, loving the power she felt beneath her palm.

He sighed. "I'm the birthday boy. Don't I get *some* say?"

She met his gaze, shook her head, felt her breasts sway slightly with the motion—and found she loved feeling so on display for him. "No. You take what we give you and you like it." She heard the condom package rip a few feet away.

"Mmm, and I do like it," he said on a growl. "But I want more, damn it."

"You'll *get* more. Right now," she added as Melanie climbed back onto the bed, the flesh-colored condom grasped between her fingertips. Erin drew her gaze from his to resume focusing on his penis.

She held it upright, waiting as Melanie rolled the rubber down onto him, and Erin smiled inwardly, glad she'd boldly bought the large size when she'd shopped earlier this week. And while one part of Erin wanted desperately to climb onto Carter's big cock and take it deep into her pussy, another *wilder* part of her wanted to watch her girlfriend do it first.

They kneeled on either side of him again, so Erin reached for Melanie's bare ass—so soft, round—and began to guide her to straddle him on the bed.

She studied the erotic vision Melanie made—her denuded slit parting as she balanced herself on the tip of Carter's cock. "Mmm," Melanie purred, running her hands up over her own breasts, then she slowly sank down, sheathing him inch by hot, hard inch. Erin's eyes were glued to where the two bodies met, and she didn't mind not being a part of it because she *was* still part of it. She'd made this happen, given this to Carter, and he knew it. She'd given all three of them this hot, forbidden encounter.

"Oh!" Melanie cried, taking him to the hilt. "*Big*. So big." Then she closed her eyes, seeming to luxuriate in the sensation of just having him inside her, moaning her pleasure as she used her hands to knead his chest, and then her breasts, too— this time tweaking the taut nipples between fingers and thumbs.

"Kiss them," Carter said.

Erin drew her gaze from Melanie to him.

He looked directly at her. "Kiss her breasts."

Despite herself, the command infused her with still more desire. He'd clearly seen her studying them as Melanie caressed herself.

Just as before when Carter demanded she do something, she considered refusing but didn't. Because the suggestion enticed her. And it *was* his birthday, after all.

After meeting Melanie's welcoming gaze, she leaned in and gently flicked her tongue over one pink nipple. Oh God. Strange. It felt…delicious, generating as much heat inside her as when she'd sucked Carter's cock. The tip of her tongue almost burned with the forbidden pleasure.

Melanie smiled lecherously, so Erin did it again, slower this time, more deliberately. Melanie let out a sound of delight, and Carter's voice dropped an octave. "Yeah, baby, kiss them. Kiss those pretty nipples for me."

Melanie had begun moving on him now, riding him, so when Erin leaned toward her friend's other breast, ready to truly kiss the beaded peak this time, Melanie's motions arched it into her mouth. She instinctively latched on, suckling softly, and Melanie mewled. Erin ended with a swirl of her tongue, then moved back to the other breast, kissing the hard little nipple once, twice, a third time, her pussy flooding.

She needed more, so she turned to Carter, any playfulness or gentleness disappearing. Her body ached with need, and it centered between her legs.

She rose up on her knees to look down at him and, following her urges once more, she stroked her middle fingertip sensuously through her cunt, over the lace panties she still wore. Then she hooked her fingers into the elastic at each hip and peered darkly into his eyes. "Do you want to see my pussy, Carter?"

He drew in his breath, looking stunned and aroused. "Hell yes."

Giving her lip a sensual little bite, Erin slowly lowered her thong, bit by bit, over her hips, until finally the lace dropped to the bed around her knees. Carter studied her even as Melanie continued riding him, even as he drove into her friend's cunt.

Melanie's breath wafted over them both, hot and heavy. "I want to see, too," she said, so Erin turned slightly, letting her friend study her most private spot as well. Melanie's gaze darkened with heat as it dropped to the crux of Erin's thighs.

A silent but intense moment later, Erin turned back toward Carter, easing the panties off, first raising one knee, then the other, until she was able to fling them away. Slowly, smoothly, she lifted one thigh over Carter's chest. "Do you want to see more, Carter? Do you want to see how open I am, how ready?"

This time, he seemed able only to nod and groan. Her cunt swelled with anticipation, leaving her surprised she didn't drip on him as she eased her way up, up, finally balancing herself directly over his face. "Do you want to lick it? Do you want me to fuck your mouth?"

"God, yes."

She began to lower herself, slowly, slowly, aware that behind her, Melanie still rode him hard.

"Do you want me to fuck your mouth while Melanie fucks your cock?"

"Unh." He lifted his head then, toward her, trying to reach since she was moving so gradually.

But she wasn't going to make him work that hard. No, she was happy to do the work here, so she finally lowered her pussy over his mouth, where she felt the heat of his breath, then the scintillating blast of pleasure when he raked his tongue over her clit. "Oh...oh God," she breathed. The sensation spread through her like wildfire, starting in her cunt but rapidly expanding outward. "Oh God, *yeah*."

Letting the hot delight grip her, she moved over him, gyrating against his ministrations. She held onto the dark headboard before her, let her eyes fall shut, and drank in each and every lick he delivered, loving the sense of control the position gave her.

Carter moved his tongue deeper into her folds as they passed over his mouth, wetting her thoroughly from front to back, but always ending expertly at her clit. "Oh God, baby, that's good," she said, her voice dark with arousal. "So good." Her body urged her to push down harder, harder, giving him no choice in the matter. That's when he began to suck her clit.

She pressed her lips tight, trying to hold herself together, but a sob of abject pleasure escaped her. She clenched her teeth, her breath coming jagged, heavy, as she fucked his mouth, as promised.

Behind her, Melanie reached around, letting her small hands close over Erin's breasts. She glanced down with a rough sigh. Saw her own nipples, taut and hard, jutting between her friend's tapered fingers. Experienced a sensation of pure hedonism, as if she were indulging in a mini-Roman orgy right here in Caesars Palace. But then her eyes dropped— to Carter's.

So green. Boring into her. Situated just above her parted flesh—the vision so forbidden and wild.

"Oh God," she said, their gazes connecting as hot waves of pleasure broke over her without warning—crashing, crashing—making it all she could do to hold on to the headboard and not collapse. "Oh God!" She let her eyes fall shut, unable to keep watching Carter licking her as she came— it was too personal, too intimate.

You thought sex with him wouldn't be personal?

She shoved the question aside and soaked up the last of the pulsations just before her body began to feel limp and exhausted, urging her to lean back from his face.

Oh Lord, his mouth, chin and jaw were so wet. With her. She pulled in her breath, still meeting his eyes.

"Kiss me, Erin. Kiss me again."

Those deep emerald eyes beckoned, so she eased her body farther down his torso, finally bumping her ass against Melanie, who still rode his cock, who still caressed Erin's breasts in her massaging hands. Now Melanie's nipples stabbed into her shoulder blades and she found herself resting back against her friend's feminine curves for a small, reckless moment of abandon, absorbing the attention to her breasts, feeling how sensual and erotic she must look to Carter this way. Given where she sat now, she could feel his pelvic thrusts, even though it was the woman behind her he fucked.

Bending as Melanie continued caressing her sensitive mounds, she lowered slow, heated kisses to Carter's chest, his neck, and then his mouth. Full tongue kisses, her hands in his hair, and she tasted herself, salty and strangely sweet. She found herself not particularly liking the taste but kissing him harder because it was so primal—it turned something inside her feral, almost animalistic.

Melanie's hands shifted from Erin's breasts to her ass, but in some way, as she kissed Carter over and over, it was easy to imagine they were *his* hands, how he would touch her if he could.

Too much emotion swirled around her—she felt too damn much. How was it possible? She'd been so careful, so sure that if she brought a third party into the mix and chained him up and made it into something totally outrageous that it would be impossible to view it—or to *feel* it—in any other way. Yet somehow, getting this close to him, sharing something so dirty with him, letting him see parts of her *she* hadn't even known existed until this moment...made her feel tied to him now, intimately connected.

She couldn't even fight it—could only bask in it. She kept kissing him, letting Melanie run those soft fingers over her body, and she realized that without meaning to, she was rubbing her pussy against his belly, seeking more attention there, needing more stimulation, whether she liked it or not.

"Oh...oh yeah," Melanie said, low and deeply aroused. She kneaded Erin's ass now, her thighs creating friction at the back of Erin's, and with every undulation on Carter, Melanie's pussy brushed Erin's backside. They all breathed heavily together, Erin letting her fingers curl into Carter's chest, wondering if she could come again just from rubbing up against his stomach with Melanie behind her.

"Oh God, here I go!" Melanie cried. "Now!"

The group gyrations nearly rocked the bed off its foundations as the headboard banged the wall. Melanie let out high-pitched sobs as she sank her fingernails into Erin's ass, making her grit her teeth at the mix of pleasure-pain.

"Oh..." Melanie breathed more softly as she came down from her climax, her movements slowing until they halted altogether. Then she slumped over Erin's back, pushing her down against Carter's chest and seeming to hug them both. "Oh my God," she said, voice languid and spent. "That was fucking incredible." Erin could sense her friend's satisfied smile.

"Now you, Erin," Carter said a moment later, his deep voice near her ear.

She raised her gaze, shocked to find their faces so close.

"Now *you* ride my cock and make this birthday present complete."

She pulled in her breath. Another command. But also another she wanted to obey. She pushed herself upright as Melanie climbed off him and moved around to the side. Mel looked flushed and pretty and giddy as she first leaned in to kiss Erin, then bent to gently kiss Carter as well. "Thank you, baby," she said to him as Erin wondered if *Melanie* could taste her on Carter's mouth, too.

A soft, throaty laugh echoed upward from the bed. "I think *I* should be thanking you. I, uh..." he glanced over his head to where he was chained to the post "...didn't exactly do a lot."

Melanie grinned, saucy and flirtatious. "I beg to differ. You have a *fabulous* cock and you *definitely* know to use it, even attached to a bed." She caressed his chest, then turned to Erin, her gaze reckless, hungry. "Do it, Erin. Fuck him. I want to watch you fuck him."

In a way, it was hard to believe this was her friend whom she lunched with on a regular basis, but Melanie was a free and wild spirit, and her attitude since they'd gotten naked had turned Erin on and made it easier for her to do forbidden things. So, just to excite all three of them a little more, she said, "Help me."

First, the two girls replaced Carter's condom with a fresh one, their fingers touching as they slowly rolled it down onto him. Next, Melanie smiled and rose up on her knees, reaching to brace her palms on Erin's hips. Lifting a light kiss to Erin's right nipple—making her shiver and Carter moan—she helped Erin lift and lean back until she hovered over Carter's crotch, her pussy maddeningly hungry for what lay between his legs.

Releasing Erin's hips, Melanie reached down to lift Carter's big, hard shaft from where it rested on his belly. She held it upright for Erin, who poised her cunt against the tip in just the right spot, then thrust down, hard. Erin and Carter both cried out.

She hadn't wanted to take him softly—she'd needed to feel him deep, all the way in, and she'd needed to take back the mental control she feared she'd lost. She'd needed to turn this into something rough and emotionless so that she felt only physical sensation, so that it would blot out anything else.

She rode him hard, bracing her hands flat on his stomach, feeling the jiggle of her breasts as she rocked, the feel of his pole-like cock sliding deep, deep, with each move she made.

Of course, he thrust, too, just as hard, and he was so big that the sensation was almost overwhelming, bordering on pain at times, but she didn't care—she just wanted her body to feel it, to fuck him, to give him what they both needed and to keep her emotions out of it.

It almost worked. She felt it, hard. With each thrust, she felt as if his shaft drove farther and farther into her, the sensations echoing up through her breasts, out through her arms, her legs. "Unh! Unh!" she cried out. He groaned along with her.

But the problem was with his eyes.

She looked into them.

And felt more than the sex.

She felt it all. The forbidden liaison...and the strange intimacy. She felt them peering into each other's souls. And bringing each other the hardest, deepest sort of physical pleasure. Her nails dug into his flesh.

"I wish I could touch you," he growled, sounding desperate.

"You are." She gazed down to where their bodies interlocked.

"Other ways," he breathed.

Where was Melanie?

Oh, right beside them. God, she was even caressing Erin's knee with one hand, Carter's chest with the other. But like earlier, for a few moments Erin had truly forgotten she was there. The connection with Carter ran too deep, too strong.

And her motions relaxed into something more wildly, deeply passionate than the hard downward plunges of a minute before.

She let her body go, let it take over.

She moved in small, rhythmic circles that let her clit rub against him in front while she caressed his cock with her slick inner walls.

Good. So good.

But she needed just a little more. Her hands left him and found her own flesh, her breasts, too big for her palms. She squeezed and kneaded and stroked, and Carter's jaw dropped with lust. "Aw yeah, baby. Do that some more. That's so fucking pretty."

Her breath came slower, louder.

And Carter said, "Come for me, baby."

Another command.

That's all it took. "Oh God!" The second orgasm was so strong it almost hurt. Her body buckled and pitched forward. "Oh God! Oh God!" The tremors shook her uncontrollably as she curled her hands into fists at Carter's chest and wished...that he could hug her. But he couldn't, of course, because she'd cuffed him to the bed. She found herself missing that natural, sure sense of security a simple hug could provide.

Yet she forgot all about that when he said, "Oh Christ, baby, hold on—here I come, too!"

And he rocked her hard, thrusting wild and deep, and she *did* have to hold on, wrapping her arms around him to stay mounted until his moans finally faded to quiet.

She lay that way a blissful moment longer, not thinking about handcuffs or Melanie—or anything but her and Carter and the fact they'd just shared intense orgasms and she wanted to rest with him this way, cuddle up against him and fall asleep.

Of course, she couldn't. Melanie was there. They'd had a *three-way*. She'd *cuffed* him to a bed to make sure she controlled the situation. And she supposed she had indeed succeeded in controlling the situation, most of the time anyway—but she hadn't exactly succeeded in controlling her heart.

"This is the best birthday present I ever got," he finally said, and she lifted her head from his chest to see a sexy, tired smile.

She let herself smile back. "It's the best one I've ever given."

"You gonna turn me loose now?" He raised his eyebrows, still grinning softly.

She only sighed. This was going to be the really tricky part. Because as tempting as it might be to uncuff Carter and snuggle up with him, she couldn't.

In fact, she had to get out of here, fast. She already felt way too much—she couldn't risk feeling any more. "Um..." she hedged, easing up off his large shaft and immediately feeling empty without it.

"Um?" he asked.

She could no longer look at his face.

Melanie, she realized, had grabbed up her underwear and scurried to the bathroom. But Erin didn't think she was going to have *time* for the bathroom, since each second from this point on felt critical, and agonizing.

Sucking in her breath, still avoiding his eyes, she hurried from the bed and spotted her panties in a twist on the carpet. She grabbed them and straightened them out and wished they weren't so soaked but put them on anyway. In one brisk move, she raised the cups of her bra back into place.

"So?" Carter said. "Uncuff me." But he sounded like he already realized that wasn't gonna happen.

Fortunately, Melanie exited the bathroom just then, back in her peach lace ensemble and somehow looking fresh and glowing despite all the hot sex they'd just indulged in. "Afraid not," she told Carter, and Erin appreciated her friend taking over.

She supposed, now that the passion had passed, Melanie could see the forlorn look Erin was desperately trying to hide. She'd never been skilled at concealing her emotions. Which was precisely why it was so vital that she not *have* too many. They just got in the way.

"What?" he asked.

Meanwhile, Erin was rushing into her shirt, stepping back into her pants—although it felt strange to put on clothes so masculine and plain at a time when she felt so wholly sensual and feminine. Like she was trying to cover it up.

But maybe she *needed* to cover it up right now, stop feeling it. Just like she needed to stop feeling so emotional about what she'd just done with him, and the fact that she wanted to do more. And that the "more" involved lots of touching and kissing and snuggling and even talking. No, no, no, this was dangerous—and bad. She couldn't have it. No way.

"We have to go," Melanie told him. Then she glanced to the clock on the bedside table. "We're due on patrol."

It was a lie, but a decent one, Erin thought. She'd told Melanie they couldn't uncuff him before they departed because then he might not let her leave easily, and she had to. She just had to do this—fuck him…and go.

"But I'm putting the key here on the table," Melanie said as she slid on her pants, then walked over to the bed, fishing a small key from her pocket. After which she bent to kiss him on the forehead. "Happy birthday."

He didn't answer for a moment, just looked at her. "You two are just leaving? Leaving me here like this?"

Erin could barely breathe. She'd grabbed up her hat and headed for the door. "Sorry, baby," she tossed over her shoulder. "But this is how it's gotta be. Just a little birthday fun for you—and for us. Now it's over and like Mel said, we have to go."

"Except…we *will* take care of this for you, hon."

Erin peeked around the corner from the entryway to see Melanie politely removing Carter's condom. Geesh! She hadn't even thought of that and was glad Melanie had. She wanted to go and she didn't want him uncuffed before she was gone— but she didn't want to leave the guy with a mess. She was officially frazzled now, not thinking clearly.

Which meant it was definitely time to make her escape.

A quick moment later, she was opening the door and trying to ignore Carter's voice behind them, saying, "I can't fucking believe you're leaving me like this!"

I'm so sorry, Carter. I have to. I just have to.

* * * * *

Half an hour later, Carter still couldn't believe it. It almost felt surreal. When it had been happening, it had been an odd mixture of pleasure and frustration — getting to have Erin and her friend, but wanting so much more of her. Hell, just wanting to touch her without being able to had been brutal.

Now his pleasure had pretty much turned to pain. And his frustration had grown. He wouldn't have believed they'd leave him handcuffed to the bed like this until they'd actually done it. Even as they'd been getting dressed and taking off, he'd *still* not really believed it. Not until the door had shut behind them, leaving the room quiet — and his predicament evident.

Jesus. Would he have to wait until a maid came to clean the room? Sometime tomorrow? And God, how humiliating would *that* be? How would he keep from going to the bathroom until then? And he'd probably be starving by then, too.

How could Erin do this to him? And she thought this was a birthday gift? Un-freaking-believable.

Just then, the door opened, making him flinch. What the hell? Had she seen the error of her ways and come back to let him loose?

That's when Marc and Diana rounded the corner to find him trussed like a pig, his pants still wide open, his dick on clear display. "Oh God," he muttered.

"Whoa," Marc said, blinking, as Diana widened her eyes and laughed.

"This is funny?" Carter asked. "You think this is fucking funny?"

Diana lowered her chin speculatively. "We just kinda thought you'd be gone by now. Or at least, um, dressed by now." Her gaze dropped briefly to his exposed cock. "But I guess it's a good thing we came to check and make sure."

Carter just shook his head. "I'd *love* to be gone by now. But as you can see, I'm chained to the damn bed."

"Dude," Marc said, glancing up above Carter's head, chuckling softly. "All you had to do was stand up and unloop the cuffs."

Trying to absorb his buddy's words, Carter followed his gaze upward—to see he was right. He shut his eyes. *Shit.* He felt like an idiot. If he'd just gotten to his feet on the stupid bed, he indeed could have gotten loose. He was hooked to a tall bedpost, but it *did* come to a knobbed end about five feet above him. He'd just been too dumbfounded and distraught to realize Erin had left him an easy way out. "Christ," he bit off.

"But don't worry, baby, I'll do the honors now that we're here," Diana said, circling the bed to reach for the key Melanie had left.

He watched as Diana slid it in the lock on one cuff and a second later his arms dropped free. Damn, they were sore, his hands numb. He stretched his fingers, trying to get the blood moving again as Diana relieved him of the other cuff, as well.

"So start talking," he said, sitting up to look into Diana's eyes. "Since you're obviously in on this whole thing." Then he narrowed his gaze accusingly. "Double agent."

She shrugged. "I prefer the term matchmaker."

He rolled his eyes and, finally regaining the use of his hands, pulled up his underwear and jeans.

Glancing downward, Diana grinned. "Guess it's a good thing I've seen you naked before or this would be embarrassing."

He let out a sigh. "Guess what. It's still embarrassing. And I still don't get what happened here."

"Well," Diana said, sitting down next to him on the bed as Marc settled into the loveseat by the window, "Erin let me know she was interested in…doing something a little wild with you. I mentioned we were all going out for your birthday, so she came up with this idea. She gave me a key to the room, just so we'd be able to check on you afterward, and like I said, I guess it's a good thing we did. I thought you'd like it, but judging from the look on your face, maybe you...uh, didn't."

"I don't get it, man," Marc chimed in. "You got to have sex with two beautiful girls on your birthday. Why do you look so mad?"

Carter ran his hand back through his hair. "Hell," he said, trying to think through it all. "I was pretty damn pissed about being left chained up like that—until just a minute ago. But that aside, I'm *still* pissed at her, because why did she have to leave at all? She went running out of here like a woman on fire, like she was scared of me. Which, uh," he gave his head a quick shake, "doesn't make any sense considering that she just chained me up and had her way with me."

"I'll admit," Diana said, "her methods were a little unorthodox, but...I got the idea she'd never really done anything this extreme before, so maybe it made her nervous. Maybe she was embarrassed afterward. I just know she seemed totally hot for you when we talked."

He looked Diana in the eye. "If she's so hot for me, why not just accept my invitations for a date? Nothing extreme about *that*. Nothing to be embarrassed about. I mean, it's not like she thought she had to chain me up to make me have sex with her—I'd already made it pretty clear I was interested."

Again, Diana shrugged. She'd always been easygoing about sex; it was her nature. And he guessed *he'd* always been easygoing about it, too—up to this moment. "Maybe she just wanted to cut loose and do something really crazy, you know?" Diana suggested. "Maybe you should take it as a compliment that she chose you to do it with. If you'll recall, once upon a time, Marc and I wanted to do something really wild and we picked you, too. Because I liked you, and because Marc trusted you."

"This is a lot different than that." He couldn't put his finger on why, but something about Erin's seduction galled him.

"Yep—two girls doing you. A guy's perfect fantasy come true." Marc shook his head, no longer seeming as drunk as he'd been down in the dance club. "I still don't get the problem here."

And that's when it hit Carter. The problem. "I really like her," he said. "I really like her, and I really wanted to go out with her and get to know her. And yeah, sure, I wanted to go to bed with her. And what happened tonight was pretty astounding when it was happening." When she'd been kissing him. When she'd been riding him. When he'd been licking that sweet, luscious pussy. Every time she'd simply looked into his eyes had been freaking amazing. "But…it's like she was just *using me*. She chained me up, fucked my brains out, then left with barely a word."

"Yeah, that's heartbreaking, dude, when a girl just uses you for sex," Marc said, his voice thick with male sarcasm.

"Well, think back to when you fell for Diana. I know the sex was great, but I also know you wanted more. I wanted more from Erin, too. And since I asked her out and she turned me down, I guess it feels like…I'm good enough to fuck but not good enough to go out with."

Diana cringed lightly, her eyes turning sad. "Okay. Maybe I'm starting to see your point. When a guy uses a girl that way, well—it can be pretty abominable."

Carter nodded profusely. "Right. And I don't do that to girls. I don't expect that kind of no-strings, no-dating, no-*nothing* sex unless it's clear that the feelings are mutual. So I don't like having it done to me, either. Especially from someone I thought I really liked."

"So then," Diana said, "you don't like her anymore."

Carter sighed. "I don't know." There had been moments when she'd looked into his eyes and he could have sworn he saw something more in them than just lust—and yet didn't her actions say it all? "I *want* to like her. I liked the girl I met at your dinner party. But the girl I met tonight..." He shook his head.

"So you think she's sending mixed signals," Diana clarified.

"Damn straight."

"Well, that leaves you two choices. Forget about her and move on. Or confront her."

But already an idea had begun to form in Carter's head, and it had nothing to do with moving on, and everything to do with getting an explanation from Erin.

Yeah, he'd confront her, all right. Two could play her racy little game.

And Carter was going to confront her in a way she'd never forget.

Chapter Four

§Ð

Erin slammed her car door, hit the button on her keychain to lock it, then started up the path that led past the condo pool. It was late Saturday night, an hour when she knew she'd never get a spot directly in front of her building, so the next best choice was to park here and take the winding walk through the garden-like pool area that led to her condo on the other side. Like the past week or so, the night was hotter than normal for Vegas in the spring, but a breeze lifted her hair from her neck and caused her nipples to perk to life beneath her cocktail dress.

But on second thought, maybe she couldn't blame her hardening nipples on the wind. Because—as usual these last few days—she was thinking of Carter; she was remembering fucking him. The mere thought made her cunt tingle.

This was getting ridiculous. Fucking him was supposed to have gotten him off her mind, out of her system—but clearly that hadn't worked. She just kept reliving each and every moment of what had happened. But mostly the parts when she'd looked in his eyes, when she'd been so drawn in by him, unable not to feel that human connection. So as a result of her actions, she was doing exactly what she'd been trying to avoid—thinking about Carter all the time.

And she'd felt positively awful about the way things had ended, that he'd literally been yelling at her in shock and anger. In hindsight, she hadn't thought through all the angles of her seduction very well. Generally, she was a good planner, but something about the guy totally knocked her off-kilter.

She hadn't bumped into him in the seventy-two hours since their handcuff encounter, but she'd seen Diana, so she knew Carter had stayed upset. "He likes you," Diana had said. "*Really* likes you. He was hurt that you wanted sex and nothing more."

Erin hadn't gone into detail with Diana, had simply told her, "I *hate* that I hurt him. But…I'm just not into the relationship thing." She didn't talk a lot about her past, her dad or her fears in life. That made it easier to just move on and be a good, focused cop. Danny was the only person who really knew the whole story about why she avoided relationships like the plague.

Just then, a large shadow—a man—stepped in front of her on the dimly lit path.

Oh Lord. She'd carried only a tiny purse tonight, to go with her slinky dress, and didn't have her gun! She pulled up short, her heart racing, and prayed her martial arts training would be enough. "Stop right there," she told him.

"It's me."

Who? Then she realized, making out his face. *Carter.*

Her body should have flooded with relief, but given that he didn't sound particularly friendly, she stayed somewhat stressed—even as she creamed her panties at the mere sight of him. "Um, hi."

Stepping farther into the light of a nearby streetlamp, he gave her a once-over. "Playing a high-priced call girl now? Frankly, I would have preferred that to the whole 'you're under arrest' thing. Man, you do a lot of pretending, don't you?"

Something inside her ran cold. *If you only knew.*

But she'd already let this man see far too much real emotion from her, so it stopped here. "I just came from a fundraising gala for the police department, if you must know. And I'm sorry about the other night. I thought it would be fun. For all of us. I never thought you'd get mad about it."

"Yeah, well," he said, still sounding gruff, sarcastic, "I get a little pissed off when someone chains me to a bed in a hotel, then walks out on me."

Her whole body remained tense. It had started with fear, but now it was…what? Desire? Hard, brazen lust? Again? Oh God, yes, *again*. She wanted him.

But she wasn't going to have him. She was going to nip this in the bud once and for all, even though it meant lying and being mean.

"Look," she said pointedly, "I wanted to party with you. That's all. A little sex, a wild time I thought we could all enjoy. It was your birthday—I figured I'd make it one to remember. I didn't mean to piss you off, but given that we're neighbors, I hope you can move past it so that we can be civil to one another if we pass in the hall."

With that, she started to move past him on the narrow walkway—but he grabbed her wrist. "Not good enough," he said.

She darted her gaze up to his. "What?"

"You owe me an explanation. A real one." She could feel the testosterone just dripping off him—and onto her.

Stay tough. Stay tough. "That's as real as it gets, baby."

He never broke their gaze, although his voice softened slightly. "I don't believe you."

She sucked in her breath. Like before, during sex, their faces were too close. "I don't care what you believe," she told him. But her voice had softened, as well—without her permission.

And she feared he'd heard it, because his eyes went darker then, looking determined. "You'd better *start* caring, honey. Because I don't like being used. So I'd advise you to start talking—telling me what your little game the other night was really all about." He still held her arm, tight, and was slowly backing her off the walkway into the grass, another step, another step, until she bumped into the chain-link fence that enclosed the pool area. Most of the fence was covered with greenery or hidden with shrubs, but here she felt the cool steel against her arms, shoulders.

"Or what?" she asked—again, too quietly.

"Or you're gonna find out the game works both ways."

Lord, what was he talking about? And why didn't he just take her explanation at face value? How did he know there *was* more to the story? Apparently, she was a better actress when it came to being a streetwalker than a sex-hungry lady cop. "What do you mean?"

"I'll show you *exactly* what I mean," he said, threat dancing in his eyes, then slid his palms down both her arms until he laced his fingers tight and smooth between her own, effectively pinning her to the fence with his body. He was bigger, broader, than she'd ever realized before—and oh, then his erection pressed to the juncture of her thighs through his jeans, making her breasts ache and her cunt weep. That's when he pressed a blistering hot kiss to her mouth—pushing his tongue between her lips, kissing passionate and hard, making her feel every nuance of it.

She couldn't help kissing back. Something about him was so powerful, intense. She didn't *want* to kiss him back—in fact, her instincts told her to run, to get as far away from such intoxicating kisses as she could. But he had her trapped against the fence, and beneath his mouth—his lush, capable, commanding mouth—and at the moment it was all she could do not to melt.

When finally the long, sensual kiss ended, they were both panting. The front of his body grazed hers, although the bulge behind his zipper achieved more solid contact. It was hard as hell not to grind against it.

"Let me go," she said anyway. It came out stronger than she felt.

"Not a chance," he replied, masculine heat from his body buffeting her. So it made no sense when he released one of her hands—until she looked down a few seconds later to see that he'd pulled something from his pocket, furry and red, a more *gentle* set of handcuffs than the regulation ones she'd used on him.

She gasped, but not before one fur-lined ring circled her wrist, snapping shut. "What are you doing?"

Just as quickly, he pressed the back of her hand to the fence at her side and snapped the other cuff shut around a couple of the sturdy, square chain-links. "What's it look like?" he said, not an ounce of amusement in his voice.

Her heartbeat tripled and before she could even summon an answer, he'd whipped out a second pair of red furry cuffs, stretched out her other arm, and cuffed it to the fence, too. She sucked in her breath, trying to think, but it was difficult given how close to her he still stood. "Carter, you can't be serious," she finally managed. Even though he *looked* plenty serious.

He tilted his head and narrowed his gaze. "Since you like to play with handcuffs so much, I figured you'd be into this."

Part of her wanted to scream in frustration. For the first time, she understood a little of what Carter might have felt in the hotel room. Her heart still beat madly, almost painfully. Yet even amid her disbelief that Carter had really just chained her to a fence, leaving her completely at his mercy, she couldn't help realizing he'd been a little more thoughtful than her, getting the furry, playful kind of cuffs so as not to hurt her wrists.

Though with that thought in mind—that these came from some adult novelty store—she yanked both her arms away from the fence, expecting one or both to break free. But they were stronger than they looked and held tight. Damn.

She shut her eyes in defeat, then opened them to see Carter peering down at her.

"Don't worry, honey—this won't hurt. At least not much."

Once more, she sucked in her breath, shocked to discover Carter could be so cold. Well, not cold. Hot as hell, actually — hot and take-charge. But calculating and tough.

She had to get out of here somehow. Not because she was frightened of him, but because she was still *deeply* frightened for her heart if she got any closer to this man. "Carter," she said, sounding breathless even to her own ears. "You have to let me go. I can't... I just can't..."

"Sure you can, baby," he said, his voice almost teasing and soothing this time, but still possessing an underlying air of domination.

And as he ran his big hands slowly, achingly, up her hips, over her waist, the sides of her breasts, she yanked at the cuffs again, an instinct, and thought of screaming. But at the same time, she couldn't deny the pleasure echoing through every single inch of her body. She couldn't deny that her breasts were heaving and her pussy had filled with heat. And she also couldn't deny that he wasn't doing anything to her that she hadn't already done to him, and that — Lord help her — her body craved more.

Carter had never planned to be so rough with her. But maybe deep down he'd known a little roughness would be required to get her where he wanted her, and maybe he thought fair was fair. The part he supposed he hadn't expected was the way he felt right now. Like an animal. A heat-seeking, hungry beast.

He'd been plenty attracted to her before their Caesars Palace encounter, but seeing her now forced him to also see her, in his mind, as she'd been then. He couldn't not remember the way she'd ridden him, that sweet, tight pussy working his cock, or the way her beautiful breasts had spilled from her bra with those pink pointed nipples before she'd caressed them in her small, pretty hands. And he discovered that he felt now much like he had then. Lust-filled — and angry.

And since she refused to give him the one thing he'd ask of her — a real, honest explanation — his body was more than ready to move on to what they already knew worked between them. Sex. And he wasn't inclined to be gentle.

So he didn't stop himself from closing his hands firmly over her breasts through her dress. And her hot moan shot straight to his dick, telling him what he'd already sensed — she could act like this offended her, but she wanted it just as badly as he did.

Kneading her breasts — pushing, squeezing, molding — he gave her another hard, punishing kiss that he hoped she felt all the way to her cunt. Then, too heated up to even think of going slow, he curled the fingers of both hands into the draped black bodice of her dress and pulled downward, easily able to catch the fabric under the shelf her large breasts created. A skimpy black bra with thin shoulder straps resided underneath, her lush cleavage looking ready to burst from it, so he helped it along, yanking down the cups of the bra, as well.

Her hot gasp fueled him, as did the way she looked, cuffed to the fence on both sides, at his mercy. He'd never been into bondage, but maybe this was a fetish waiting to happen, because she looked too delectable this way — chained, her voluptuous breasts bared.

He dove on them, unable not to. Letting both hands close back around the abundant curves, he feasted, sinking his mouth firmly to one hard pink peak. She sobbed softly, the sound wafting through him like sweet music as he suckled her hard.

"Oh God," she moaned. "*Oh God.*"

He molded and sucked harder. Then moved his ministrations to her other breast, latching on just as tightly, savoring how amazingly rock-hard her nipples had grown for him, like pearls between his lips.

Freeing one hand, he reached down, under her dress, easing his fingers directly between her thighs. Her panties were soaked and it made his cock strain in his jeans. Oh yeah, she wanted this, all right—she wanted it with just as much ferocity as he did.

"Your pussy's so wet," he growled between suckling her breasts.

She answered by thrusting against his hand.

He moaned in response, rubbing the damp, swollen mound in a hot, hard rhythm he hoped she felt in her clit. "That's right, baby," he told her between heated breaths. "Fuck my hand."

Her heavy breathing replaced the night's silence, hot and beautiful. Carter had never realized how quiet it was where they lived late at night—in Green Valley, an outlying suburb twenty minutes from the Strip. But he noticed it now, because Erin's beautiful panting noises were all he could hear and they filled his senses as she moved on his fingers.

Needing more of her—damn, it was heaven to finally be holding her, finally have the control to do what he wanted with her—he shoved her silk panties roughly aside and sank his touch to her wet folds. "Oh God, yeah," he said, his fingers instantly drenched with her desire. He rubbed her, really *felt* her, exploring her cunt the way he'd wanted to the other night. He raked his fingers deep through the warm, damp furrow, enjoying her noises of pleasure, then he traveled farther, farther, until he sensed the spot where she opened. His blood ran hot as he thrust two fingers up inside.

"Oh!" she cried, louder than before, so he quieted her with another hard kiss. He moved his fingers in and out of that hot, wet passage where his cock had been only a few nights ago, but somehow this felt more intimate to him—because he could touch her now, make her feel things, *make* her respond.

He loved how she met the rough kisses he slanted across her mouth, loved how her breasts jiggled against his chest, loved how damn wet she was for him. "Dirty girl," he whispered heatedly.

"You *make* me dirty."

169

"I *like* you dirty."

She met his gaze, her lips swollen, eyes wild. "Then fuck me," she said.

He'd never imagined she would ask under the current circumstances, but he liked it, and he told her so with another bruising kiss. Reaching under her dress, he found the elastic at her hips and yanked it toward her knees in a rush, until it fell in a small heap around her ankles, over top the sexy black heels she wore. Glancing down, he let the sight increase his arousal, and he worked at his jeans until he could shove them down, spread them open, his hard shaft bursting free.

"Ohhh…" she purred at the sight of it, and he could have sworn he grew another inch.

"You like this, baby? You want it?"

She clenched her teeth lightly, her brown eyes so wide and hungry in that moment that she looked just as reckless as he felt. "You know I do," she said, her voice sounding a little strangled. "Take me. Fuck me. Now."

Oh God—that was all he needed to hear. And she was so wet and ready that he could smell her, the sweet scent of her pussy wafting to greet him as he pushed her slinky dress up around her hips. She automatically hooked one leg around his thigh, the pointed heel of her shoe digging into his flesh in back as she used the leverage to pull him closer. He locked both hands onto her sweet, round ass and thrust his cock inside her.

They both cried out and he hoped to God no one had heard.

And then he looked into her eyes.

He'd planned to fuck her hard, be relentless, give her the most brutal pounding she'd ever had.

But somehow things slowed then, turned more rhythmic. It was the way she moved so deliberately, the way he sensed she *needed* to feel him. It was the languid, sexy, needful look in her eyes. It was how she arched against him, her body seeming to roll against him like a wave against the shore, again, again. Hot, slow—a sexy cadence he couldn't fight.

He picked her up, lifting her ass in his palms. "Wrap your legs around me," he instructed, breathless.

She did as he'd said, their gazes never breaking. He kissed her once more—pure instinct.

With her back pressed to the fence, she undulated against his cock in a tempo that felt ancient, timeless, hypnotic. Her breasts ebbed and flowed against his chest until finally he reached down and captured one pink peak in his mouth. "Oh, oh God," she murmured. "Good. Good."

He suckled, at once hard yet gentle, and used his tongue to tease the very tip of her nipple inside his mouth. Her hot sighs filled the air and drove his thrusts slowly deeper into her welcoming cunt. He wanted to fill her, possess her. And mostly, he wanted to make her come.

"Unh..." Her hot rhythm changed then, just slightly, speeding up even as her gyrations became more drawn out. "*Unh...*" she moaned again.

He squeezed her ass, suckled her breast harder.

"Yes," she whispered. "Yes, baby."

In back, he splayed his fingers wider over her bottom, using the longest on each hand to reach toward her anus. Then he curled his fingertips deep into her flesh, knowing she'd feel the sensation in her asshole, that the movement would draw it slightly open, making it tighten in response. He'd never heard a sweeter sound than the shocked, ragged, high-pitched little sob that left her.

He made the same movement, stretching his fingers across her ass over and over, each time taking her deeper into a swallowing sort of bliss he was pretty sure she'd never felt before. The noises that left her were new and she seemed lost to sensation, her head falling back, eyes dropping shut as she thrust, thrust, thrust in those hot, jagged little moves against his cock.

Soon her lips trembled beneath the rays of the streetlamp and Carter studied her face as she edged still further into ecstasy.

"Come, baby," he whispered. "Come on me."

"Oh, I...unh..."

He sank deeper into the rhythm she'd set for them, trying to make her feel him more. "Come hard, honey. Come so fucking hard on me."

"*Unh!*" Her body jolted, once, twice, then she rocked on him, bucking like a wild rodeo girl, and she looked so fucking beautiful in the throes of passion, her arms stretched out at her sides, held in place by those red fur cuffs, that Carter couldn't hold back.

"Jesus," he groaned, then gave her what he'd planned from the beginning, those rough, brutal strokes that he wanted her to feel in every pretty limb of her naughty little body.

She cried out at each hot stroke, and he rammed his cock into her moist little cave over and over, back to feeling like an out-of-control animal.

"Yes! Yes!" she sobbed. "Do it! Fuck me!"

That last hot, dirty plea from her swollen lips pushed him over the edge into an all-consuming orgasm that rocked his whole body. "Ah, God!" he moaned, shocked by the power of it, trying like hell to keep holding them both upright as the waves of heat pulsed through him like thunder.

When finally they faded, he leaned forward, resting them against the chain-links until he could regain his strength. Finally Erin unwrapped her legs and he lowered her gently to the ground, easing out of her.

He never moved away, though—he stayed close, just looking into her brown eyes, and like the other night, feeling they'd shared something more profound than mere sex. Lifting his hands to her face, he gave her one last kiss, this one not quite so hard as the rest, but more desperate and searching.

That's when it hit him. He'd fucked her brains out, filled his animal urges—but he still didn't know why she wanted to keep this connection only a physical one.

So what had he accomplished here?

Okay, yeah, some really great sex and a couple of *insane* orgasms. But what had changed?

Nothing.

"Are you gonna leave me here like this?" she asked softly. "Cuffed to the fence?"

The question almost amused him, but she looked so worried that he couldn't enjoy her fear. "No, honey. I wouldn't do that to you." That simple. He'd never even considered it.

And, glancing down at her still-bared breasts, he lowered a kiss to the curve of one, then pulled her bra and dress back up over them before zipping his jeans. Reaching in his front pocket, he extracted the little key that had come with the cuffs, and went about unhooking her from the fence and freeing her hands.

When she drew her arms down and took turns rubbing her wrists, he said, "Are they okay?"

She glanced up, nodding. "Fine." Then guilt flashed through her eyes. "What about yours—the other night?"

He shrugged. "Had a couple red marks—no big deal."

She sighed. "I'm sorry, Carter."

Carter swallowed, just peering down into her eyes, feeling the depth of her emotions. He understood she was apologizing for more than just the marks left by the cuffs. So he decided to take another, *calmer* stab at the problem here. "You want to talk awhile? It's nice tonight, cooling down a little now."

At first, she looked hesitant, and he feared she would bolt, but after a moment, she gave in. "All right."

Carter turned to lean against the fence, letting his back slide down it until he was sitting on the grass, his knees bent before him. He reached up to take her hand. "Come on down."

Kneeling next to him in her sexy dress, she finally situated herself at his side, her back against the chain-links, as well.

He wasn't sure where to go from here, but decided maybe kindness would work. Erin had seemed so nice at Marc and Diana's party—maybe he could find that girl in her again.

"If I've been a jerk tonight, I apologize," he said. It was just hitting him that he'd been crazed enough to handcuff a woman to a fence and fuck her, right in the middle of a bunch of condos. And not just any woman, but a *cop*.

"I was the jerk," she replied quietly, looking straight ahead, toward the concrete walkway and the ornamental trees and tall, decorative grasses beyond that had made the location feel more private than it really was. "The other night, I mean. I…didn't think it through well enough when I planned it." Then she turned her head to look up at him, her eyes earnest. "And for what it's worth, I don't usually… I've never… I'm, uh, not generally that wild. It was my first threesome."

"That part I didn't mind," he confessed with a smile. Fresh heat rose in his groin, his cock perking back to life that quickly at the memories. "I have to tell you, Erin, you were fucking beautiful being that bold, that hot, touching your friend, kissing her. That part was amazing."

She lowered her gaze, still looking hesitant, appearing to choose her words carefully. "Then…what part did you mind exactly?"

"Mainly the part where you left," he answered bluntly.

She sighed. "Yeah, that's the part I didn't think through."

"Why did you do it that way? Why did you rush off?"

He saw her swallow, clearly nervous. "I…I'm just not into having relationships, Carter. It's just…not my thing." She shook her head, back to staring straight ahead now.

"That still doesn't explain it. You don't have to want a relationship to act decent after sex. And who ever even *said* anything about a relationship?" He was interested in having one with her—he couldn't deny that to himself—but he'd sure as hell never told her that. "All I did was ask you out."

Next to him, she sighed. "Well, dating often *leads* to relationships. So...I just didn't want to go there."

He stared at her pointedly. "There's more to it, more you're not telling me. Because nobody acts this weird about sex and dating without a reason. Now out with it, Erin. Tell me the truth. What's really going on here?" Maybe he was pressing too hard, but at this point, he didn't care. She was the one who'd seduced him without his consent and turned things so odd and intense between them. He had every right to find out why.

And when she didn't answer, simply sat there staring quietly upward at the crescent moon overhead, he only grew more resolute. *So* resolute that he picked up the furry handcuffs from the ground where they had fallen and quietly put one end around his right wrist, clicking it shut, even though it was too tight on him and needed to be loosened. Then he grabbed her left wrist and snapped the other red cuff around it, locking them together.

She gaped down at the cuffs and the silver chain between them, then raised her eyes to him. "What the hell is *this*?"

"Consider it gentle persuasion," he said. "You're gonna sit here with me until you give me a real explanation that makes sense. And guess what, honey. I've got all night if that's what it takes."

Chapter Five

ଛ

How had this happened? Erin could only stare in disbelief. She never could have known he'd be so damn upset about her leaving him or so hell-bent on understanding why. The plan had seemed so simple in the beginning—the perfect way to get close to him *sexually* without getting close to him *emotionally*. What a disaster she'd created.

"Well?" he prodded. "Gonna tell me?"

She stayed silent, unable to summon an answer, still too stunned by this whole thing. Not only his reaction—but the sex just now. It had been…overwhelming. The best she'd ever had, by a long shot.

She'd been angry at the beginning, of course, feeling trapped and cornered—suffering that loss of that control she valued so much.

But the truth was, there had been moments when she could have gotten away.

She could have fought him, but she hadn't, not even a little. And she could have screamed—they were in the middle of a condo complex, someone would have heard.

But she hadn't done those things, or *any*thing—besides succumb.

"I've got all night, Erin, but if you just tell me now, we can both go inside and get some sleep. On the other hand, if you want to sit out here with me, watch the sun rise, and let some of our neighbors find us cuffed together, with your panties on the sidewalk," he pointed to where they'd landed when she'd kicked them off, "that's fine by me."

Okay, she was crazy about the guy, but he was getting on her nerves about this. And he'd just pushed her over the edge. "You want to know why I left? And why I won't go out with you?"

"Please," he said brusquely.

She glared at him. "Fine. It's because I can't date a guy like you without getting emotionally involved. And I can't afford to get emotionally involved—with anyone. And I thought I could at least have sex with you without getting emotional, but that didn't exactly go my way, either. So I left before I felt any more emotions than I already had. So there. I *feel* something for you. That's the answer. Happy now?"

His eyes widened, then narrowed, until he looked completely bewildered. "Kind of. But what the hell are you talking about—saying you can't afford to get emotionally involved? What does *that* mean? That some jerk hurt you and you never got over it? Because I know girls are like that sometime, and let me tell you, it's dumb to waste your life worrying about getting hurt by people."

Oh, the gall of him. "It's not like that," she snapped. "But even if it was, I wouldn't appreciate you telling me I was dumb."

He didn't apologize. "Then what's it like?"

She huffed in frustration. God, he was insufferable. She didn't want to tell him. Because she didn't like thinking about this, let alone talking about it. But if it got her uncuffed from Carter—if that's what it took to end this—fine, she would spill her guts a little more.

"It's like…" Her voice softened. "My father died."

He blinked, concern filling his green gaze. "I'm sorry."

But she shook her head. "It was a long time ago, when I was in high school. Only, the thing is, he was a cop, too, and he died on the job. And the reason he died on the job was…he was too emotionally wrapped up in my mother. She was sick at the time—cancer—and he was having a hard time dealing.

His focus shifted from his work to her health, and he lost his edge. Then got shot by some idiot because of it."

She didn't think she'd ever heard Carter speak so gently, with such care, as when he said, "I'm really sorry about that, honey. It's awful. But...what does that have to do with *us*?"

Another heavy sigh escaped her. She bent her knees, not caring that her dress dropped to the tops of her thighs with the move. "I can't lose *my* edge, Carter," she explained slowly. "The day I chose to be a cop, I knew it meant placing the job above all other things, for my own safety. I made a conscious decision that I couldn't get too attached to anyone from that point forward. Guys, I mean."

He was looking at her like she wasn't making any sense. "Well, forgive me for pointing this out," he said, still speaking with care, "but don't most cops have...pretty normal lives? Like don't they get married, have kids, that sort of thing?"

She pursed her lips, glancing over just enough to meet his eyes. "Most cops, yeah. But...I guess I'm not most cops."

He shook his head. "I don't get it."

She let her head drop back, exasperated. She didn't necessarily expect him to *get* it—she just wanted him to accept it. But since he still didn't, she felt forced to dredge up yet one more personal truth. "I...feel things *deeply*, Carter. My father always said so. He said I had a 'sensitive soul'. He told me once that he was afraid my life would be more difficult because of it—because I get hurt easily, because I feel pain too long, too deep. And the truth is...he was right."

She paused, bit her lip, peered up again at the moon as if it held some deep secret she could interpret. "But my strength is that I know my weakness. I know how to combat it. And I need to ask you to respect that, even if you don't understand it."

"But..."

Ah hell, he was still going to argue. She'd just poured her heart out to him completely, and he was still going to fight her.

"Are you saying your plan, for your whole life, is to never, ever get involved with anybody? To...always be alone?"

She cautiously lifted her gaze, trying for a smile, even though her voice came too small. "It's not a death sentence. It's just how I choose to live."

"Aren't you afraid..." His eyes narrowed, and she tried to ignore how lush and kissable his mouth looked in the shadowy light. "Aren't you afraid of getting lonely? Maybe not now. But at some point, later? You really want to spend your whole life alone?"

Erin could have argued that she had friends and co-workers and a cat—but the ugly picture he'd just planted in her head, the thought that someday she might really feel alone in the world without a soul to turn to or a shoulder to lean on, sank down into her bones and made her defensive. "Why can't you get it?" she snapped at him. "I don't want to die! And I don't want to leave behind someone who loves me to mourn! It's selfish and I won't do it!"

She sucked in her breath as soon as the words left her. Then dropped her gaze, shocked. "Oh God," she murmured.

"It's okay," he said.

"No, it's not." She shook her head, staring at the ground, the grass between their bodies, Carter's blue jeans, her own bared thighs.

"You're mad at your dad, but that's okay. It makes sense—it's natural."

She was still shaking her head, wanting to deny it, but at the same time, deeply buried emotions bubbled to the surface. "Why did he do it? Why did he keep going out there, night after night, risking his life, when he wasn't up to the job? Why didn't he just take a break, take a leave of absence or something?"

Carter's free hand rose to cup her cheek, warm and strong. "Maybe he didn't see it. Maybe he just wanted to keep on going, acting normal."

She gazed into his eyes, trying not to let tears leak free. She never cried, never. And she could scarcely wrap her mind around all this. "I don't want to be mad at my dad. I loved him. He was my world." She shook her head, confused.

"It's okay," Carter said again. "It's okay for you to be mad even though you loved him. And it's okay for you to *feel* things, Erin. I mean, you've obviously been keeping a lot of shit bottled up inside—it's probably good to get it out."

She nodded, feeling numb, her heart beating too hard.

Was Carter right?

She could still hardly believe or understand it—but had she really been angry with her dad? All this time? She'd loved him so much.

And yet…maybe it was true. Maybe she was mad that he hadn't been careful enough when he was under so much stress, in so much emotional pain.

Or hell—for all she knew, although she'd never wanted to admit this to herself, maybe his death had truly been unavoidable. No one had seen it—his partner had been approaching the house from the back while he'd been in the front. Maybe he'd made no mistake; maybe there was nothing he could have done, no way to be more careful. She'd never wanted to believe that because she liked to believe a person, even a cop, was in control of his or her own life—just like she needed to believe she was in control of hers.

She didn't know the answers. She didn't know anything right now.

Except that the man attached to her at the moment with furry handcuffs was too sweet. Too kind and understanding. And too, too hot for words.

And she wanted to run away—from all these memories, all these fears, everything bad. And from Carter, too, because she'd let him see *way* too much of her tonight—hell, he'd drawn things from her that she hadn't even known were there. But she *couldn't* run…because of those damn soft red cuffs that tickled her wrist each time one of them moved.

"Are you okay, baby?"

The work-roughened fingertips of his free hand gently caressed her cheek as their gazes connected. Then his palm skimmed down her arm, his wrist barely grazing her breast, until his hand closed high on her outer thigh, shifting her legs across his, gathering her to him closer. The sheer comfort the move delivered nearly immobilized her. *This is what it is to be held by a man who cares for you.* She'd nearly forgotten how good it felt. She'd *made* herself forget.

But then she looked deeper into his eyes, her whole body sensitized as his hand slid slowly onto her ass—bare beneath the silky dress. And as another soft night breeze wafted over them, her pussy rippled, and a glance down revealed that the fabric had risen past it now, putting her on display.

She never answered his question. Just leaned closer to him. She never decided to—it just happened, her body led her there.

He leaned closer, too, until the warmth of his skin seeped into her. His mouth hovered not an inch away, and her whole body hungered. And when finally he kissed her, slowly, thoroughly, in a way she felt between her thighs, she melted deeper against him, and his hand eased farther around, over her ass, his fingertips teasing the tiny fissure in back before sinking down into her cunt.

"Ohhh…" she moaned, her chest swelling with arousal. This man did things to her she couldn't understand—or fight.

And then came the sweet, hot intrusion—two fingers, at least, thrusting up into her wetness. "God," she breathed. "Oh God." She let her eyes fall shut.

He kissed her again, beginning to move his fingers in and out, and she heard her breathing match his rhythm, and her pleasure.

"Stand up," he rasped against her lips.

She should argue. Stop this. Somehow.

But instead she eased slowly up onto her heels, those fingers inside her guiding the way, pushing her where he wanted her to go. Her whole body pulsed with need, and at the moment she was too weak to resist.

Still cuffed together, her left wrist to his right, she found herself dragging his hand with her, the soft weight of it pulling on her furred bracelet and sending a gentle frisson of passion up her arm and down through her breasts.

And then she was facing the fence, leaning toward it, locking her fingers through the chain-link squares. And his tongue was slicing up into her pussy, making her willingly spread her legs farther as she met his mouth with her mound.

"Oh Lord," she breathed. "So good."

She gripped the fence tighter, pressed her breasts to it and shut her eyes as Carter licked deep into her folds, his fingers still fucking her from behind.

"Yeah," she murmured throatily. "God, yeah."

She quit thinking, just letting her body absorb every sensation. She moved harder against his mouth. She cried out when his tongue traveled higher, raking over her clit—again, again.

Despite herself, she loved that their hands were locked together—the feeling of being confined, even just slightly, was weirdly arousing. She'd felt it when he'd chained her to the fence earlier, too. The friction at her wrists when she'd pulled at the cuffs, the way it spread through her whole body.

She met his skilled tongue, practically felt her clit swelling with blood beneath his ministrations, and slowly sank a bit lower, lower, bending her knees against the hard fence to better fuck his mouth.

"Yes, yes," she prodded through clenched teeth as the pleasure rose inside her, growing, blooming, getting bigger and bigger until the orgasm tore through her like a storm. She sobbed as the pulses thrust her pussy hard against his face and her body against the fence. "Oh! Oh!" she cried, until it waned, and she sank down into his lap, straddling him.

Like in the hotel room, he kissed her, tasting of her own juices, and she kissed him back just as feverishly, drowning in the rank intimacy of it. At the same time, they both struggled to undo his jeans, the furry cuffs not hindering them since they both worked at the same task.

When his enormous cock burst free, Erin sighed with pleasure, wrapped her loose hand around it and impaled herself without a second's delay. They both groaned at the impact, and she said, "Oh God—big," her voice rife with pleasure.

In one smooth, strong move, Carter anchored his free arm around her and laid her back on the soft, cool grass without his shaft ever leaving her. The moon shone behind his head as she looked into those intense eyes and, despite herself, relished having him on top of her. She loved her control, craved it, needed it, thrived on it—but being under this man was undeniably good. Feeling his strength, how much larger he was than her. Feeling the power of his erection as it drove into her so deep.

His cuffed hand rose to her breast, dragging hers with it as he yanked down her dress and bra to reveal one stiffened pink peak beneath the streetlight's glow. He licked it hungrily, leaving it to glisten, then tingle with pleasure as the soft breeze cooled her skin.

He massaged the mound in his hand as his shaft filled her with deep, hard strokes that echoed to her core. She wrapped her legs around his waist to pull him deeper and somehow felt even more hedonistic than she had during their three-way with Melanie. In that moment, she didn't care if anyone came upon them—she didn't care if the whole condo complex gathered around to watch them fuck.

That's when he found her hand, the one chained to his, and placed it full on her breast beneath his palm, and began to squeeze. She looked into his eyes and let him, let him make her touch herself. The chain connecting their cuffs scraped coolly across her soft flesh, adding to her excitement as he pummeled her with hard thrusts that pressed her ass into the ground.

"Harder," she said through clenched teeth. "*Harder.*" Needing to feel him more and more, needing to take every ounce of what he had to give.

His rough drives soon came with deep groans and she knew he was getting closer and closer to exploding in her. "Come, baby, deep inside me," she urged him, remembering how, despite herself, his demands for *her* to come had helped push her to climax.

"Oh fuck, yeah," he said, voice deep, filled with a hard, masculine pleasure, and then he pounded into her still more roughly, brutal and hot and good, and she knew he was spilling his come inside her, and she'd never felt so physically satisfied.

He kissed her again, his mouth still flavored by her cunt, and they lay quiet for a long moment, recovering.

Finally, he rolled off her, lying beside her in the grass, their wrists still connected. "Damn," he said. "You get me so hot, baby." Then he turned his head to look at her and caught her already peering at him. "And I like you, Erin. So much."

His earnest tone made her feel the words in her gut. Shit. She hadn't expected him to come right out with it. She thought it was pretty clear that they were strongly drawn to each other, and that, yes—like it or not—there were emotions involved, a lot of them. But having a guy as hot and handsome as Carter come right out and simply say that he *liked* her hit her hard.

She turned her gaze back toward the sky and decided not to respond.

Because as good as this had been—as unbelievably intense and pleasurable—she had to get back to business here, the business of making him understand this had to end.

"I fucked up by letting myself be attracted to you," she said frankly. "And I fucked up worse by trying to…to stop it with sex. And I apologize for that."

She looked back to him, but couldn't read his expression until he said, "All right. Apology accepted. And thank you. For telling me everything you told me tonight."

She gave a short, precise nod, and realized it was her "cop nod", something she used on the job. And that was good—because she had to close the emotional floodgates now. Once and for all. "And I wish I could have something more with you, Carter, because…well, it's clear you're an amazing lover and also…a really nice guy." She blinked. "What I'm saying is…I like you, too. A lot."

Oh hell, stop it. You're supposed to be closing the floodgates, not opening them wider.

So she again withdrew her gaze, focused on the moon. "But like I told you, I can't allow myself to feel the things you make me feel. If I'd had to go to work the other night after we had sex at Caesars, I'd have been toast. I felt too much. I was thinking too hard. And I can't do that, Carter. It literally puts my life at risk."

"You're soft underneath," he said gently, simply.

"What?" When she looked at him this time, those green eyes were enough to bury her.

"You're soft underneath your sturdy cop exterior, and I love that, Erin."

She sucked in her breath, again felt his words in her chest.

Then forced out the ones *she* had to say, to make him finally grasp the situation. "But the two don't mix—soft girl, hard cop. So I have to choose. I have to be the hard cop all the time." And the further truth, although she didn't tell him, was that the contrasts between her true personality and her profession *did* make her do a lot of pretending—she'd realized that when he'd accused her of it earlier. Only maybe a lot of it was to herself—pretending it was easy to be so tough all the time, pretending she never needed anyone to lean on or a guy to love. And she talked herself into *believing* it most of the time, too, but Carter was wearing down her defenses.

"So," she went on, "I answered your questions. Honestly. I've told you things I've told no one else. That's what you wanted—an explanation for my behavior, and now you've got it."

She sat up then, thinking it was high time they got off the ground. "So now you can keep your end of the deal and unlock these cuffs, and this can be over. Because it has to be."

He sat up next to her, but she didn't look at him, just went on. "You get that now, right? It's over. You need to let me go, Carter."

"Give me a night," he said.

She shifted her eyes to his. "*What?*"

"Give me one night to show you that you don't want to be alone. And that what you feel for me isn't bad. And that losing control of yourself can be a very good thing."

Chapter Six

❧

Carter focused on the concrete beneath his feet, which he was drilling into with a jackhammer, the noise deafening to most people, but he used earplugs to protect his hearing. They were just getting started on the strip's next mega-hotel, which required destroying some old concrete on the large, otherwise empty site. The Las Vegas sun beat down hard, but he was used to it and wouldn't have traded it. He'd migrated from Boston some years back and only went home to see his family at the holidays. He would have liked seeing his parents more often, as well as his brother and sister and their growing broods, but Las Vegas provided an endless stream of work, mostly nice weather, and lots of beautiful women.

Not that he was noticing many beautiful women lately—other than Erin.

Saturday night had been unbelievable. He'd planned to confront her, get that answer and seduce her with those furry handcuffs he'd bought—but he'd never imagined how intense things would get, or that she'd end up confiding in him so deeply.

The truth was, he couldn't stop thinking about that soft girl he'd uncovered inside her. And he had the scary feeling that maybe he was…falling in love with her. He knew it was quick, but wasn't that how love worked sometimes?

He stopped the jackhammer with a sigh. Leave it to him to fall for the one chick in Las Vegas who wanted nothing to do with guys. He still thought her reasoning was pretty insane, but apparently the loss of her dad had affected her in a lot of deep ways that even *she* didn't completely understand. And he hoped like hell he could convince her, make her realize that caring for somebody could make you stronger, not weaker, if you let it. But she was so stubborn that he had his doubts.

A tap on his arm made him remove one earplug to hear the words, "Knock off for lunch, dude."

He looked up to see his buddy Drew—construction worker by day, college student by night. Although in his late twenties, Drew had just decided to pursue a degree in psychology last year. He and Carter weren't longtime friends, but they usually walked up the strip together each day at lunch to grab a burger or some tacos, so Carter had gotten to know him pretty well. He was majoring in sexual psychology—mainly, Carter suspected, because he was a horny bastard—and he generally had more wild stories to share than Carter. But he was a smart, friendly guy, too, and Carter liked him.

Laying the jackhammer down, Carter wiped his hands on his old jeans, then tossed his hardhat aside, leaving only a navy bandanna tied around his forehead. Drew followed suit, ditching a white hardhat in the gravel to reveal straight but shaggy blond hair above the five o'clock shadow already darkening his face even though it was only noon. Carter scratched his own darkly stubbled chin, aware he hadn't shaved the last couple of days. Erin was so constantly on his mind that he'd grown tired, lazy, lost in the haze of wanting her and not being sure he was going to get her.

"How's your wild lady cop?" Drew asked as they hit the sidewalk at the edge of the empty, sprawling lot.

It was only Monday, so Carter hadn't had a chance to fill Drew in on the latest. However, as they headed to a nearby McDonald's, decked out in extra neon due to its Las Vegas Boulevard address, Carter hit the high points, focusing not so much on the sex as the end result—that she'd reluctantly agreed to give him a night to make her want a relationship with him more than fear it.

"Damn," Drew said, shoving a couple of fries in his mouth as they sat at one of the brightly colored outdoor tables watching the traffic go by. "You got it bad for this girl, don't you?"

Carter wasn't too proud to be honest. "Looks like I do."

"So what's your plan? How do you convince her?"

Carter took a bite of his Big Mac and grinned. "More of what we've already been doing. Good, hot sex. Because as much as I like her with her clothes *on*, the sexual chemistry between us is..." He blew out a breath, remembering. "Fucking outrageous, man. So that's what I'm relying on."

"It's not enough," Drew said with a short, precise head shake.

Carter blinked. "Huh?"

"You haven't won her over with hot sex *yet*. You have to do something that pushes the envelope. Her issue is that she thinks losing control is going to endanger her, right?"

Carter nodded, curious to hear what Mr. Psychology Major was going to say.

"Then you have to play into her fears, turn them around."

Okay, nothing too insightful there. "Dude, I've got a brain—I already got that far on my own. Give me something new."

Drew ate a few more fries, finished his own Big Mac, then slurped on his Coke while Carter waited. Finally he said, "Look, you know the girl, I don't. But here's my advice. Whatever you do, you have to take it to extremes. You have to show the girl that surrendering can be...really hot."

"We've already used handcuffs, twice."

Drew flashed a pointed look. "Then guess you're gonna have to go *way* extreme. To the very edge. Take her where she's never been before, where she's never even thought about going—and make her love it."

As Carter sipped on his Coke, two sexy girls in short skirts and high heels, with "tourists looking to party" written all over them, smiled at him and Drew. He smiled back just to be nice, but he was thinking about Drew's suggestion.

The girls left the sidewalk and approached, looking like carbon copies of the Hilton sisters. The blonde reached up to lower big sunglasses just far enough that she could gaze seductively overtop of them. "So, boys, is it true what they say? What happens in Vegas stays in Vegas?"

"Sure is, beautiful," Drew said with a wink. "If you want to make some memories together, I'll be happy to let you leave 'em here with me when you go home to your boyfriend."

Carter zoned out into his own thoughts as one of the girls wrote down their room number at the Bellagio, and they probably thought he was a bore, but he didn't mind letting Drew take both of them. What he'd just said had Carter's mind spinning. People who visited Vegas could do wild things here, then after they left pretend they hadn't happened and didn't matter. But when you *lived* here, you didn't have that luxury. *Erin* didn't have that luxury. So maybe Drew was right. Take her to the edge, take her someplace she'd never go otherwise— someplace the soft girl inside her would feel *deeply*—and make it feel good, and right, just by virtue of the fact that he was the tour guide. Do that and how could she forget it—how could she *stop* feeling it when it was over?

Yep. Make her give him absolute and total control—and she'd see that letting someone take care of her a little would make her stronger, happier and more complete, even as a cop. Make her know that he was gonna be there for her, loving her, whether she liked it or not.

* * * * *

"So tomorrow night's the night, huh?"

Still in her hooker garb after another long night outside the Desert Oasis, Erin glanced across the car toward Danny. They'd made three busts through the course of the evening and she was exhausted, both physically, from standing on those fuck-me platform heels all evening, and mentally, from trying to do her job while all this chaos with Carter hovered in the back of her mind. "Unfortunately," she replied, still unable to believe she'd let Carter talk her into a whole night alone with him.

"I still don't get you on this," Danny said, shaking his head. "You're crazy about the guy, and he's ga-ga over you, too, but you don't want to be around him."

She hadn't given Danny any details—basically, she'd told him they'd ended up getting involved and that despite trying to keep emotions out of it, she felt more for the guy than she was comfortable with and had called a quick end to it. Oh, and that now she'd also agreed to give him a chance to change her mind. "We've been through this before and you know how I feel about it."

Danny shrugged. "It was easier to take when I thought you were happy that way, by yourself, no one in your life but your mom and a few friends. Now I see you're really into this guy and trying to fight it, and it bugs me."

"Well, bug schmug—it's *my* life. Now can we please change the subject? What are *you* up to tomorrow night?" After working three nights in a row, they were both off tomorrow and the next day.

"Oh, you know, real exciting stuff. Dinner with Ann and the kids. Maybe rent a movie, maybe play some X-Box with Johnny."

Erin always enjoyed listening to Danny talk about his family. Even when he tried to sound bored, like now—implying that compared to her night, his would be a snorer—a contented little smile always played around his lips when he spoke about them. She let him go on talking—Johnny was playing a soccer tournament this weekend and Megan had gymnastics. The gymnastics were expensive as hell, but she loved it so much they didn't want to pull her out of it. And on it went, that little smile she could almost hear in his voice as they headed toward the downtown bureau.

Of course, once she got in her own car and headed toward her place, she no longer had Danny's life to distract her from her own. Driving through the neon jungle toward home, she couldn't help reflecting on her anger at her dad. She'd had a few days to work through that now, to understand and accept it. She couldn't believe she'd not recognized it all this time, carried it around inside her—but as Carter had reminded her, she'd gotten good at pretending, in more ways than one.

She'd even gone to her dad's grave yesterday afternoon before work, taken flowers, and told him she forgave him for leaving her and her mom alone in the world. Despite herself, a tear had snuck out. "Maybe it made me stronger," she'd told him, kneeling there. "I hope it did. I've tried like hell to be strong, Dad." Of course, lately, her strength had felt depleted by her lust for a certain construction worker.

But she'd also made a decision—or made it more *firmly* anyway. As far as Carter was concerned, she was going to indulge in one more night of full-blown pleasure and that was it. She was going to let herself go completely during her evening with him, going to throw herself into it with reckless abandon—because the man knew how to please her and if she was going to do this, why not make it a night to remember, maybe the best of her life.

But then, after that, it was over—for real this time.

She knew now that she was simply incapable of fucking him without feeling an emotional link, yet she would just have to deal with the fallout of her brief, passionate time with him. Tomorrow night would be the last encounter in their short, tumultuous affair, and the next morning she would start the task of getting over him.

Of course, she'd still see him all the time, in the halls, looking all hot and sweaty and dirty good, but...well, maybe she'd move. She liked it here, she thought, pulling into the quiet Green Valley condo community, and she liked the friends she'd made in the building, but she knew the condo had already appreciated in value since buying it last year, and if she felt the need to put more distance between them, she could always move away. They were building *new* condos right up the street, after all.

She found parking directly in front of the building, and as she got out, she heard a familiar female voice call, "Hey, girlfriend."

She looked up to see Diana—and Marc—curled up in a lounge chair together on their balcony, situated between hers and Carter's. "Hey," she said, then glanced down at herself. "Uh, don't mind the sleazy outfit. I'm still on hooker detail."

"Mmm-*mmm*," Marc said, teasing her. "How do I get Diana on that?"

It was only then that she noticed Diana appeared to be wearing nothing but a slinky, silky robe, and as for what Marc wore, she couldn't tell, but it wasn't much. She forgot sometimes what she'd slowly picked up on about her neighbors—they were freer spirits than her when it came to sex.

Disentangling herself from Marc's embrace, Diana got to her bare feet and took the few steps to the balcony's railing, resting her arms on top. Her short kimono draped open in front, flashing nearly as much round, sexy cleavage as the skimpy tank top Erin had on. She smiled down at her. "Hear you got a hot date tomorrow night with a hot guy."

Geesh, the whole world wanted to talk about this, didn't they? Well, she was going to nip this in the bud. "Yeah, but this thing with me and Carter—he's a great guy and all *and* totally hot, but…it's not gonna go anywhere."

Diana tilted her head knowingly. "Because you need to stay tough and keep your guard up and not get involved with anyone?"

Erin only sighed. "Carter has a big mouth. I keep forgetting how close you and he are."

Diana just shrugged. "He only told me because I kept asking him about you when he came over for pizza last night.

And I know you probably don't want my advice, but I'm going to give it to you anyway."

Erin sighed, tried to smile. She truly liked Diana, so she would listen politely then say good night. "All right."

"Once upon a time, I, too, tried to wish away a part of myself, tried to close it up and pretend it wasn't there. Then I met Marc. And he made me realize how unhappy I was that way, and that I had to be who I really was and that it was okay to want the things I wanted. The right guy, Erin, can change your life forever, in lots of wonderful ways, if you'll only let him."

* * * * *

The following night at seven, Erin stood at Carter's door holding a bottle of wine. It seemed crazy as she thought about it, since this wasn't a dinner party—it was a date for sex. But she'd never had a date for sex before—well, other than the weird one she'd set up without his consent last week at Caesars Palace—so she wasn't sure what to do, what to bring or how to dress.

"Hey," he said with a smile, opening the door, taking the wine. God, he looked good. His dark hair was only slightly less rumpled than usual, late-day stubble shadowed his jaw and his muscular body filled out his t-shirt and jeans just right. "Come on in," he said. "You look great."

She'd finally opted for a thin pink sweater with dark blue jeans, but his eyes roamed her body with the same look he wore when she was in her hooker costume. Of course, that made her tingle—all over. Which was good since she knew she had a crazy night of sex ahead, but bad since she knew this was the last time. She took a deep breath and tried to smile back as he showed her to the dining area off the kitchen—the condo having the same floor plan as her own.

She watched, feeling oddly shy, as Carter uncorked the Chardonnay and poured two glasses, passing her one. Their fingers touched as she took it, and he made a toast. "To...tonight. And possibilities." His eyes were playful—and possessive. And as usual with Carter, her pussy spasmed just from the way he looked at her, the forbidden promise in his gaze, as she swallowed her first sip of wine.

"By the way," he said, pointing to a pair of handcuffs— *her* handcuffs—that lay on one corner of the counter, "thought you might want those back."

Blushing slightly, she nodded. "Now that you mention it, yeah—if my sergeant knew what I'd used them for, I'd be dead meat."

"Well, I'm officially returning them. Consider it a peace offering," he told her. And her heart warmed a little—maybe this meant they were going to put all the kinky stuff behind them now.

A few minutes later, they sat down to barbecued pork chops from the grill on Carter's balcony, along with baked potatoes, corn, and rolls. "I hit up Marc and Diana for dinner ideas," he told her across the table as they both dug into the food. "But next thing I know, they've got out this recipe book filled with complicated Italian dishes from Marc's mom. She's from Italy, so it's the real thing. And I'm not much of a cook, so I finally just threw up my hands and said, 'You know what? I'm just gonna go with something simple that I can make without screwing up'."

And in that moment, Erin nearly stopped breathing. Because he was so...real. Such a normal, simple, nice guy. So meat and potatoes, literally. Like her own dad had been. Of course, he was also impossibly hot, and every look at him had her cunt swelling more, her breasts feeling sensitive and heavy.

And the reason she couldn't breathe was—he was perfect. Her perfect man. He had it all—everything she wanted in a guy. Even when he was rough, demanding, when they were fucking, something about that became perfect. She'd never thought she could want that in a man, but when it came from

Carter, it was the ideal attribute, complementing all the others he possessed.

"You okay?" he asked then.

She sucked in her breath. Got hold of herself. Nodded. "Yeah, fine. The pork chops are great," she assured him. And wondered how she'd survive the rest of the night without saying the words that were gathering inside her, almost pummeling her heart right now. *I love you.*

Did she? Love him?

Oh God, she feared she really did.

Which meant getting over him and moving on was going to be a hell of a lot harder than she'd realized. But she still had no choice—she had to do it. The way she saw it, Carter and her job couldn't co-exist in her life peacefully—one of them had to go. And her job meant so much to her—until Carter had come along, it had been pretty much *everything*, and she just couldn't give it up.

As the meal continued, Carter told her how he'd grown up in a whole family of construction workers, but when the seasonality of the business in his native Boston had gotten to be too uncertain for him, he'd decided to make a drastic move west. He'd been to Las Vegas on vacation before, and for a couple of bachelor parties, and he'd liked it enough to make a home here.

With some prodding, Erin told him a little more about *her* life—growing up nearby, the daughter of a cop. She explained that she'd always straddled the line between tomboy and girly-girl, even having to choose one year between being a cheerleader and a track and field star.

"What'd you choose?"

"Track and field. I like to win," she told him, smiling.

"About your dad," he said then, speaking more quietly, "I hope you're okay. I mean, after the stuff we talked about the other night."

She nodded, sorry they'd delved that quickly back into a serious topic, but she appreciated his concern. "Yeah, I'm fine, don't worry."

"Do you see your mom a lot? Is she...I mean, did she get over losing your dad?"

Erin stiffened a little, because the answer, she understood now, related to her personal relationship issues. "It took her a very long time for her to adjust to life without him. They were...pretty crazy in love. But..." She let her tone change to a more hopeful one. "She got remarried a couple of years ago to a nice guy named Tom. And yeah, I go over for dinner once every couple of weeks, and she and I go shopping or out to lunch pretty often. We're...close, she and I."

"I'm not surprised," he said with a gentle smile.

"Why not?"

He shrugged. "Gotta be close to somebody." The unspoken part was, *And you sure don't let yourself get close to anybody else.*

After dinner, Erin helped him clear the table, but standing near him in the kitchen got her hot, quick, all over again. And the moment they bumped arms at the counter, Carter looked down at her and their eyes met, and he swooped in for a kiss. She nearly dropped the plates in her hands, and a second later, his strong arms were easing around her from behind and he was whispering in her ear, "Put those down."

Her whole body flooded with warmth as she lowered the dishes into the sink and fought the urge to lean back into the erection she could feel growing in his pants.

"I have to tell you," he said, leaning closer to her ear, his voice as intoxicating as the wine, "I loved talking to you over dinner, just spending time with you. But I'd also be lying if I said I haven't been waiting all damn day to get close to you again, to get inside your sweet, perfect pussy."

She gasped, that particular part of her body grown heavy with anticipation. Then she turned in his arms, because she could no longer resist. Besides, she'd decided to throw herself into this, right? For this one last night? So she was ready—oh so ready.

Looping her arms around his neck, she pulled him down for a long, deep kiss, tongues swirling slowly as she pressed her body to his. Mmm, he was so hard—not just his delectable cock, but his stomach, his broad chest, the thick arms that closed around her. Construction work had built a very nice body on this man.

His hands dropped to her ass then, pressing her tighter against his crotch. Oh God, he was so big. She hadn't forgotten, yet it somehow felt brand new just to have that rock-like column stretching up her center.

"Do you remember the rule for tonight?" he asked.

She swallowed. God, had she really agreed to this? Unbelievably, in a moment of weakness, she had—so she had no choice but to nod.

His deep voice colored the dark words, making them sound just as forbidden—and frightening—as they were. "You let me have you however I want you. You don't say no to *anything.*"

She couldn't seem to speak—there was a lump of trepidation in her throat—so she only nodded again. Agreed again. To let him. Do anything. And *everything*.

And it occurred to her that she had the power to stop it—she could disagree right now, tell him she'd changed her mind. But the cold, hard truth was, she didn't want to. For this one night in her life, she wanted—amazingly—to have the control taken away from her.

Chapter Seven

ॐ

"Wrap around me," Carter said, then hoisted Erin up into his arms, her legs twining around his thighs, her ass in his hands. He kissed her, angling his mouth first one way, then another, as he carried her down the hall into a bedroom done in light but masculine shades of beige and sage green. The window was open, admitting a gentle breeze, but darkness had fallen, so the only light in the room came from the overhead, which she decided must be on a dimmer switch.

And only as he lay her back on the bed did she realize that a crisp, white sheet stretched beneath her, standing out from the rest of the room's décor and clearly placed here especially. Her man, it seemed, had a plan—dimmer switch, white sheet—she just had no idea what the plan entailed or how worried she should be.

Easing between her legs, he lay down atop her, kissing her over and over, each kiss taking her deeper into desire. She liked this, just kissing him, clothes on, like normal people—not like crazy cops arresting him and cuffing him to a bed, or him chaining her to the fence a few nights ago. The crux of her thighs grew just as hot from this, simply making out with him.

She didn't mind at all when he pushed her sweater up, sliding the soft fabric over her breasts. "Mmm, look at this," he said, peering down at her cleavage as he brushed his thumbs over her nipples. "A pretty pink bra under your pretty pink sweater."

She smiled, then rose slightly, letting him take the sweater over her head. "Pink panties, too," she volunteered, feeling more comfortable now, less afraid of what the evening would hold.

He raised his eyebrows. "Let me see." Then unzipped her jeans.

She lifted her rear from the white sheet to let him pull them down until they were around her bent knees. He lay on his side next to her now, propped on one elbow, running his palm over the panties, just above her mound. "Perfect," he whispered, and she bit her lip, feeling pretty and sexy and ready for more.

"Take yours off, too," she said.

He made a tsking noise and reminded her, "Who's in charge here?"

She rolled her eyes playfully. "Forgot." Then let her voice go silky, seductive. "But I want you naked. I want to see that big, beautiful cock."

He grinned, both teasing and lascivious. "I like when you talk that way. Keep that up, and I might have to give you what you want."

She just giggled, kicking off her jeans the rest of the way and delighting as his hands closed over her breasts, squeezing, molding, making her cunt surge with moisture. "Mmm," she purred throatily.

"You like that?" he whispered, his voice taking on a naughty edge.

"Mmm, yes."

"I'm gonna make you feel so good tonight, baby. I'm gonna make you feel things you've never felt before. I'm gonna make you…mine."

Her toes practically curled at the promise. Or was it a threat? Either way, her entire body tingled as Carter drew the bra straps from her shoulders to begin kissing his way across her chest, and by the time he drew the cups away from her breasts, it felt like a glorious release, like she'd been trapped but was now free.

Cupping the outer sides of the two mounds in his big, rough hands, he licked and kissed first one taut nipple, then the other. She liked watching, and threaded her fingers through his thick hair to make sure he knew she wanted more of his hot mouth there. Licking her upper lip as she let herself get lost in the simple pleasure, she arched her breasts higher, thrusting one nipple deeper into Carter's mouth. He suckled her, soft at first, but then hard, in a way that shot straight to her cunt. She writhed on the bed, rubbing against him, hungry for more stimulation, everywhere.

Still kissing her breasts, he reached behind her to smoothly unhook her bra, then drew it down her arms and flung it away. Next he rose to his knees and lowered her pink panties. "I've never had you completely naked," he told her, all playfulness gone from his voice. "Tonight I'm having you naked."

The panties hit the floor, too, and he used both strong hands to part her thighs wide. She wondered if he could see how wet she was, and if her pussy was parted, open for him.

He studied her for a moment then smiled wickedly. "More pink."

Question answered.

Erin was as on fire for him as she'd ever been, and waited for him to sink his mouth to her cunt, or to finally open his pants and maybe sink his nice, stiff shaft there instead.

Which was when he eased his body up onto hers once more, skimmed his palms up her arms, urging them over her head, giving her the feel of being stretched out and on display beneath him—and proceeded to handcuff her to the damn bed.

She felt the fur, heard the clicks, and looked up above her to see that his bed possessed convenient twists of wrought iron, perfect for cuffing. It shouldn't have surprised her, but it did. And it also *reminded* her—he was in control here, he *did* have a plan, and they weren't just making out like "normal people" anymore. They were about to travel back to the land of "beyond normal" again, and that both bothered and unwittingly aroused her.

Now that she was cuffed, Carter leaned back on his knees and studied her, from her fur-bound wrists to her pretty little toes. Like it or not, he *was* developing a light bondage fetish—she looked too hot this way—and it was all her fault.

Dropping his gaze to her pussy, his mouth watered. She was open and glistening for him, ready for all the dirty surprises he was about to give her. He planned to pull out some pretty serious stops here in hopes of finally making her understand that control could be vastly overrated. And now to let the games begin.

Stroking one thumb gently through the open pink folds between her thighs, he listened to her pretty sigh. "You have a beautiful little cunt, honey," he said, his voice deep with the lust thrumming through his veins. "And I'm gonna make it even *more* beautiful."

With that he reached over the far side of the bed, raising the tray he'd placed there up onto the mattress. It held shaving cream, a razor, a bowl of water, aloe gel, a small towel and a shaving mirror usually stuck on the wall in his shower. She gasped at the sight and it made his dick harder. This was why he'd put the white sheet under her—things were about to get a little messy.

She seemed barely able to speak. "You're going to, going to…"

"Shave you," he finished for her.

"But I…I…"

Maybe he was a bastard, but something in him enjoyed her fear just now. "You what?"

He liked that it took her a minute to figure out what she was afraid of. "What if you…cut me?"

He just shook his head. The truth was, he'd shaved a woman before. It had been one of the most erotic things he'd ever experienced. And he knew he could be gentle enough not to hurt her. "You have to trust me here, baby. Because you have no other choice."

He knew it was a harsh thing to say, but tonight was going to *be* harsh. A harsh sort of pleasure designed to break through her irrational fears. Maybe it was a gamble, but hey, this was Vegas. He'd decided it was a risk worth taking.

She didn't answer — but she also didn't close her legs, still lying before him on the bed, thighs spread wide, those slender arms stretched to the headboard above her.

And she didn't flinch when he began to smooth the fluffy white shaving cream onto her dark, curling pubic hair — even if he *did* feel her muscles tighten a little. With fear? Or arousal? He hoped it was a good dose of both.

He took his time, covering her thoroughly, enjoying the feel of her mound beneath his fingertips and thinking of the soft skin he was about to reveal. He'd chosen a disposable ladies' razor during his trip to the drug store, and now held it up for her to see. "Pink," he said, teasing just a little. Only a hint of a smile crossed her face before she looked tense again.

"Hold still now," he warned as he took the first gentle stroke over her pussy.

She sighed in response, and his chest went tight as the first tuft of hair came away, revealing the smooth white skin underneath.

Dipping the razor in the water to rinse it, he returning for another smooth, soft swipe over her most sensitive area. The move drew another sigh from her, and her body relaxed a little. He kept his eyes on his task and continued working, stroke after stroke, unveiling her cunt a little more with each. And soon, just as he'd known it would, her sighs came deeper, and her expression softened into more arousal than fear.

He shaved her completely, leaving not even a strip of hair above her slit. When he'd said he wanted her completely naked, he'd meant it. By the time he was done, his arms and hands felt weighted, tingly — from careful movements and an excitement that had built more with each swipe the razor had made.

Dropping it in the dish of water at his side, he took the towel to wipe away the remnants of white shaving cream still streaking her flesh. She shivered as he did it, and — oh God — when the towel dropped away, she was fucking beautiful. Truly bared for him now.

Pulling in his breath, and trying not to come in his pants at the mere sight of her naked feminine flesh, he next reached for the aloe, squirting some on his fingertips, then sensually rubbing it in, all over her pretty cunt, until her smooth skin glistened with it.

Her voice came shaky as she tried to look down at herself. "Are you done?"

He nodded.

"Can I…look?"

He'd almost forgotten, but loved her request and reached over to grab up his shaving mirror with the little suction cups on back. He held it between her still-spread legs, angling it slightly upward. "Can you see it?"

She nodded, then visibly swallowed. Said nothing, but looked as impassioned as he felt. "Why did you do it?" she finally asked, sounded perplexed.

He cast a wicked grin. "The better to see you. The better to eat you. The better to fuck you."

She sucked in her breath. "Oh."

And now that he had seen her, he decided it was time to eat her.

Setting mirror and tray aside on the floor, Carter bent between her legs, still studying the freshly revealed flesh there, and used his hands to part it wider. So hot and pink and wet, her scent a mixture of shaving cream and the salty-sweet smell of her own wetness. Dragging his tongue up her deep, moist slit now was like a journey through a slick, smooth valley, nothing to get in his way. So he licked her from the very bottom of her pussy all the way to the swollen pink nub at the top, again, again, listening to her hot sighs evolve into high, breathy moans.

He stroked his fingers over the denuded skin at each side of her cunt, loving the soft feel of it, and through it all, he gazed up over her mound, through the beautiful swells of her breasts and into her eyes. She looked lost in passion now, just how he wanted her. Just how he needed her. Because she was going to have to surrender a lot more than just her pubic curls before this night was over. And he was more determined than ever to make her see things his way.

He licked her vigorously, soon pushing two fingers up inside her, into the swallowing warmth of her passage. "Oh!" she said when they entered her, and he wanted more now, more than her gentle responses—he wanted to *make* her feel him, get her good and ready for the various forms of fucking to come.

So he drove his fingers hard and deep, as deep as he could plunge them into her, and he licked her hard. It got him hot to take those long languid trips through her pink valley, to feel her wetness all around his mouth, to sense her pussy trying to swallow him, wrap around him—but he soon rose to concentrate on her clit, because he wanted to make her come now.

He took it between his teeth, biting lightly and making her cry out. Then he swirled his tongue around it, listening to her pant and moan and struggle against her cuffs. Finally, he locked his mouth onto that hungry little knob of flesh and sucked, sucked, the same way he would her nipple. And the thought urged him to reach up with his free hand to tweak one hard little bead, pinching just lightly as he pushed her harder toward climax.

Her low moans and eager thrusts at his mouth told him it was near, and a tremendous cry left her as the orgasm broke. He kept sucking her clit, riding it out with her, her whole body undulating as she came. He only let loose with his mouth when she went limp beneath him, her breath coming like someone who'd just run a great distance.

He kissed her right above her slit and peered up at her beautifully flushed face. "I love to make you come."

She seemed capable only of nodding, but looked well-pleasured, making him smile. Lazily caressing her hips, thighs, tummy, he let her recover, eyes shut.

But soon she opened them again and spoke softly. "What now?"

Now, he thought, things were gonna get really good and dirty.

Now he was gonna take her places she'd never been. This was the point of no return.

But he didn't tell her that. In fact, he didn't answer at all. Instead, he reached back over the side of the bed and drew out…what looked like some kind of strange whip.

Erin gasped, jerking her handcuffs against the wrought iron. "What the hell is *that*?" Still recovering from an orgasm that had blasted through her like a rocket, she could scarcely believe Carter had actually shaved her cunt—and now *this*? Some kind of medieval-looking cat-o'-nine-tails thing? It was made of black leather, with a long, thick, rounded handle that led to loose-hanging leather strips reminiscent of a horse's tail.

"It's called a flogger, honey."

She swallowed, strange dread rolling through her. "Are you…going to beat me with it?"

Much to her confusion, Carter laughed. "No, baby," he said, a kind look taking over his dark features. "I would never hurt you. Not *really* hurt you."

"What does *that* mean?"

His face went more serious again. "Sometimes a little pain can produce a lot of pleasure. But I would never hurt you, Erin, I promise."

Uh-huh. On one hand, she was relieved, but on the other, it was hard to believe him while he sat there holding that thing. "Then...what are you going to do with it?"

"Just this," he said, then extended the tail end of the flogger out over her body, lowering it so the strips of leather came to rest at her breastbone. He dragged the tool gently downward, between her breasts, over her stomach, and she shuddered at the shivery pleasure it produced, like being tickled with great, heavy feathers.

"And maybe this," he added, then brushed the leather stripping over her clit. This time, the effect was so strong that she gasped, the sensation bursting sweetly through her.

"Maybe other things, too," he went on, his voice dropping an octave, "but I'll make you like them." He set the flogger aside on the bed and said, "Now tell me what you want, honey." And as if there was any doubt, he glanced down toward the prominent bulge in his jeans.

Everything inside her thickened at the demand—despite her orgasm, despite her worries over the flogger, she remained completely turned on, because she'd been waiting for this so long now. "Your cock," she said. "I want your cock."

Masculine pleasure passed through his green gaze as he finally reached down to yank the t-shirt over his head. She loved the sight of his muscular chest, but was still waiting, watching, as he stood up, unzipped, and let his jeans fall to his ankles. He pushed his briefs down, too, and *finally* that perfect male specimen came into view, stretching up past his navel, solid and ready for her.

Without meaning to, she licked her upper lip, then lifted her eyes to find Carter watching her. "Glad you're still hungry," he told her, and her chest tightened.

Climbing back onto the bed, Carter lifted one knee over her chest, and she remembered straddling *him* the same way during their Caesars Palace liaison. And to have his majestic shaft hovering directly above her now was intimidating as hell—because she was chained up, and he was going to push it into her mouth, going to *fuck* her mouth, and she'd have no choice in the matter, no way to back off if it was too much. But, despite herself, she also *wanted* it. She hungered, not only to suck his cock, but to let herself go to that darker place, to know what it felt like to give up *that* much control.

First, though, Carter angled his body so that his erection pressed directly to her chest, between her breasts, then he used both hands to push the mounds up around it. "Oh..." she sighed, shocked by the raw pleasure. Melanie had wrapped Erin's breasts around him, too, but she'd already forgotten the indescribable delight of having something so hard against a part of her that was so soft.

As he fucked her that way, his gaze shifted from her breasts to her eyes and back. He made longer, deeper strokes until the tip of his cock came close to her mouth with each drive, until he said, "Open up, honey."

She did, letting the head of his shaft enter her parted lips.

Oh God, yes, he felt so good there, and she welcomed it each time, sucking the head, then letting it back out. Carter dragged the wet tip down between her breasts with those long, smooth moves to moisten her there and make his passage easier, slicker, like gliding into her mouth or her pussy.

Finally, though, he eased his way farther up her body, his knees balanced astride her arms where they stretched over her head, and he slid his length full into Erin's mouth.

He didn't go too far, expect too much, just pushed in halfway, then drew back out, again, again.

Erin had never felt dirtier—in a thrilling way. To have let a man chain her up. To let him put her beneath him and fuck her mouth. Her lifelong instincts, of course, urged her to scream out, protest, somehow break free. But her body, and the lusty woman at her core, discovered she loved being at his mercy, loved having to surrender her control, loved being like a sex slave to him. She couldn't understand why—she only knew she'd never felt as wholly like a sexual being as she did in this moment, by letting herself go, letting herself explore these new sexual waters with a man who, like it or not, she cared for.

He moved his shaft in and out of her mouth for a long while, until her lips were stretched, sore, and tired. But their eyes met the whole time, and she could only imagine how she must look, and something about the power in that, the freedom to be that dirty, that obscene, inspired her to continue for as long as he wanted.

Finally, he pulled out—only to carefully turn around and straddle her once more, facing the opposite way.

"What—"

"Shhh," he said, then reinserted his cock between her lips, effectively quieting her.

Strange, her mouth was so tender, but she welcomed it back anyway, wanting to pleasure him still more.

He leaned forward over her until he was on hands and knees. Still sucking him, she could see through the space between their bodies, and she thought he might lick her pussy some more. The poor thing was starting to feel neglected, so she found herself lifting, arching her ass slightly toward him— a silent request.

But then he reached for the flogger.

Oh. She sucked in her breath. He was going to rub her with it. Okay. Fine. She didn't even care, so long as she got some stimulation down there.

And yet...why was he turning it around, holding onto it by the tail?

His cock still thrust in firm, even strokes between her lips as he—oh God, he was positioning the leather handle at her cunt. Like a dildo!

That's when she saw it—the end was shaped that way, and just the right size. Not a lifelike representation and it was not quite as big or thick as Carter, but indeed, someone had designed it with dual purposes in mind.

"Ohhh!" she cried around his shaft as he pushed the handle into her, all the way.

Without responding to her reaction, he began to fuck her with it, to slide it in and out in the same rhythm as he moved in her mouth.

Oh Lord, it was too much stimulation. One cock in her mouth, and something very *like* a cock in her cunt. It was too much and too *good*.

That quickly, she was lost to it, consumed by it.

She sobbed around his shaft as he filled her at both ends. She shut her eyes and simply absorbed the pummeling pleasure that was enough to overwhelm her. It drove away thought or worry or wonder or decision—and it left only sensation. Hot, consuming sensation like she'd never experienced before.

She had no idea how long he fucked her that way, only that when it stopped, she felt almost numb with pleasure. She no longer even thought about the fact that she was cuffed to the bed. She no longer thought about being at his mercy. She no longer worried about what would come next. She simply *was*. She was his willing, content sex toy.

And unlike other times, he didn't ask if she was okay. He didn't say anything soothing or sweet. He only withdrew the handle after a long while and said, "Turn over, on your knees."

She hadn't realized it, but having the cuffs looped only around one little bit of wrought iron made it so that she could easily flip in the bed without them being removed.

"Good girl," he said deeply as she turned. "Now draw your knees up under you."

She did so.

"That's right," he told her. "But lift your ass some."

She followed the instruction, still aware of little more than obedience and pleasure.

That's when he brought the strips of the flogger down across her bottom in a soft but stinging slap. She flinched, yet felt the surge of heat rippling through her, centering in her pussy.

"Tell me you're a bad girl."

She never thought of not doing it. "I'm a bad girl."

He smacked her with the flogger again—the other side of her rear this time. "Tell me you're a bad girl for ever fighting me."

"I'm a bad girl for ever fighting you."

Another snap of the leather on her ass. Mmm, yes—so hot, delicious. "Tell me *you* want what *I* want, whatever I demand of you."

"*I* want what *you* want, whatever you demand."

And then things got blurry, strange. She couldn't see him any longer, so she had closed her eyes and now only absorbed. He used his hands to knead her bottom—and then, then, he dragged one finger down the valley of her ass, ever so slowly, and when he reached her anus, he stopped…circled…*rubbed.*

She bit her lip. What an odd sensation. It almost felt good.

He rubbed some more and…it *definitely* felt good. Who knew?

And then…wetness there, something cool and gooey. The aloe from before?

Whatever it was, he was rubbing it into her, lots of it, and after that, oh God! He pushed one fingertip into the fissure and she sobbed with the shock of pleasure. Behind her, his breath came heavier, audible. She realized both of her cuffed hands gripped the wrought iron of the headboard, tight.

His finger slid deeper, deeper, all the way. Oh Lord. So good. Strange. A bizarre sort of intrusion where she'd never

211

really imagined one before. But a *welcome* intrusion. She even heard herself whimper, "Yes."

He slid his finger in and out, in and out, as Erin sank deeper into the strange, murky delight the penetration delivered. Maybe the wine earlier was finally setting in, making her feel fully drunk now, or maybe *surrendering to Carter* had made her drunk. Whatever the case, she was no longer in control of her responses.

When his finger disappeared, she didn't worry—she knew something else would come, and she waited patiently to see what it would be.

Yet, for some reason, she hadn't expected what she got— the leather handle of the flogger nudging at her ass. "Oh Lord," she heard herself whisper when she realized.

"Relax, baby." His voice was soothing now, but that was all he said.

So she tried to relax. It wasn't hard—she was so aroused now, and so into him, into whatever he wanted to give her.

At first, she thought it wouldn't fit. He prodded, gently, then began to move it rhythmically against her, and it felt impossibly thick for that particular hole—until, suddenly, it went in.

"Jesus," she said, assaulted by a head rush that accompanied its entry. And like before, with his finger, the pleasure was...strange. New and different. She was experiencing it *because* of him. And *for* him. "Yes," she said again, just to let him know she truly wanted this. Yesterday, she wouldn't have. An hour ago, no. But he had intoxicated her, and now it was easy to just let go and *feel*.

"Oh...*ohhh*..." she moaned as the handle edged deeper into her ass, filling her impossibly. Behind her, Carter groaned, too.

Every nerve ending in her body tingled, tensed, as he began to move the flogger in and out, and she wondered— strangely—if she looked like she had a tail. The leather strips tickled her from behind. "God, oh God," she sobbed, pushing gently at the tool, amazed when Carter was able to thrust it in and out with relative ease.

"So good, baby," he murmured hotly over her. "Your sweet little ass is taking this so good."

I love you.

Shit—she almost said it. Now, of all odd times. She bit her lip, shoved the words back, resumed only feeling, not thinking. Maybe that was safer for a *lot* of reasons.

And then…he pulled the flogger out. And she moaned at the emptiness it left behind, but once more felt patient, waiting to see what came next from her lover.

"Now," he said, suddenly close to her, and she opened her eyes to see him right next to her, his face on the pillow near hers, "is where you really have to trust me, honey." He looked so serious. And so hot.

Her first thought was, *Anything, I'll do or be or give you anything you want.*

But the break in the action had brought back at least a small pinch of sanity, so she stayed quiet, only met his gaze, only gave a small nod.

"Good," he whispered. And then he covered her eyes with a black blindfold.

She sucked in her breath, but he said nothing to reassure her, only tied it tight behind her head.

Then she sensed him leaving the room. Oh Lord. Where the hell was he going?

Her heart beat wildly in her chest, but she told herself to calm down. She'd kept her eyes shut through a lot of this anyway. And she'd wanted to be his slave, his toy, hadn't she? That was hard for her to accept, but she couldn't deny it now. And the reality of it girded her for whatever was to come. *You want to be his sex slave tonight. He said he would never hurt you. That's all you need to know.*

That's when she sensed him joining her in the bed again, when warm hands closed firm but gentle at her bare hips.

Carter said, "Get on your hands and knees," but his voice sounded farther away than he actually was.

She pushed up onto her knees, and she couldn't brace her hands on the bed due to the cuffs, but found leverage by gripping the wrought iron again. She arched her ass upward, so ready to be fucked she wondered how she'd withstood waiting for it this long. "Please," she begged. She knew she shouldn't ask, knew he was calling the shots, but she couldn't help it. "Please give it to me. Please fuck me."

The hands on her hips flexed, tightened, then his large cock eased smoothly inside her cunt. She moaned deeply, always stunned by how big he was inside her, the way he filled her body so wonderfully.

"Is it good, baby?" His voice still sounded strange, distant.

She nodded beneath her blindfold. "God, yes."

"Good. That's so good."

And then he began to move, to pound in hard, deep strokes that stretched all through her. He felt different than before somehow—in some way she couldn't explain—but still powerful and oh-so pleasing. Her body felt hypersensitive—her orgasm seemed a long time ago now, and she'd had so much stimulation to every part of her body since then that she simply wanted to be fucked, wanted to take it as hard as he could give it. She mewled and cried out with his strokes, listened to his breath and her own, and thrust back against him.

Until he went still and...and...oh God, what was happening?

A pair of hands closed over her shoulders. Only...Carter's hands were still on her ass. Weren't they? What...what *was* this? How could this be? There were too many hands.

Then she sensed a leg grazing her side, the curve of her waist—but Carter's cock was still inside her, his thighs still stretching along the backs of hers, so this made no sense.

"Carter?" she asked.

"I'm here," he assured her, his voice suddenly near her ear, the warmth of his body stretching across her back. "Don't worry."

"But what's—"

"Shhh," he told her like once before. "This is so fucking good, baby, and you're so damn beautiful. Don't be afraid. Just trust me. That's your job right now. Trust me. And let yourself feel good."

Erin could hardly breathe. She began to understand then...the man who'd just been fucking her, who was *still* fucking her, wasn't Carter!

Who the hell was it? Was he young, old? Would she find him physically appealing? Was he using protection? God, how could this be?

And now Carter was going to...what was he going to do? What were the *two of them* going to do to her *together*? This was insane! How could Carter do this to her?

The controlling part of herself thought of screaming, fighting, stopping this. He'd said he wouldn't hurt her, so if she freaked out, he'd stop—she knew it.

So maybe she should do that. Stop this somehow. Because it was insane. Impossible.

And yet her body roiled with sensation.

What she'd just found out had startled her, but it hadn't killed her excitement.

And the truth was, with two men's hands now on her, and with one cock in her pussy and another rubbing stiffly against the small of her back as Carter reached around to caress her breasts, her arousal blossomed anew. It blossomed

215

immeasurably, her body going crazy hot at the wild and unexpected turn things had taken.

She heard her own moan and knew as she arched, thrusting her cunt against the cock inside it and her breasts into Carter's grasp, that she wasn't going to stop this. Instead, she was going to do what Carter had told her to—what she'd been doing all night. She was going to trust him, and she was going to *feel* this.

Because she *could*. She *could* trust Carter. She *wanted* to. And she knew in her heart that his promise was true—he'd never hurt her.

And this was still just as insane as it had been a minute ago, but the insane part now was that she wanted it. For *herself*. *And* for Carter.

The mystery man behind her fucked her deeply as Carter continued touching her, kissing her shoulders, her back. His cock rested in the valley of her ass and she grew nearly overwhelmed with envisioning what they must look like on the bed together and wondering how close Carter's cock was to his friend's and if he took any pleasure from being close to another naked guy right now.

But her focus shifted and such pondering ceased when the head of Carter's big shaft pushed at her asshole.

Oh Lord. He'd been getting her ready. Ready for *this*. Ready to fuck her ass while another man fucked her pussy.

Jesus God, would they both fit? Would she be able to stand it?

She drew in a ragged breath, tense, heart pounding, wanting this—wanting them both in her—like she'd never wanted anything before. She yearned to be reckless and hedonistic for Carter, because he made it okay for her to express her most forbidden desires, things she'd never even wanted before meeting him.

Behind her, he moved slowly, gently, and she could tell he'd rubbed more of the aloe on his shaft because when it began to glide in, it felt slick and cool and then went instantly deep. "Oh!" she cried.

"Is it okay?"

"Mmm," she said, nodding. More than okay. It was unbelievable. Astounding. Impossibly filling.

And when they both began to move, pumping their cocks in and out of her—oh! She felt it in every inch of her body— she pulsed with pleasure from the top of her head to the tips of her toes. Sensation buffeted her everywhere. From the pressure of the blindfold around her head to the fur rubbing on her wrists to the many hands that roamed her skin. She cried out as they pummeled her most sensitive areas with thrust after hard thrust, feeling at once high, lost, dizzy, heady and consumed with heat. Her sobs turned to screams. How could a body feel this much?

But then, oh God, came even more—when the tail of the flogger was thrust between her thighs from underneath. She didn't even know which man wielded it and didn't care—she only knew that the leather strips rubbed and teased her pussy, and oh! Oh! She was going to come. That fast. "I'm coming!" she yelled. "I'm coming!"

And as the release blasted through her, more powerful than anything she'd ever experienced, she heard Carter say, "Christ—me, too," and felt the strange wonder of him spilling his seed in that newly opened orifice. She'd barely recovered from that when the other man let out a huge groan and drove deep, deep, deep into her pussy.

After which she collapsed on the bed, unable to bear even one more sensation.

* * * * *

Erin didn't know how much time had passed, only that she'd slept. And that Carter was slipping the blindfold from her eyes and then unlocking her handcuffs.

She drew her arms down, feeling strange to be untethered. Her lover lay next to her, close, his eyes focused tightly on hers. They were the only two in the room. "I'm just going to say this, Erin," he told her, his voice deep and serious. "I'm in love with you."

Oh. Oh God.

"I made you give up your precious control tonight, and I know you loved it, so don't deny it. And I proved that losing control of yourself can bring you more pleasure than you ever even imagined."

He looked at the red fur handcuffs in his fist and said, "So now you're free. To stay or to go. I hope you'll stay."

Chapter Eight

ɞ

When Carter woke up in the middle of the night, she was gone.

He knew the outrageous sex had really happened because the evidence remained—the red cuffs on the bed, along with the flogger and the tray of shaving supplies on the floor. But Erin and all her clothes were gone.

Shit.

He'd done all he could do. And hell, maybe he'd gone *too* far, too extreme, bringing Drew in to give her the ultimate fuck without giving her a choice. But he'd known she would never agree if he'd asked her and he'd also known she would relish it—and she had. And, all things being equal, he didn't see it as being much different than her and her girlfriend fucking him at the hotel, which is what had started all this.

It had been…the most profound, intense sexual experience of his life. Up until meeting Erin, that honor had lay firmly with the night he'd spent with Marc and Diana a few years ago—but Erin had changed everything.

He'd fallen in love with her, fast.

And she'd run from him, just as fast.

And the fact that she'd left now, tonight, after all they'd shared…hell, he'd tried his best to be patient and help her overcome her hang-ups, but he wasn't gonna beg anymore.

Part of him was tempted to—part of him didn't want to give up on her, ever. But with a girl as stubborn as Erin, he had a feeling he could beg all his life and until she decided to change, be brave and take a chance on love, nothing he could do would change *anything*.

He loved her, and he feared this was gonna kill him — but he was done chasing the lady cop.

* * * * *

"You're an idiot," Danny said when Erin slid into the beat-up Nissan next to him.

She just glared. But he was right. She'd gotten too close to a guy soliciting her tonight — trying too hard to make him say the words, offer the money — until he'd grabbed her arm and tried to pull her into his car with him.

"Do you have any idea how fucking stupid that was? What if he'd gotten you in that car, Sparks? What if I hadn't been able to get to you? What then?"

She let out a huff of breath. "Look, I know, okay? I screwed up." *Just like my dad once did.*

And she'd been preoccupied, just like her dad once had.

She'd been quietly mourning how much she missed Carter, and how she'd hurt Carter, and how much she still *lusted* for Carter — and when a car had pulled to the curb, she hadn't been ready, hadn't had her game face on. It had thrown everything off — and she'd soon found herself in real danger. Thank God Danny and the guys had been quick to respond.

"If anything happened to you…" Danny said, then shook his head. "I couldn't take it, Sparks. So you gotta be careful out there, got it?"

She sighed, nodded, feeling contrite.

"And you gotta get that guy off your mind, since I know good and well what you were thinking about out there tonight instead of your job."

And that's when it hit her.

Square in the face.

Plain as day.

Bright as the neon lights that lined the Las Vegas Strip.

"I've been so stupid," she said quietly, amazed.

He raised his eyebrows. "Oh?" He sounded as taken aback as she felt.

"All these years, I've been angry at my dad for letting worries over someone he loved cloud his brain when he was on the job. And I'm doing the exact same thing."

Now Danny blinked and went smug. "And this is news to you?"

She blinked back. "Yes. Because...I thought by staying out of a relationship, it would protect me. But instead, fighting it so hard is causing the same exact problem."

"No shit, Sherlock."

She scowled at him slightly, but then sank back into her thoughts. She was endangering herself just as much by denying her love for Carter as she'd feared she would if she got into a relationship with him.

Which kinda meant she'd be just as well off in a relationship with him.

At least then—well, if everything went all right, if he didn't break her heart—she'd have a pretty good chance of being happy, *really* happy. And a happy cop surely meant a safe and alert cop.

"Can you do me a favor?" she asked Danny, her heart beginning to beat erratically. "Can you drive me home? Not back to the bureau for my car—just straight to my place? I need to get to Carter—now. In fact, floor it. This can't wait."

Danny smiled over at her and said, "Sounds like you finally got your head out of your ass, Sparks." Then he pulled the blue dome light from under the old car's seat, set it on the dash, turned it on and sped toward Erin's condo.

For the whole ride, Erin's mind whirled. She'd just decided to declare her love for Carter and—oh Lord—nothing had ever felt so overwhelmingly right. So good. So...*safe*. He would make her safe, in every way, she just knew it. It was suddenly so, so clear.

"Honk the horn," she said when Danny screeched the car into the parking lot, racing toward her building.

"Are you sure?"

"Honk it!" she insisted.

He honked, two long blares of the horn, and Erin jumped out of the car, looking anxiously up at Carter's balcony. "Carter!" she yelled. "Carter Brooks! I love you!"

A moment later, Carter's balcony door opened and he stepped out, looking confused as he peered down, then said, "Erin? What the hell's going on?"

"I love you!" she cried again. "I've been so stubborn, hanging on to insane fears, but I've just figured out—there are no guarantees in life, Carter. Maybe you'll hurt me or maybe you won't. Maybe the sky will fall tomorrow, too—who can say? But it's stupid to waste my life worrying, right? I love you, and I'm not afraid of it anymore. Will you give me another chance?"

Her lover appeared dumbfounded—and beautifully handsome in a pair of flannel pants, no shirt, hair scruffy, face unshaven. "Of course," he finally said, his voice quiet. "Of course, baby."

A tear rolled down her cheek then, and she was no longer afraid of that, either. Crying a little didn't mean you were weak—it meant you were normal. And more than anything right now, that's what Erin wanted to be—a normal woman in love.

"And I *won't* hurt you, honey," he told her, shaking his head. "I promise." Just like he'd told her in the bedroom the other night. But this was different—bigger. It was about their love, about their whole lives.

"I believe you."

"Can I make a suggestion?" he said.

"Anything you want." She meant that, too. He'd taught her that giving and trusting could be amazingly intimate, and she was so ready to give to Carter, and to trust him, too.

"Why don't you come inside so all the neighbors don't think I've hired a hooker to come here."

She looked down at herself in her tight red mini-dress and stripper shoes. "Oh." She'd kind of forgotten how she looked right now. "Yeah, okay."

Then she waved goodbye to Danny, thanking him for the ride and seeing him wink as he drove away—then she sprinted for the stairs, hoping she didn't break an ankle in her heels.

A few seconds later, Carter met her in the hallway and she threw her arms around his neck. "I'm so sorry," she said. "So sorry I'm an idiot."

He grinned. "I love you anyway. And you're forgiven." But then he drew back slightly. "As long as the idiocy is over for good."

"Cross my heart," she said, drawing a big X across her chest.

His gaze dropped there. "You know what I think I'm really gonna like?"

She tilted her head. "What's that?"

"Having a girlfriend who pretends to be a hooker for a living. I foresee definite after-hour perks."

She grinned playfully. "Oh? And they would be?"

"Well," he confided, "since I met you, I discovered I've got a little bondage fetish going on. And right now, I think I just found out there's a shoe fetish in the mix, too. Because I'm picturing you naked except for those shoes, and I'm getting a major erection." He leaned against her, and *mmm*, the man wasn't lying.

She eased her arms provocatively around his neck, rubbed her breasts against his chest and went into her hooker routine. "Want a date, mister?"

"How much?" he asked, skimming his palms over her ass.

"For you, a freebie."

"Are you opposed to being handcuffed?"

She smiled. "Not at all."

He motioned toward his door, a few feet behind them. "I predict a long and naughty night ahead."

"I predict *lots* of them," she promised.

Erin had spent a long time pretending she didn't need a man, a relationship, someone to love, trying to make herself believe she was stronger without those things. But now she realized that love, with Carter, was going to make her stronger than she'd ever been before. So from now on, pretending would only take place when she was on the job, catching smarmy guys—or in the bedroom, seducing her man.

Enjoy an excerpt from:
HOT IN THE CITY: KEY WEST

"What can I do for you, beautiful?"

Carrie Marsh pushed a ringlet of hair from her face and made eye contact with the cute, tan guy who'd just addressed her from behind the counter. The sun beat down relentlessly, but something compelled her to lift her sunglasses and take a better look. He had a smile that could melt an iceberg, although his ocean blue eyes made her think he fit much better with his current surroundings than with anything cold. Both of his ears were pierced with small silver hoops, and to her surprise, she found that sexy. His light brown locks were streaked with gold, no doubt a result of tropical living, and the messy hair made him look like the proverbial beach boy.

No, she thought, make that beach *god*. The mere act of meeting his gaze turned her fluttery between her thighs. Definitely not her normal reaction to a guy, so that instantly qualified him for god status in *her* book.

"I…have these tickets," she said, lowering her glasses back over her eyes and digging the vouchers from her purse, "but they were part of a vacation package, and if possible, I'd like to trade them in for something else."

The beach god took the tickets from her, his fingers brushing lightly over hers, sending another surprising skitter of awareness tingling up her arm and down into her breasts, which suddenly felt a little heavier than they had a moment before. He had great hands, she thought. Large, as tan as the rest of him, and…it was insane, but just that brief touch left her feeling as if he'd know exactly what to do with those hands when it came to sex.

He raised his eyebrows and offered a small grin. "You don't want to go on the sunset wine and cheese cruise? The Sea Wind is a great boat."

When was the last time a mere smile ran through her like little rivers of pleasure? She couldn't remember. In fact, at the moment, she couldn't remember much about *anything*. She was too busy taking in his tan, muscular arms and the broad shoulders that threatened to bust through his t-shirt. A sexy tattoo—some sort of Celtic knot design—banded his upper arm. And, as much as she enjoyed looking at the top half of him, she couldn't help being sorry the kiosk he stood behind prevented her from seeing his bottom half, as well.

Only when he raised his eyebrows did she realize she hadn't answered him. And while, once upon a time, the sunset wine and cheese cruise had sounded spectacular to Carrie, now such a romantic excursion was the last thing on her mind. The cruise was clearly for couples and she was no longer part of one. "I'm…here by myself, so I don't need two tickets to the same cruise. And besides, I think I'm in the mood for something a little different." It seemed the easiest way to say, *Nothing moonlit and romantic, please.*

"Different, huh?" He gave his head a sexy tilt. "How about the Party Barge? It's a sunset cruise, too, but a whole different atmosphere. Loud music, lots of people looking for fun, and all the rum punch you can drink."

Yesterday, Carrie would have turned her nose up at "the Party Barge" in a heartbeat. Today, though…well, even if it sounded a little wilder than her usual fare, she was tempted.

"And if you want to go tonight, you even get *me*."

Why an electronic book?

We live in the Information Age—an exciting time in the history of human civilization, in which technology rules supreme and continues to progress in leaps and bounds every minute of every day. For a multitude of reasons, more and more avid literary fans are opting to purchase e-books instead of paper books. The question from those not yet initiated into the world of electronic reading is simply: *Why?*

1. *Price.* An electronic title at Ellora's Cave Publishing and Cerridwen Press runs anywhere from 40% to 75% less than the cover price of the exact same title in paperback format. Why? Basic mathematics and cost. It is less expensive to publish an e-book (no paper and printing, no warehousing and shipping) than it is to publish a paperback, so the savings are passed along to the consumer.

2. *Space.* Running out of room in your house for your books? That is one worry you will never have with electronic books. For a low one-time cost, you can purchase a handheld device specifically designed for e-reading. Many e-readers have large, convenient screens for viewing. Better yet, hundreds of titles can be stored within your new library—on a single microchip. There are a variety of e-readers from different manufacturers. You can also read e-books on your PC or laptop computer. (Please note that Ellora's Cave does not endorse any specific brands.

You can check our websites at www.ellorascave.com or www.cerridwenpress.com for information we make available to new consumers.)

3. *Mobility.* Because your new e-library consists of only a microchip within a small, easily transportable e-reader, your entire cache of books can be taken with you wherever you go.

4. *Personal Viewing Preferences.* Are the words you are currently reading too small? Too large? Too… ANNOYING? Paperback books cannot be modified according to personal preferences, but e-books can.

5. *Instant Gratification.* Is it the middle of the night and all the bookstores near you are closed? Are you tired of waiting days, sometimes weeks, for bookstores to ship the novels you bought? Ellora's Cave Publishing sells instantaneous downloads twenty-four hours a day, seven days a week, every day of the year. Our webstore is never closed. Our e-book delivery system is 100% automated, meaning your order is filled as soon as you pay for it.

Those are a few of the top reasons why electronic books are replacing paperbacks for many avid readers.

As always, Ellora's Cave and Cerridwen Press welcome your questions and comments. We invite you to email us at Comments@ellorascave.com or write to us directly at Ellora's Cave Publishing Inc., 1056 Home Avenue, Akron, OH 44310-3502.

MAKE EACH DAY MORE *EXCITING* WITH OUR

ELLORA'S
CAVEMEN
CALENDAR

☥ WWW.ELLORASCAVE.COM ☥

erridwen, the Celtic Goddess of wisdom, was the muse who brought inspiration to storytellers and those in the creative arts. Cerridwen Press encompasses the best and most innovative stories in all genres of today's fiction. Visit our site and discover the newest titles by talented authors who still get inspired - much like the ancient storytellers did, once upon a time.

Cerridwen Press

www.cerridwenpress.com